MERCURY RETROGRADE

MERCURY RETROGRADE

A Dark Alchemy Novel

LAURA BICKLE

HARPER
VOYAGER
IMPULSE

An Imprint of HarperCollins Publishers

Cover art © by Shutterstock Images.

EPub Edition OCTOBER 2015 ISBN: 9780062437617

Print Edition ISBN: 9780062437624

10 9 8 7 6 5 4 3 2

To my wonderful husband, who always hears me.
I love you.

MERCURY RETROGRADE

CHAPTER ONE

DUST

No matter how decent Petra Dee's intentions were, things always went to shit.

Sweat dribbled down the back of her neck, sliding down her shoulder blades and congealing between her skin and the Tyvek biohazard suit. The legs of the suit made a *zip-zip* sound, snagging on bits of prickly pear as she walked through the underbrush of Yellowstone National Park. She clutched her tool bag tightly in her gloved grip, the plastic of the suit rustling over the hiss of the respirator in her ears. Her breath fogged the scuffed clear mask of the suit, softening the edges of the land before her with a dreamlike filter.

"You don't have to do this," Mike said.

"Consider it a professional favor, okay?" she said. "And you said it was weird. Now, I'm curious."

The park ranger in the suit in front of her stopped, turned, and awkwardly grabbed her sleeve. "Look, you don't have to. The hikers who found it said it was pretty gruesome." Mike's voice was muffled behind his own mask, but his brow creased as he looked at her. It was clear to her that he now thought better of bringing her here. Maybe it was his dumb, misplaced sense of chivalry, or maybe things really did suck as badly as he suggested. With him, it was hard to tell.

"You can go back," he suggested. Again.

"Mike. You need a geologist. There isn't anybody on your staff who can tell you if it's safe to be up here. Weird seismic shit has been happening in the last couple of weeks—new springs and fumaroles and mudpots opening up in this area, stuff that isn't on the maps. And you're stuck with me unless you want to wait for the Department of the Interior to show up and tell you what you need to know." She didn't want to be having this discussion out in the open. There were more men and women in suits behind them, far behind, waiting to see what Mike and Petra would do. They might not be within earshot, but it offended her sense of professionalism. "Besides, I owe you."

And she did, big-time. Petra had a knack for causing trouble for Mike. Since she'd shown up in town two months ago to take a quiet-sounding geology gig with the federal government, she'd managed to stumble into an underground war between a cattle baron and the local drug-dealing alchemist. A shitstorm of administrative paperwork had been generated for Mike when drugs and bodies turned up in his jurisdiction. Pizza and beer only went so far to balance the scales of debt.

Mike rubbed the back of his hood with a crinkling sound. "Yeah, but . . ."

Petra nodded sharply. "I can do this." Her voice sounded steadier than she felt.

"If you need outta here, just say the word." Mike started walking again, pushing aside a branch blocking her way.

She moved forward to the edge of the tree line, beyond where blotches of color swam in her sweaty vision. A campsite. A red tent had been pitched in a clearing, though it tilted in a lopsided fashion on a broken pole, like a giant spider someone had plucked a leg from. Nice tent—a deluxe model, with mesh windows and pop-outs. A dead fire with cold ash was surrounded by a ring of rocks. Laundry dangled from a clothesline: T-shirts, jeans, socks.

And beyond it, a gorgeously pink mudpot. Iron in the underlying slurry likely yielded the soft rose color. The acidic hot spring burbled mud, steaming into the cool air. She was reminded of the steam rising from mountains as the dew baked off in the spring. There were thousands of these mudpots dotted all throughout Yellowstone National Park, too many to catalog, despite the hazards they posed.

Petra ducked under the clothesline, wrestling for a moment with a pair of child-sized purple leggings that seemed determined to get snagged around her respirator hose. After fighting them off, she turned her attention back to the scene.

A dark-haired man sat upright at the edge of the dead fire, hunched forward, his arms tangled in a blanket as if he'd been trying to protect himself from the cold.

Her breath echoed quickly in her mask. Mike moved forward to kneel before the man. Pulling the blanket off, he reached for his neck to take his pulse.

Early morning sunshine illuminated the man's face. It was slack, jaw open, violet tongue protruding from his lips. Broken capillaries covered his cheeks, the red contrasting with mottled grey skin. His eyes were frozen wide open, and the sclera were bright red instead of white.

The blanket fell away to reveal a red flannel shirt. Oddly enough, it looked as if part of it had been bleached, as if he'd brushed up against a gallon of white paint. A knife glinted in his right hand, trapped in a claw frozen by rigor mortis. Petra squinted to get a good look. The knife was a piece of junk—the blade had been melted.

The body rolled over on its side, landing like an action figure holding its pose in the dirt.

Mike swore and grabbed his radio. "This is L-6, be

advised that we've confirmed a male victim. Tell the medics to . . ."

Petra turned. That was a big tent. Too big for just one guy. And then there were the little girls' leggings that she'd tussled with . . . damn it. Steeling herself, she crossed to the tent, her suit creaking. Sweating, she grasped the tent zipper. Its teeth stuck in the PVC-coated canvas, and she tried three times before she gave up. Part of the tent had come unstaked on the right side, letting daylight creep in. She worked that seam and pulled it open.

She stumbled back, falling on her ass.

A woman sat bolt upright in a sleeping bag, with speckled and broken skin like the man at the fireside. She stared at Petra with the same blood-red gaze under a tangle of brown hair.

Petra leaned forward to touch her shoulder. The woman didn't move, frozen in some unfathomable moment of shock. Heart hammering, Petra fumbled for a pulse. Through her gloves, the woman felt cold, and her chest didn't move. Her skin felt swollen, as if stretched over an unseen trauma.

Mike crawled into the tent to stare at a bundle beside the woman. He peeled back a sleeping bag on a little girl, maybe five or six, clutching a dinosaur plush toy. Her eyes were closed, seeming very peaceful under bruised skin.

"Please let her be alive," Petra whispered.

Mike shook his head. "No pulse. But . . . not a mark on her."

Petra backed out of the tent into the clearing. Blinking, she reached for her equipment bag and dug out a handheld yellow gas monitor. Stabbing at the buttons, she waited for the sensors to start analyzing the air.

She glanced at the mudpot, that beautiful pink jewel barely the size of a bathtub. The warmth it radiated condensed against her plastic suit. When the call came in that a man had been found dead near a mudpot in Yellowstone, the rangers had all assumed that the culprit was poisonous gas, carbon dioxide or hydrogen sulfide. And that would make sense, but . . .

While waiting for the gas monitor to calibrate, Petra stood to peer into the bubbling mud. It was possible, but poisoning by those gases was a relatively rare phenomenon. She fished some tongue depressors out of her pack to dip a glob of the mud out into a specimen bottle for analysis.

A sharp drumming sounded overhead, and she looked up.

A woodpecker drilled into a pine tree above her, making a sound like a jackhammer. Birds had much more delicate respiratory systems than humans. If poisonous gas had seeped up from the mud here, then the bird should be showing ill effects. But instead it had found its breakfast, plucking bugs from bark, ignoring the humans below.

Her gaze scraped the perimeter of the camp. The vegetation was all wrong here—brittle and yellow and spotted, as if burned by something acidic. She knelt to pluck a piece of curled grass to stuff into a specimen bottle. Low-level amounts of hydrogen sulfide were likely to enhance plant growth. High levels could kill plants, but not quickly.

She glanced down at her gas detector. "Huh."

Mike had backed away from the tent. "Well?"

"No carbon monoxide. No sulfur dioxide. Normal amounts of carbon dioxide. No appreciable levels of hydrogen sulfide right now, which is what I assumed the culprit would be, since that's the most common airborne poison spewed by mudpots." She pulled the hood of her suit back to take a sniff of the air. It smelled like pine needles, not like rotten eggs. "I think that it's safe for your people to come in. Just . . . tell them not to touch anything they don't have to. Gloves and suits."

Mike nodded and began barking orders into his walkie-talkie.

Petra lifted her freckled face to the sky, feeling the blessedly cool breeze against her cheeks. She spat a bit of dark blond hair out of her mouth and reached to take another soil sample. Maybe there was some other toxin here? Something more exotic that would need more tests run. Arsenic could be here, but it wouldn't have killed these people so quickly. The ground was opening up in pockets in the whole Pelican Creek area. Geologists had been detecting midlevel quakes in previously quiet land. In a place like Yellowstone, the geology was always changing, but this was unusual. And it needed to be investigated.

Mike mopped his brow. "Maybe there were high

levels here overnight, and the wind swept it all away," he mused. "Or the mudpot belched. A one-time thing."

"Could be." Inspiration struck her, and she stood to examine the man's body by the dead fire. He lay where he'd fallen, rigidly on his side. "Could you help me with him?"

"Sure. What do you need?"

"I need to check his pockets for change."

Mike rolled the guy over. The body didn't turn over with a normal thick, human sound. Petra heard sloshing, as if they were moving a cooler full of melted ice. Mike came up with a set of car keys and a fistful of change, which he handed to Petra. She stared at the debris, pushing aside the quarters, nickels, and dimes in her palm.

"Whatcha lookin' for?"

"Pennies . . . ah." She held a penny up to the light. A 2015 penny, bright and shiny and new. "It wasn't hydrogen sulfide poisoning."

"How can you tell?"

"If he'd been exposed to hydrogen sulfide, the copper in the penny would have oxidized. No evidence of that, here. When hydrogen sulfide was used as a chemical weapon in World War I, copper coins in the pockets of victims turned nearly black."

"Great. Maybe the coroner's toxicology report will tell us what it was. I'm mostly just concerned that we've got an ongoing hazard situation here."

"I'll run some soil samples," Petra said. "In the meantime, you should have your rangers cordon this off for at least a hundred yards until we know for sure what it was." She wrinkled her nose and reached for her respirator. "What the hell is that smell?" It wasn't the rotten-eggs smell of hydrogen sulfide. This smelled worse, like roadkill.

Mike turned to the body. "It . . ." The smell hit him, and he struggled to pull his hood over his head. "It's the body."

Where the camper's corpse had been turned over to the earth, a black, viscous substance oozed. Two medics had arrived in full gear and grasped the body, one at the arms and the other at the feet. As they lifted, it seemed as if some fragile surface tension held by the man's skin failed. The skin split open, and dark fluid soaked the dirt to splash against the white suits of the medics.

"Christ," Mike said behind his mask. "Only a floater would behave like that."

"A floater?" she echoed.

"A body that's been in a river for weeks. The gases build up while the organs rot. But . . . these guys can't have been here that long. We'll know for sure when we get an ID."

More plastic suits showed up with body bags into which to pour what remained of the camper. They discussed how best to remove the woman and the child from the tent without rupturing them. It was decided to start with the child.

Petra turned away. She just didn't want to see that. She began picking at samples around the edge of the campsite, trying to fade into the background. But the scene burned behind her eyelids. It wasn't just the people that were dead. Death had spread to the vegetation around the campsite in a circle, as if someone had sprayed the plants with weed killer. As she ventured farther and farther away, she found a trail of rust-colored grass vanishing into the forest.

Ignoring the chatter and radio static behind her, she began to follow the trail. It spanned an area a little over three feet wide, a perfect path of brittle vegetation that contrasted sharply with the early autumn grass that still thrived. She paused before a pine tree that seemed to have had its bark scorched away by some kind of chemical reaction.

She began to regret removing her hood. Holding her breath, she chipped a piece of bark away with an awl and dropped it into a sample bottle.

The track ended abruptly at a spine of rocks that composed the next ridge. There were no plants to speak of here, only fine milk quartz pebbles and sandstone gravel.

She blew out her breath, frustrated at having lost the trail. Had there been some kind of chemical accident here? She ran through the desiccants and herbicides she knew, most of which were not good for people, but the most likely short-term effects would have been simple respiratory distress or skin contact allergies. Nothing that could cause the amount of squish and slop that the medics were dealing with.

No rational explanation.

Maybe there was an irrational one.

She glanced behind her. No one had followed her this far, to the edge of the forest. She fumbled in her gear bag for the last bit of equipment she'd brought: a golden compass. Glinting in the sun, it lay flat in the palm of her hand. Seven rays extended to the rim, with an image of a golden lion devouring the sun in the center. The Venificus Locus, a magic detector that she still wasn't entirely sure she believed in, but couldn't discount. Maybe it would have something to say. Maybe it wouldn't. But not asking the question would be stupid.

She stripped off her glove, wiggling her sweaty fingers in the air. A hangnail that she'd neglected to trim kept annoying her. She ripped it off and hissed when blood welled up around the cuticle. Clumsily, she sloshed a bright drop of it into the groove circumscribing the outside of the compass. The blood sizzled on contact, then gathered itself into a perfectly round bead. It circled the rim of the compass once, twice . . .

Petra held her breath, as much in anticipation as not wanting to spill the blood. The bead of blood swung back and forth in an agitated fashion, then settled on north, pointing to the campsite right behind her.

"Great," she muttered. That was pretty decisive. The compass would have just sucked up the blood if no magic was present.

This was weird land. The nearby town, Temperance, had been founded by Lascaris, an alchemist who'd conjured gold from dead rocks. Some of Lascaris's old experiments still wandered the countryside. She'd encountered a few of them in her short time here: the Hanged Men, the Alchemical Tree of Life, and the Locus itself—which she'd been told had been made by Lascaris's own hands.

A shadow flickering through sunlight caught her eye, and she looked up. She half-anticipated it to be the woodpecker foraging for more insects, but froze when she spied a raven watching her, balanced on the edge of a branch. His eyes reflected no light, his shadow mingling among the flickers of needles and branches of the lodgepole pine.

She stared back at it. It might be an ordinary raven. Or it might be one of the raven familiars of the Hanged Men. She turned the compass toward the bird. The drop of blood spiraled halfway around the disk before the bird, alerted, took wing and vanished.

Things around here were rarely ordinary.

Clear now.

The raven pumped his wings, pulling himself into the blue sky, as far as he could get from the smell of blood in the compass and the aura of poison clinging to the campsite. He caught an updraft from the sun-warmed land, skimming along the south edge of the mountains, over the dark ribbons of road and the dry grasses of autumn fields.

This draft required little effort from him. He stretched his wings and allowed his eyes to drift shut.

The sun felt gloriously warm on his back, seeping through his feathers into his light body. In the sky, things were simple. There was no magic that could touch him here. No blood. No pain. There was just sun and air and sky.

He sailed along the current until it weakened. He twitched his feathers, gave in to the instinct to flap his wings, and opened his eyes to look down.

A vast field spread below him, gold and grassy and glinting with dew. A massive elm tree stood at its center, and below its shade stood a man in a white hat.

The raven made a slow spiral, relishing the last bit of air through his feathers. He skimmed around the tree in a lazy arc, approaching the motionless man on the ground.

The man opened his arms, as if inviting a lover back. His amber eyes glowed brighter than the dawn.

The bird slammed into his chest. Feathers melded with flesh, fluttering into a pulse and soaking into skin.

Gabriel let his hands fall. The bird twitched through his consciousness as he absorbed all it had seen.

Above him, leaves rustled. Some were living leaves, some dead. The tree stood, scarred and ancient, but its shadow had grown thin. He reached up to pluck a brown leaf from a branch of the Hangman's Tree. This wasn't the only withered branch; the tree's leaves had begun to curl at the center, as if autumn's breath had come weeks earlier.

He turned the leaf over in his hands. The tree was dying. He'd felt it even before the leaves had begun to drop, as the magic in it faltered. Even the Lunaria, the Alchemical Tree of Life, couldn't survive forever. Not after what it had been put through, creating generations of undead to haunt the Rutherford Ranch.

Not after what he had been put through. If he closed his eyes, he could still remember bleeding into the roots of the Lunaria and the tree's frantic efforts to put him back together. He'd been torn to pieces in the explosion of a collapsing house. Wood had pierced and rent his body to bits. It would have been best to leave him to dust.

But no . . . the other Hanged Men had brought him back here, out of sheer instinct. And the last raven had been brought back to him, the last fragment of himself. Through excruciating pain and light, he'd been revived.

Though not wholly. He was conscious of vast gaps in his memory, as if time had eaten away at an old tintype photograph. He'd forgotten his middle name. He couldn't remember the exact year he'd come here, though he knew it had happened over a century ago. He recalled bits and pieces of alchemy, arcane bits of ephemera about dissolution and phoenixes. His right hand shook when he wasn't concentrating on it, and he'd developed a somewhat mechanical twitch in his left eye. An irritating limp came and went, even if he parsed his feet away as ravens and brought them back again.

Revived. But at terrible cost. The light running through the veins of the tree grew more sluggish with each sunrise. He could feel it choked off, as if some force had girdled it beyond retrieval. The end of the tree would be the end of all the Hanged Men. He remembered that much.

Behind closed eyes, he thought about that possibility of oblivion. Nothingness was seductive. No more striving to see another day. Just dust. He'd had a taste of it, when he'd lain in pieces within the Lunaria's embrace.

He crumpled the brittle leaf in his fist and opened his eyes. His gaze traveled to the south fence, where the rest of the Hanged Men toiled, herding the cattle to the north pasture. This wasn't just about him; there were the others to think of. The others, who had no voice, who would simply cease to exist along with him if the tree died. He could choose to give up—but the decision was not his alone.

And yet . . . perhaps he had seen a solution. The part of his consciousness he'd sent out as a bird had detected something strange.

Something that might save the last thing he held dear.

CHAPTER TWO

BREATH OF LIFE

"Just breathe."

Petra squeezed her eyes shut. Light pressed against her eyelids, creating distracting red dots on the darkness in her skull. Her breath whistled in the back of her throat as her pulse pounded in her neck. The pounding crept up from her throat to her temple, thudding like the beginning of a migraine. She tried to push away thoughts of hydrogen sulfide, black pennies, and dead eyes.

"There is nothing, emptiness within and without. Feel the void opening in your heart."

In response to the gravelly voice, Petra shifted her awareness to her chest. Her heart thumped in time with the pulse in her head. She squinted into the darkness behind her ribs, searching . . .

Searching.

Something twitched across the field of her vision. The red lights faded to a thin streak of grey. She could make out a meandering stripe of beach along an ocean, faint in color, like an overexposed photograph. At the edge of the water stood a silhouette—a man in a black coat with his hands clasped behind his back. Long grey hair was tied back from his face, and he gazed out over the ocean, as if expecting a ship or a bottle to wash in. The figure turned. His eyes were hazel, the only color in this landscape.

"Dad?" she asked.

She said it not only in her head, but aloud. Her throat tightened around her pulse and her words, and her concentration slipped. The image vanished.

Her eyes snapped open. The sky stretched overhead in dazzling blue, and the sun pressed warm on her face.

An old man sat before her, cross-legged on a stone. He cupped his chin in his hands, braced on his elbows like a garden gnome statue.

"You suck at meditation," he told her.

"No kidding, Frankie." She pressed the heel of her hand to her head. She wiggled her toes to generate some feeling. The coyote asleep in her lap grumbled and kicked her.

"The coyote has no problems getting to the spirit world," Frankie observed.

Petra rubbed Sig's belly. "Sig is much more spiritually evolved than I am." The coyote knew exactly what he wanted from life and exactly how to get there. It had been true since the first day he'd shown up on her doorstep. He'd had to make some compromises, though: He now wore a flea collar, with ID tags attached.

"Did you see anything at all, this time?"

"Just a glimpse . . . a glimpse of my father." She shook her head. "It could have been just wishful thinking or an imagining. I can't . . ."

"You can," Frankie insisted. "You just *aren't*."

"I know. I have to." Petra blew out a frustrated breath. She stared down at the ground, plucked at a limestone pebble. Sun had begun to burn her freckled shoulders, reminding her that this was likely the last day of autumn that would be over sixty degrees. Wearing a tank top and cargo pants, the scars on her arms were exposed: a handprint-shaped mark around her right wrist and slashes on both. The old handprint had faded to white, while the slashes remained pink and new. The handprint was a burning reminder of the lover she'd lost on an oil rig at sea, and the slashes were a gift from the drug-dealing alchemist, Stroud, who had wanted her blood to run the Venificus Locus. She would never allow these to be seen in public, but hanging out with Frankie wasn't really what she considered "public."

The pendant her father had given her glinted at her throat: a medallion depicting a lion devouring the sun. She knew now that it was an alchemical symbol, but it was her last tangible tie to her father. It had soaked up the heat of the day, feeling leaden in the hollow of her throat.

A shadow interrupted the sunshine. Maria, Frankie's niece, stepped through the field, the grasses scraping her long skirt. The breeze worked loose tendrils of her long dark hair caught up in a complicated series of braids around her head. She held a basket under her arm. For a moment, it seemed that she could have stepped out of time, from an earlier era.

Sig rolled over, instantly awake. He scrambled up to greet Maria, twitching his nose toward the tantalizing basket.

"Are the two of you finished plumbing the mysteries of the universe?" Maria reached into the basket to hand Frankie and Petra bottles of water. Frankie tore into his greedily. She offered Sig a dish, and Petra poured half of hers into it for the coyote to drink.

"Not many mysteries have revealed themselves," Frankie said, wiping his mouth with the back of his hand. He stood, stretched, and walked toward a pool of spring water, dyed a Technicolor blue by algae. He knelt by the edge of the water and began skipping stones across its glasslike surface.

Maria perched upon a sandstone rock, tucking her skirt beneath her. From the basket, she distributed sandwiches and containers of potato salad. She'd made a stack of meat for Sig, who took it delicately from her hand and wolfed it down as if he hadn't eaten in a week.

"So . . . you're looking for your father in the spirit world?" Maria poked at her potato salad with a fork, not meeting Petra's eyes.

"He's there. I mean . . . he's somewhere. Maybe just in my head," she confessed. "His body is in the nursing home. But the thing that makes him . . . his soul, I guess . . . is somewhere else. I spoke with him the very first time I came here."

Frankie chortled in the background. "This is the Eye of the World. Drinking the sweetwater is the key to the spirit realm."

Petra glanced at the pool of water. "You said you tried it?"

Maria laughed. "Of course. But it didn't take me anywhere." She gazed out at Frankie, who dangled his feet in the water and sang to himself.

Petra's mouth flattened. "I've drunk it three times since then. Nothing." It caused her to wonder: Had she hallucinated it?

"So now the meditation practice?"

"Yes."

"I'm sure that meditation will be helpful to you. I would never discourage you from that." Maria said. "And I know Frankie can lead you where you want to go."

Hearing a splash, Petra glanced at the pool. Frankie's clothes lay on a rock, and he swam in the water like a wrinkly, pale eel.

"I sure hope so."

"He'll get you there. He will. You just need to be sure."

A smile played on her lips. "Are you social working me over?"

Maria laughed. "Maybe a little. Nobody leaves work at work for long."

Petra looked away.

"What is it?"

Petra took a deep breath and told Maria about the scene at the campsite—the little girl and her dead parents, the mysterious poisoning, and the red eyes of the bodies.

"You think it was the mudpot?"

"I don't think so. Mike's people cordoned off the area, and the bodies are at the morgue. I assume that the coroner will have a better idea. Though . . . I did take some samples and sent them off to the federal lab to see what's in that mud. To be certain."

"Nothing's certain around here." Maria fed another piece of meat to Sig.

"I did another test," Petra confessed. "I used the Locus."

Maria lifted her eyebrows.

Petra shrugged. "I figured that it was able to detect Stroud's magic, when he was still screwing around with living mercury. It could find the Lunaria, and . . ." She forced herself not to mention Gabe's name, and plunged forward. ". . . . I thought it might tell me if there was something not normal going on there. And the compass did detect something. What, I'm not sure . . . I saw a trail of dead grass that made me think of something like Agent Orange as the culprit. But the Locus woke up and was spinning away."

"Maybe those campers were into something strange," Maria mused. "Did you see any Ouija boards or salt circles? Any summoning Cthulhu with a pop-up gate to hell? I hear the Dark Lord loves toasted marsh-mallows."

"I didn't see anything more out of the ordinary than camping gear. No copies of the *Necronomicon* or black candles. I'll check with Mike to see if he found any-thing odd in their packs." Petra doubted it; aside from the miasma of death, the family seemed as wholesome as corn flakes. She picked at her sandwich. "But the Locus felt there was something there. I can't tell if it was the campsite, the trail of dead grass, or if maybe it was . . ." She trailed off, not wanting to give voice to what she really thought.

"Maybe it was what?"

"There was a raven there, watching."

Maria stilled. "You think it could have been one of the Hanged Men? Watching you?"

"I don't know. If it was one of them, if they had any-thing to do with it, or know what did . . . they won't talk to me. Not with Gabe gone." She swallowed and looked down at her hands. She hadn't admitted to Maria that she'd begun to feel something for Gabe, but she knew that the other woman guessed.

Maria came to sit beside Petra on the same rock,

putting her arm around her. Sig rested his chin on Petra's knee. The only sound was the wind stirring the grass. A tear slipped down Petra's nose and landed in her sandwich wrapper.

"I don't know how to feel about this," Petra said at last. "He died, trying to help me. It was my fault. "

"No. He cared for you," Maria said, brushing a piece of Petra's dark blond hair out of her face. "He came to find you. You found something human in him. You did a good thing."

Petra sniffled ungracefully. "It sure doesn't feel that way. It feels like I fucked up his . . . his unlife. Whatever he had. Like I fucked up Des's life." She traced the palm print burn scar on her wrist. He'd reached for her as he was dying, burned to death in an oil disaster. The scar still felt warm when she thought of him.

"Give it time. Meditate with Frankie. Give yourself permission to look for more than your father in your time in the spirit world."

Maria gathered the remains of the picnic and walked back in the direction of her house. Petra watched her go, envying her certainty.   In the short time she'd known Maria, she'd never seen her look backward at anything.

And looking backward seemed to be Petra's specialty. She sighed and stood, looking to the pool for Frankie.

Frankie had finished his swim. He lay upon a flat rock the size of a Volkswagen Beetle, stretched out in the sun with a straw hat covering his face. Petra wondered if he journeyed in the spirit world without her, but a snore fluttered the brim of the hat.

Petra walked through the gravel to the edge of the pool. Sig slipped past her and plunged into the water, dogpaddling in the blue mirror that reflected the autumn sky in perfect detail: the cirrus clouds, a formation of geese moving south.

She knelt at the edge and lowered her empty water bottle below the surface. Bubbles gurgled against the plastic as it filled. She lifted the full bottle to the sun. It was the color of sea glass, bits of cloudy algae floating inside.

Bringing the bottle to her lips, she drank. The water tasted cold and with a hint of something sweet, like linden flower. She chugged the bottle, feeling rivulets of it dribbling down her chin and soaking her shirt.

Clutching the bottle, she sat back on her heels. She closed her eyes and slowed her breathing. Her yearning to speak once more to her father flowed through her, from the soles of her feet to her eyes, heavy with unshed tears. She had so much to ask him.

The sun pressed down on her; she sought the darkness behind her eyes, tried to slip into one of those trances that Frankie seemed to so effortlessly fall into at the bottom of a breath or the bottom of a bottle.

A cold shadow passed over her. Petra tried to ignore it, squinched her eyes as tightly as she could, so tightly that she saw sparks behind them. She could get there, she *knew* it, if she only pushed hard enough . . .

Frankie's voice drifted down to her, as gentle as an autumn breeze:

"You know, I just peed in that water."

Her eyes snapped open, and her tongue involuntarily scrubbed the roof of her mouth. She made a face and was about to tell Frankie to go to hell when forty pounds of wet coyote bounded into her lap and began to shake himself off.

So much for fucking enlightenment.

There was no way out of this hell. None that he could see.

Cal pressed his fists to his temples. The thundering in his head. *Would. Not. Stop.* It was so loud he couldn't think. It didn't stop after he took an entire bottle of ibuprofen. It didn't stop after he drank a whole bottle of vodka. It didn't stop when he threw both of those up and screamed at the top of his lungs. It was chewing him up inside, and he knew it.

He moved his hands to his face, pressing his knuckles to his eyes. They came away smeared with liquid silver. With mercury.

"Fuck," he moaned.

The mercury seeped back into his palms and twisted in his arteries. He could feel it moving, crawling up his arms. Its cold fingers wrapped around his heart and his lungs, tapping out a rhythm that was too fast, too fast for any drug he knew of. His heart was gonna fucking explode if he didn't get help.

"Fuck you," he growled at the mercury. And he cursed its creator seven ways to Sunday, with every permutation of the f-bomb he could summon: Stroud. The stringy old alchemist was dead, but he'd left Cal with this fucking experiment that was chewing his guts out. He'd been shitting silver for weeks, trying to purge it out with laxatives and prune juice. It just left him weak and furious. Furious at Stroud for not taking his own magical creepy crawlies to the grave with him. The motherfucker's house got blown up when the DEA and Petra's creepy ranch hand friends had come for him. Wasn't that enough to keep all of his bad juju down?

Cal pressed his fingers into the dirt and staggered to his feet. He stumbled through the filthy remains of his camp: a tent made of trash bags set up in the shade of a clump of scrub trees, boxes of Twinkies, and empty energy drink bottles. It was getting too cold at night to sleep on the ground, cold enough that his breath steamed and frost was coming. He left it all behind and moved through the falling darkness toward the road in the distance. His boots clomped in the dust before him, feeling as heavy as concrete blocks. Wrapping his hands around his black jacket, he shivered. The road seemed to twist and slither in his vision, and he struggled to keep it in view.

The road. Almost there. His boots crunched in gravel, and he nearly fell when he arrived at the shoulder. Bracing his hands on his knees he looked north and south at the empty, wavering asphalt. The sun had set, and stars prickled out above the mountains, swimming in his vision. He couldn't make out which one pointed north; they all spun overhead like a bad acid trip.

Somebody had to come. They just *had* to.

He waited for what seemed like forever until he saw headlights in the distance. He straightened, brushed futilely at the filth on his jacket, and stuck out his thumb like he knew what the hell he was doing.

The headlights came closer, washing over him. He closed his eyes.

Pleasestoppleasestopplease. . .

An engine ground to a halt, and he opened his eyes. A tractor trailer slowed beside him, the passenger's side window rolled down. By the dim green light of the instrument panel, Cal could make out a flannel-encrusted dude with a goatee.

"This is a long way from anywhere, kid," the trucker said. "Where you headed?"

"I'm trying to get to Temperance. My motorbike ran out of gas, and I got no way to get there."

The trucker paused to light a cigarette. The ember danced like a firefly. "I'm going that way. Get in."

"Thanks, man."

Please don't let this guy be a perv. Cal cringed inwardly. But he opened the door and scrambled up the running board to get inside. The cab smelled like cheeseburgers and corn chips. A glow-in-the-dark figurine of a plastic alien danced from the rearview mirror.

Cal slammed the door, scooted as close to the

window as he could, and wrapped his hands around his stomach to stifle the gurgling. He didn't want the guy to think he was gonna shit in his truck. That would be epically bad.

The driver put the truck in gear, and the semi growled down the road. The cigarette bobbed in the dark, but the driver didn't say a word. His right hand reached toward Cal.

Cal squealed and clawed at the door handle. The truck had to be going at least forty, if he jumped . . .

"Relax, kid." The trucker reached down to the littered floorboards and lifted a bag of potato chips. "Have some."

Cal gingerly accepted the crinkling yellow bag, and the trucker's hand returned to the steering wheel. Cal's shaking fingers wormed inside, and he lifted a chip to his mouth. It tasted stale, but the salt soothed his swollen tongue. "Thanks."

The truck driver looked at him sidelong. "Temperance. Small town. Is your dealer in Temperance?"

Ah, shit. Well, maybe it was best if the guy thought Cal was going through some hellish withdrawal. That would be the most benign explanation, anyway. "Something like that."

"Mmm-hmm." The driver didn't sound especially inclined to make it any of his business.

Cal glanced out the window, at the miles flashing by. His pale face was reflected back at him in the glass, superimposed over the dark landscape . . .

. . . and mercury leaked out his nose.

He rubbed at his nose with his sleeve, smearing it away. He glanced back at the trucker.

The dude was watching him.

Shit.

Sweating, Cal turned back to the window. Silver beads of liquid began to spring out on his forehead. He wiped them away with his shaking hand, but he could feel the metal squirming under his skin. The mercury licked up over his eyes, covering the whites and the irises. He could see through it, as if he were looking through tinted sunglasses, and he gasped.

"Hey, what's wrong with you?"

The truck swerved. Cal twisted around to see the trucker pulling a gun out from under the driver's seat. The driver shoved a pistol against Cal's nose, and Cal shrank back up against the door of the truck, holding his hands up.

"Be cool, man, be cool!" he squeaked.

"What the hell is wrong with you?" the trucker shouted at him, while the cold metal slipped from Cal's nose to his upper lip.

The rig swerved into the left lane. Headlights shone in the bug-smeared windshield before them. A tinny horn sounded. The car in the left lane ran off into the ditch without making contact.

"Don't do that, man!" Cal rasped. A tear leaked out from his eye. In fascination, he watched as the mercury reached out, spiraling around the barrel of the gun.

"You're one of *them*, aren't you?"

"One of who? What?"

"Them! One of the Greys!"

Cal's eyes flickered to the alien figurine bouncing against the windshield. Oh, fuck . . . this guy was a true believer. "Oh, shit. No, man I'm from Earth, I swear. I come in peace!"

The trucker pulled the trigger.

Cal shrieked, expecting his brains to blow out all over the seat. But the mercury had wrapped itself around the gun, absorbing the concussive impact with a belch-like bubble and a sound like a blown tire.

The driver sawed the wheel back. The tires screamed, and the cab of the truck tipped up on two wheels. He dropped the gun to struggle with the wheel, but it was too late. The back end of the trailer came around, and they were sideways in the road, sparks showering against the pavement and metal shrieking.

Cal pitched forward against the windshield, then lashed back like a rag doll as the truck jackknifed and skidded across the road. The cab landed in the ditch with a force so great that the roof wrinkled like aluminum foil. Steel and glass howled.

Cal whimpered against the floorboards. He clawed his way up through the debris of old newspapers and spilled potato chips, peering at the driver's side. The trucker slumped over the wheel. His hands dangled motionless, but Cal couldn't see his face.

Cal clambered up to the seat. A huge spider-shaped crack spread across the windshield right across from him, roughly where Cal's head had hit. Cal touched his forehead. His fingertips brushed what felt like the cold chrome of a car bumper, not warm flesh.

"Damn it," he cried. He reached to open the passenger door, but it was wedged against the side of the drainage ditch, wouldn't open more than a couple of inches. Cal worked the crank of the window, succeeding in getting it partway down. He wriggled his lanky frame through and out onto the bank.

He lurched forward into the safety of the weeds before he turned back. The truck had folded in on itself on the road, and he smelled gasoline.

Pain lanced through his stomach, and he doubled over, spitting a string of mercury out on the ground.

He squinted ahead, seeing light. The truck's headlights illuminated an arrow-shaped road sign: TEMPERANCE 3 MILES.

Maybe the crazy guy had gotten him close enough.

He limped off into the darkness.

Darkness was split by a low growling.

Petra bolted upright in a tangle of blankets. Moonlight filtered through the blinds of the Airstream trailer she called home, striping her futon bed and the linoleum floor in streaks of black and white.

A shadow crossed the floor. Sig. He'd climbed off the futon and stood before the door. The dim light outlined the fur raised on his back. His lips were drawn back in a snarl, exposing white teeth.

"Sig . . . what is it?"

Sig continued to growl, eyes fixed on the door. Petra heard nothing, but that didn't mean that nothing was out there.

She didn't have much worth stealing. Her 1978 Bronco was parked out in the gravel in front of the trailer, all buttoned up for the night. Somebody would have to be out of their mind to try to boost that ride. Her geology picks, GPS, and other tools were in a duffel bag inside the trailer. Aside from the gold pendant her father had given her, and the Venificus Locus, they were the most valuable things she owned. She kept some cash stuffed behind the paneling of the walls, but that would be hard to find.

Under a blue tarp near the door was her latest project—the one thing she couldn't hide well or lock up. At one of the reservation swap meets she'd gone to with Maria, she'd picked up a motorcycle frame and an accompanying heap of parts on a whim. She'd cleaned the rust off of the WWII-era BMW R75 frame and had just begun tinkering with the ignition plate and draining rainwater out of the odometer to see if it could be salvaged. The sidecar was a rust-eaten disaster and would likely need to be reconstructed entirely from scratch, but she liked the idea of seeing if Sig would take to a sidecar. The restoration would likely take her years of cobbling together bits and pieces. She hadn't ridden since college, but it felt like she needed something to do at home to take her mind off things. The pile of rusted junk was probably also a prime target for thieves looking to make a quick buck.

She reached under the futon for her gun belt and drew one of the antique pistols from the beat-up leather. She climbed out of bed, padding across the floor in bare feet. Her toes curled, feeling unprotected against the floor, but she felt secure enough to answer a threat at the door in the sweatpants and T-shirt she slept in.

His head low to the ground, Sig crept closer to the door, stalking in slow motion.

A shadow crossed the window of the screen door. Someone *was* there.

The shadow knocked. In the silence of night, the sudden sound made her jump.

Her grip slick on the pearl grips of the gun, Petra crept to the door.

The knock sounded again, harder and faster. Sig barked, snarling like a dog ten times his size.

"What do you want?" she shouted, loud enough to be heard beyond the door.

A thin voice seeped around the cracked weather stripping: "Petra. It's me, Cal."

Cautiously, she sidled up to the door. She pushed the blinds apart with the gun barrel. The silhouette of a gawky teenage boy dressed in black stood on her step, hands stuffed in his pockets.

Petra swallowed a lump in her throat. "Are you alone?"

That was the key question. She felt somewhere in her gut that Cal could be a decent kid, but shit had gone pear-shaped when he got in with the wrong crowd. Last time she'd seen him, he'd been deceived into luring her to Stroud's Garden for a bloodletting. She trusted him about as far as she could throw him.

"I'm alone. Unarmed, too. Please . . . I need your help."

At her feet, Sig gave a feral yip.

"You wanna tell me why I shouldn't call the cops? They're still looking for you."

"Please. I got nobody else." He sounded plaintive, like a lost emo puppy.

Against her better judgment, she unlatched the door. She stood back, aiming the gun before her.

"Come in. Hands up."

Cal nudged the door open and stepped inside. In a flash, Sig had backed him against a wall in a flurry of fangs and fur.

"What do you want?" She fumbled behind her for the light switch, keeping her gun trained on Cal.

The light clicked on, and she gasped.

Beneath a shock of black hair, Cal's eyes were silver, silver like coins on a dead man's eyes. Liquid metal tears oozed from them, dribbling down his chin.

"Oh, shit," she breathed.

CHAPTER THREE

MERCURY RISING

"What happened to you?"

Petra held the gun before her in a quavering grip. She hadn't seen anything like this . . . not since Stroud's Alchemical Garden, when Stroud had been holding himself together with duct tape, chewing gum, and a whole lot of sorcery.

"I'm not sure." Cal shifted unsteadily from foot to foot. He took a step toward Petra, and Sig snapped at him. He backed up against the wall.

"Where's Stroud?" she demanded. It was impossible to believe that he didn't have something to do with this. She believed him dead when his house blew up, but . . .

"I don't know. I swear. I was digging around in the ruins after the Garden burned down, and saw this . . ." He turned over his hand and opened it. The skin of his palm rippled with grey shadows underneath. "It grabbed me. It wouldn't let me go."

"The mercury," she breathed.

"Yeah. Yeah . . . and it hurts." Silver tears spilled from his eyes. "You gotta help me."

"Jesus, Cal." She holstered the gun.

Cal slumped against the wall, his eyes flickering closed. Petra caught him before he fell.

"We gotta get you to a hospital."

His eyes opened. "No! No hospital."

"You're sick, Cal. You've got heavy metal poisoning and God only knows what else." She grabbed his wrist for a pulse, and it thundered under her fingers. "Your heart can't take this."

"No." He shook his head as Petra lowered him to a chair. "Stroud could handle it. It didn't kill him. You gotta find a way . . ."

Petra retreated to the back of a trailer for a bra, a beat-up military jacket, and a pair of boots. She snatched her keys, wallet, and cell phone from the kitchen counter.

"No. Stroud was magic. *He* might have known what he was doing, but he clearly didn't share that with you. I'm driving you to the ER."

Cal tried to climb to his feet. "I'm not going."

And he fell to the linoleum like a ton of bricks.

"Cal!"

Petra hovered over him. His pulse still thudded strongly. She pried his eyelid up, and the mercury cataract had retracted. Maybe that was good. Maybe bad. But figuring out which was beyond her pay grade.

She ran outside to unlock her rust-colored Ford Bronco. She popped the passenger's side door and had to fight Sig out of the passenger's seat.

"You can't come," she insisted. She reached forward for his collar and dragged him out.

She went back for Cal. She saw no sign of the leaking mercury. It was as if it had trickled back beneath his skin. Grasping him under his arms, she managed to drag him through the trailer door. His legs bounced on the steps, and his heels dragged in the dust as she hauled him to the truck and shoveled him in. Throwing his torso across the bench seat, she flung his stringy legs in after him. A seat belt was a waste of time on that pile of goth spaghetti.

Sig paced outside the truck, growling. As she opened the driver's side, he lunged inside, heading for the darkness of the backseat of the Bronco.

"Sig . . . I don't have time for this."

His eyes glowed in the back. He was resolved.

She jammed the key in the ignition and cranked the engine. She flipped on the lights and peeled away down the gravel road, conscious of the gold coyote eyes boring a hole in her back. She was certain that Sig thought she was the stupidest human who had ever lived.

"What do you want me to do? Turn a sick kid away?" Sig huffed.

"This isn't going to end well, is it?" She knew that shit was going bad, could feel it creeping up on them.

Sig didn't comment, just let her stew in her frustration.

Miles whipped by in the dark, marked by faded stripes on the pavement and the gathering of clouds on the western horizon that scrubbed out the stars. She pushed the old Bronco to its limit, the engine roaring underneath the hood like a dinosaur with a head cold.

Petra chewed her lip as she glanced down at Cal. He'd picked up something from Stroud, something awful. She rubbed her hand on the side of her jacket. Some of Stroud's magic had sneaked up on him. She had no idea how contagious it was, but she sure as hell didn't want to find out.

Stroud had a freakish relationship with mercury. As an alchemist, he'd had the ability to work the element as an extension of himself. She'd seen him wear it as liquid armor, seen it deflect bullets. She'd even heard it rumored that he'd used it to choke a cop nearly to death. It was powerful magic, but Stroud had had many years to harness it. Maybe he invented it himself; maybe it was something he'd cooked up following a recipe from Lascaris. Maybe he inherited it; she'd heard that Stroud could trace his lineage back to the founder of Temperance and the local madam. However Stroud had come by it, it was bad news for Cal.

The nearest hospital lay twenty miles away, at the county seat. This time of night, and this far out in the middle of nowhere, Petra had expected that the tiny ER would be empty, perhaps occupied by a solitary drunk or a pregnant woman in labor.

But the emergency room was packed. The two-story cement building was surrounded by a nearly-full asphalt parking lot. As Petra parked and hopped out of the Bronco, an ambulance with flashing lights screamed by. A knot of cops and civilians swarmed by the front door. Slamming the Bronco's door on Sig, Petra threw Cal's arm over her shoulders and dragged him toward the yellow-painted berm.

"Hey!" she shouted. "I need some help over here!"

A cop and a man in scrubs rushed toward her.

"Is this another victim?" the cop asked.

"Victim of what?" Petra echoed, then shook her head. Clearly, these folks were having a bad night, too. "This guy's got heavy metal poisoning. Mercury."

The man in green scrubs shouted through the glass doors of the ER for a stretcher.

"How long has he been like this?" the man in scrubs asked, checking Cal's respiration with gloved hands.

"I don't know. He just showed up at my doorstep. He was covered in mercury, and he passed out." That much was true. Petra struggled with how much to explain. She opened her mouth to say more, but a gurney arrived. More people in scrubs flopped Cal onto it like a sack of potatoes and whisked him into the fluorescent glare of the hospital lobby.

Petra made to follow. She glanced at the ambulance. Another stretcher was being pulled out of the back, with a blood-smeared burly man in flannel strapped to it.

"Incoming!" one of the paramedics yelled, pushing inside with the stretcher.

"Busy night?" Petra mumbled to the cop beside her.

"You have no idea." The cop shook his head. "Crackpots, brawls, auto accidents and . . . ah, shit."

A news van bristling with flying saucer antennae on the roof pulled up to the curb. A man with a camera and a blond woman in a red coat holding a microphone hopped out. The woman was clearly ready for television: Her teased hair had been parted in the back and sprayed on the sides to resemble a cobra's hood.

The cop retreated, and Petra slipped in the doors to the lobby. Whatever they were here for, she sure as hell hoped they wouldn't find Cal. He'd make one hell of a story: "Local Teen Cursed with Living Mercury, Clings to Life."

She made her way to the admitting desk, through a lobby that looked like a box of human misery had been upended on the green tile floor. A family huddled together, weeping, while an angry man shouted into a cell phone. An old man sat in the corner with his hands covering his face, while a little girl knelt on the floor, trying to reach up inside the Coke machine. A look of utter concentration had spread across her face, her tongue protruding from her lips.

Petra spoke to the nurse behind the Plexiglass-shrouded desk. "I brought the emo kid in. He's got heavy metal poisoning."

The nurse nodded. "Please come with me. I need to get some information." He led Petra through a pair of double doors back to the bowels of the hospital.

"The doctor wants to speak to you," he said, pulling aside a pink-patterned curtain.

Cal lay in a hospital bed, looking like an overcooked vegetable. They'd cut his shirt off, and his skin held a greyish cast as it stretched over his ribs. A nurse was starting an IV, muttering about the needle tracks in his arm, while another stuck heart rate monitor leads on his chest. His eyes remained closed, and an oxygen mask covered his face.

"I'm Dr. Burnard," a woman in scrubs with a stethoscope slung around her neck said, nodding at Petra. "Are you a relative?"

"No . . . I don't know him very well, at all," Petra admitted. "He just showed up at my trailer, in a bad way."

"What did he say?"

"That he'd been poisoned with mercury. I saw it—it covered the sclera of his eyes and was moving . . . under his skin."

The doctor squinted at her. "How do you know it was mercury?"

"I'm a geologist. I know mercury."

"How much of it did you see?"

"Visible on him at the time? I'd guess about twenty fluid ounces."

The doctor turned and told the nurse: "Let's get some blood to confirm. See if we have some Demercaprol on hand, or if we need to get it from the university."

"Did you touch him? Skin on skin?"

"Yeah, I brought him here."

The doctor hooked a thumb at her and nodded at a nurse. "Check her and scrub her down."

"Hey, wait a minute . . ." Petra protested. A nurse grabbed her arm with a latex-covered hand and led her away to the second floor, while an aide trailed with a clipboard.

"Is he gonna be okay?" Petra asked, though she knew that there was likely no good answer to that question.

The nurse beside her said: "We'll do everything we can do for him. And for you, if you got contaminated." She pushed Petra into a tiny exam room and yanked out a red bag with a biohazard symbol on it. "You'll need to put your clothes in here."

The aide with a clipboard clicked a ballpoint pen. "The young man you brought in. What's his name?"

"Cal. His name is Cal."

"Last name?"

"I don't know."

"Age?"

"Sixteen, maybe?"

"Address?"

"I don't think he has one."

"What's your relationship with him?" she glanced over the clipboard.

"He's a . . . friend."

"Any family or legal guardian?"

"I think he's on his own."

"Do you know if he has insurance?"

"Probably not."

"Any known medical conditions? Allergies?"

"None that I know of, but . . . I don't really know."

"Is he taking any medicines? Legal or illegal drugs?"

"I don't know about medicines, but he used to occasionally smoke meth. And that drug that killed a couple of people last month. Elixir."

The aide frowned and scribbled.

Petra sighed. She didn't know enough about Cal. Not enough to help him. Maybe not even enough to keep him alive.

People in scrubs poked and prodded and quizzed her about her own identity and medical history, which she was able to answer adequately enough. Another nurse herded her into a room with a shower and brought her a hospital gown and socks to change into.

Petra scrubbed her skin until it was raw. She wasn't worried so much about mercury itself—she could watch herself closely for symptoms, and would likely have refused to be clucked over if it had been an ordinary chemical spill. She told herself that it *was* reasonable to worry about the magic underneath it. While the hospital staff were scrupulous about gloves, she had not been. A phlebotomist came by to take her blood, saying that they'd test for heavy metal poisoning and get back with her.

They let Petra keep her keys, wallet, and cell phone in a zipper plastic bag. She sat in the smaller waiting room for the second floor with the bag in her lap, waiting for news of Cal and her own blood work. The television overhead was tuned to a local station, and she glanced up to the screen to see the same blond newscaster she'd seen at the ER entrance. The reporter stood outside, with the parking lot behind her. Petra could make out the Bronco in the background and Sig's face in the back window. Drawn by the lights of the camera, he seemed intent on photobombing the shot, licking the back glass. Petra rested her head in her hands, rubbing her temples.

" . . . report that they saw a giant snake after the rest of their party went missing. Steven Moore was at the scene." The woman shoved the microphone at a young man standing uncertainly beside her. He sported an expensive-looking down jacket and an impressive amount of facial hair that he couldn't seem to stop playing with.

"We were, uh, partying by the creek when Tamara heard a noise. At first, we thought it was maybe a beaver or something. I heard hissing, but . . . yeah. Beavers don't hiss. I don't think. Anyway. Ed shined a light down on it, and it wasn't no beaver. It was big . . . like the Loch Ness Monster. Had to be at least thirty feet long and as big around as a barrel. Yellow eyes, it had yellow eyes. It disappeared into the water. Tamara got some video on her phone."

The television image changed to dark, blurry footage of . . . something. Petra leaned forward and squinted at it. Something writhed sinuously in the water while a woman shrieked in the background.

It could be a log twisting in a fast current. Maybe. But it had some curve to it. And she could make out two yellow points that could be eyes, under the right conditions. The eyelike lights vanished as the camera was dropped.

The reporter returned to the front and center of the screen. "Two members of Steven's group were found ill beside the bank of the creek, suffering respiratory distress, and one is still missing. They were taken to Park Community Hospital. No news is available yet on their conditions." The reporter looked a bit irritated at that, her crimson mouth turning downward. Petra guessed that since she was reporting from the parking lot, she'd gotten her ass booted out of the hospital. "The missing person is Amber Taylor. She's nineteen years old, blond hair with blue eyes, five feet five inches, and 130 pounds. She was last seen at the west side of Pelican Creek, east of Sulphur Hills. Amber is wearing jeans and a white hooded sweatshirt."

Petra's brow wrinkled. That was less than five miles from where the dead campers had been found. She wanted to believe that it was a coincidence.

A picture of an attractive young woman flashed on the screen. She looked like a girl next door, with bits of pink chalk in her hair and flashing a peace sign to the camera.

"If you've seen Amber, please call the county Sheriff's Office or Park Police. Stay tuned to Channel 4 for more updates on this breaking news."

Petra leaned back in her chair. She wasn't inclined to believe in anything she couldn't touch and measure. In all likelihood, the snake was as real as Bigfoot, and the illnesses had been brought on by whatever they'd been smoking or drinking.

Still. She wondered.

And shuddered.

There was dead, and then there was *really* dead.

Gabe flipped on the overhead light at the hospital morgue. The fluorescent lights buzzed to life in the chill, illuminating a small basement room covered with glossy olive-colored tile and battered stainless steel tables. He remembered an earlier time when bodies were dressed and carried downstairs, around coffin corners cut into the stairwells. They were taken to the parlor of a house to be laid out until they started to reek or the last relatives had shuffled through—whichever happened first—but times had changed. Not that he could remember the exact year he'd last seen it. But it had been awhile.

He reached to the counter for a pair of latex gloves.

He glanced at a body on a table, tugging open the zipper of the body bag to reveal the wizened face of an old man, peaceful in repose. Gabe guessed that the corpse was probably half his own true age. After a moment's hesitation, Gabe zipped him back up. Not what he was looking for.

He crossed the room to a wall of stainless steel cabinets with six doors. He opened one, pulling out a drawer containing a nude body decorated with a toe tag. Wrong body—a middle-aged woman missing a leg from the knee down.

Third try was a charm. He yanked out a drawer that crinkled with plastic. Shrouded in a bag, the body was wrapped within several layers of plastic tarp. Gabe dug into the plastic. The coroner clearly hadn't gotten to these bodies yet . . . or was planning on shipping them away to the state lab.

It didn't smell right. Dead bodies had a particular unforgettable smell about them, soft and final. This smelled acidic. Dead, but chemical. Gabe stared into the bloated face of the man his raven had seen at the campsite. The corpse's eyes were blood red, open. Gabe pulled back the eyelid. Dark liquid had begun pooling at the back of the cavity, and the eye wobbled like gelatin. The nose and mouth were bright red inside.

The body's skin was soft, leaving dents where Gabe's fingers prodded. He traced a tire tread pattern that had eaten through the corpse's shirt into the flesh. It had a rough texture, like abraded road rash. He poked the ribs, where bones should be, but could feel nothing solid beneath the skin. That small amount of pressure yielded a black, viscous fluid that pressed out of the corpse's mouth.

Gabe's mouth thinned. If the coroner didn't do something with these bodies soon, he suspected that any usable evidence would liquefy. No one would ever know what really happened to them. Not that it would be a bad thing.

The woman and the child looked to be in a slower state of decomposition than the man. The woman's fingernails had fallen off, and the child's teeth were loose in her palate. The interiors of their noses and mouths were the same vivid crimson. Gabe guessed that the poison had been inhaled by those two, and that the man had come into direct contact with it. That could explain why he was turning into sludge a bit faster than the others.

Gabe wrapped the bodies back up and closed the drawers. Stripping off his gloves and discarding them, he glanced through the files in a wire basket on the desk. Very preliminary notes. They'd been identified as the Carrollton family: Rob, Sue, and their girl, Melanie.

Gabe closed the folder and dropped it back in the basket. The raven he'd sent had tasted magic at the scene of the crime, and his observations here had confirmed it.

Something murderous was loose.

He slipped back into the hallway and took the freight elevators to the patient floors. He limped by the nurses' station, pretending to be reading a sign while he eavesdropped.

"Have you seen that guy's throat in three? It looks like that carnie who got admitted last spring."

"Finn the Fire-breather?"

"Yeah. It's like he inhaled a tank of napalm or something."

"Is he one of the giant snake guys?"

The nurse snorted. "Oh, the tox panels came back on that. Looks like a winning bingo card."

Gabe frowned. There was no way that he could sneak in to see them—new patients were always tightly observed. And uniformed police milled about the halls. Perhaps he could try tomorrow.

He made his way to the bank of main elevators to leave, but paused.

In the waiting area near the floor nurses' desk, a motionless figure lay curled up in a chair. Dark blond hair had fallen over her freckled face, and her arms were crossed over a hospital gown. Her eyes were closed, and by her breathing, she seemed to be asleep.

His heart hammered.

What was *she* doing here?

A bright shard of memory bubbled up in the back of his brain, sharp and blistering as a bullet.

No. He couldn't remember that. She'd hurt him, hurt him badly. It wasn't safe to go near her. Deep in his undead bones, he knew that she would kill him.

Gabe noiselessly stepped beside her. He reached out to touch her hair, but stopped an inch above her temple. Fear and fascination twisted in his gut. He forced himself to stop, to take a step back, and walk away.

CHAPTER FOUR

WEST OF THE MOON

"The beginning is the end. The end is the beginning."

Voices rose in a hypnotic chant, through flickering firelight and smoke scented with white sage. Darkness enfolded a circle of shadows gathered around a bonfire. The shadows turned in the light, seething, seeming less substantial than the fire.

"In the mouth of the serpent lies the tail of time."

Fire picked out faces surrounding the flames, eyes closed, lifted to the ash and stars in the sky above. All thirteen were women, dressed in dusty motorcycle leathers. Sparks glistened, intermingling with bits of ash drifting to settle on the shoulders of their jackets. The women pressed their hands toward the fire. Flame reflected in the chrome of motorcycles clustered just beyond them in the desert. It was an eclectic collection of bikes: a handful of ex-military KLR650 bikes in matte paint, a Triumph Tiger 800, a BMW F800GS, a pair of S13 Suzuki DR-Z400S motorcycles, and a couple of Yamahas that had begun life as more dirt bike than street bike, but had been customized for the road. There was good metal there, and fine coin in all of them to make them road and dirt machines that chewed up the landscape. But they'd been carefully painted with low-key finishes to draw as little attention to themselves as possible. Someone who knew bikes would be impressed; a casual onlooker would walk on by. And that was what they intended: to be invisible on the street and the forest.

"As above, so below."

"As within, so without."

The fire burned swiftly, the blue of gasoline at its core, acrid when the wind pushed the smoke just right. Tangled in bits of a broken pallet, scrap wood, and scrub brush was something that hissed like fat. A human skull popped off the stem of its neck and sizzled in the heart of the fire, flames rimming an eye socket. This was a fine sacrifice that had fallen into their laps. The man had attempted to attack one of the women at a gas station restroom. She'd broken his hand, and the others had fallen on him like a swarm of bees. He was dead before the toilet had finished flushing. A worthless human being, but a fine sacrifice.

Belinda lifted her hands to the sky. Her arms, bared by a tank top, were covered with massive tattoos of snakes spiraling from her shoulders to her hands. The tail of each snake wrapped around her throat, with the body of a snake curling around the length of each arm, like a black caduceus. The heads of the snakes were inked into the thin skin on the backs of her hands, and her silver-ringed fingers flashed like fangs. The heat of the fire pressed close against her skin, summoning a sheen of sweat that glistened on the ink.

Bel's voice lifted above the others, beseeching the dark sky above and the still ground below: "The Sisters of Serpens ask for the blessing of the Great Serpent, the Great Mother of all things hidden, in all her guises." As she spoke, long silver earrings brushed her shoulders, and wisps of long dark hair worked free of a ponytail at the nape of her neck. She closed her eyes, feeling the sear of the fire on her eyelids and the palms of her hands as she reached up. Her boots pressed deep into the dust, and she felt her soul taking root in the land. Her fingers tickled the stars, and the power of night formed a complete circuit, flowing between her hands, down her spine, into her feet. The warm energy of the fire uncoiled along the base of her spine, crackling along her vertebrae. She was conscious of the shadows of her sisters around her. They were paler shadows than the long, dark shadow she cast, but still stronger than any ordinary man or woman; their black auras radiated night.

"I summon thee, with all thy names: Medusa, Ariadne, Astarte, Python, Wadjet, Renenutet, Tanit, Manasa, Melusine, Ishtar . . ."

She sucked in her breath and closed her eyes. Her head lashed backward on her neck, lifting her chin to the sky. Power buzzed between her shoulder blades, vital and alive, as the kundalini energy of an ancient and powerful goddess snapped her awake. Behind her eyes, red shadows seethed and boiled.

"Priestess?"

One of her sisters called for her, but they dared not touch her. Bel shivered, and the energy cascaded down her arms like snow shaken from a coat. Her eyes opened, falling upon her followers. A joyous smile filled her face, and she lowered her hands, shaking, to the level of her shoulders.

Bel found her voice, deep behind her ribs. "She is here. She's calling. The Great Serpent has awakened."

Something deep within the bonfire collapsed, sending a twisting finger of fire roaring toward the sky. A bystander might have thought it a log breaking, or a pocket of gasoline immolating the last bit of marrow in the bones of the body that burned within it. The bones had gone black, splintering open in the heat. But Bel knew it for what it really was: magic.

Whispers circled around the fire, sobs of joy, and brilliant smiles flashing white in the darkness.

"The Great Mother is here!"

"She has returned to Earth."

"What shape do you think she's taken?"

"She will be a force to be reckoned with!"

"What now, boss lady?" Tria, her lieutenant, asked. Petite and blond as a doll in a toy catalog, her waist was circled with a belt full of knives. When she crossed her arms over her chest, her fingers unconsciously dipped down to trace the hilts. A twitch formed above her right eye, as always happened when she was anxious. The man who had attacked her at the gas station was not the first to have done so, and it had opened an old wound. Still, it had been cathartic for her to cut him into pieces to be carried away for the fire.

Bel reached out and touched Tria's chin, activating a decade-old hypnotic suggestion that she'd implanted in Tria's psyche. The magic in Bel's touch crept up her face and sank deep into her brain. The twitch softened and faded, and Tria smiled.

"Better?"

"Better. Thank you."

Bel turned to the space in the sky where the sun had set hours before. She pressed her hands to her heart to contain its racing.

"West," she said, with certainty. "We head west."

"Ms. Dee?"

Petra jerked awake, nearly falling out of the hospital chair. She'd been dreaming—dreaming of a shadow too remote to touch stretching over her like a storm cloud. It smelled of grave dust and sunshine and made her chest ache.

She struggled to hold on to her plastic zipper bag of personal effects and twisted around to see the doctor from the ER sitting down in a chair opposite her.

"Yes?" Petra tucked the hem of her gaping hospital gown around her knees and leaned forward. "Dr. Burnard?"

"We have your lab work." She flipped a page on her clipboard. "No traces of heavy metal poisoning, so you're clear."

Petra nodded. "Thanks. That's a relief."

"You should make an appointment with your primary care physician at your earliest convenience, though. Your white blood cell count is abnormally high."

Petra's brow crinkled. "What does that mean?"

The doctor shrugged listlessly, and Petra thought that this must be the time of night that nothing got sugar-coated. "Might be nothing. Most likely a routine viral or bacterial infection. But you should get that checked out, just to rule out immune disorders."

Petra nodded quickly. "Okay. But . . . how is Cal?"

The doctor's left eye twitched. Petra wondered how long she'd been on duty. Her scrubs looked like they'd been slept in, and there was a rusty stain on her pant leg that Petra chose to assume was coffee.

"He's not well. We found mercury in his system . . . so much that I don't know how he's still alive."

"But can you help him, can't you?" Petra hugged the plastic bag to her chest.

"No. I can't. We've done all we can to stabilize him, and we're going to transfer him to the university. There are some experts who deal with heavy metal poisoning there, who might be able to properly filter his blood. But we just can't do that here."

Petra nodded. "I understand. Can . . . can I see him?"

Dr. Burnard seemed to hesitate. "Yes. But only for a few minutes. MedFlight will be here for him soon, and we have to be ready to move him right away."

"Thank you."

She led Petra through a warren of green-painted halls with swinging doors. Personnel in scrubs scurried right and left, pushing wheelchairs, linen carts, and stacks of paper. The doctor weaved around the flow like a fish in the water, while Petra clutched her plastic bag and tried to ignore the sticky feeling of her slipper socks on the waxed tile floor.

Dr. Burnard paused before an open doorway. "He's here."

Petra's heart dropped down into her slipper socks. Cal lay in a cocoon of plastic. A clear plastic tent surrounded him, head to foot. Hoses and tubes snaked from IV poles into his scrawny arms. A tube had been installed in his throat, taped to his mouth. He lay motionless, eyes taped shut under the glaring fluorescent light.

"Can I go in?"

"You can, but don't open the isolation tent."

Petra went inside. She stared down at Cal. His skin was grey, pallid as canned tuna left in a refrigerator too long. The machines whirred and buzzed and beeped around him, and his chest flexed in a mechanical rhythm.

She brushed her fingers against the plastic, swallowing hard. "Cal. I don't know if you can hear me. It's Petra."

Cal's artificial breath continued its regular rhythm, with a *whoosh* and a *click*.

She went on: "They're going to take you to the university hospital, where there are people who can help you. They're *going* to help you." She bit her lip and her vision blurred. She didn't want to lie to him. But she kept going: "It's gonna be okay. Really."

She didn't believe it. But she wanted him to.

If he didn't, if he didn't believe enough to fight, he was good as dead.

Something was choking him.

At first, Cal thought it was something out of a bad hentai movie. A dark, viscous tentacle had wrapped around his neck. He struggled, gasping, trying to unwind it from his throat. But the creature had his body enveloped in its cold, slimy grip. The tentacle around his throat slipped up over his lip, and he whimpered, fingernails clawing into its slick skin. As his fingers dug into it, the flesh congealed like concrete. The viscous substance forced itself past his teeth and crawled down his throat, frigid and twisting.

Oh, God. Oh, God. Oh, God.

Cal gagged, trying to hurl it back up like bad sushi. But it wormed deep in his throat, behind his ribs, rising behind his eyeballs . . .

He tried to howl around the arm in this throat, but couldn't make a sound. A flash of silver dribbled over his vision—the mercury—loosening the tape over his eyes. Bright light flashed over him—fluorescent lights, and a murmur of voices. He was lying down but moving, moving fast, and a dozen tubes and wires and hands were digging into his skin, jammed down his throat.

Oh, God.

He struggled and thrashed, but he couldn't move his hands and legs. He rolled his eyes downward, and he could see Velcro restraints around his wrists. Someone was shouting at him, over him, and hands were pressing against his shoulders. A woman in green was struggling to uncap a needle. The cart on which he was tied clattered along, through a hallway and into darkness, deafening darkness.

He smelled fresh night air, felt the roaring of a machine and impossibly strong wind. He thrashed again, panicked, trapped, and helpless. It was the feeling he'd had at Stroud's Garden, at the mercy of the drug-dealing alchemist who'd made him his errand boy. It was the first feeling he woke up with in the morning and the last one at night.

Something cold twisted within him. The mercury.

He could feel it unwinding in his veins, seeping through his pores. It leaked through his hands, soaking the Velcro restraints. Cal whimpered, flopping like a fish.

And one of the restraints popped free.

He reached up for the tube in his throat. Someone was screaming at him, and bodies in green and blue scrubs were struggling to pin him back down. But the mercury climbed over his arm. A woman shrieked and backed away.

He gagged and spat out the tube, gasping in pain. Jesus . . . how had they gotten something like that down him? Someone had let go of the gurney, and it spun at a lazy angle, pushed by the wind from what he saw were helicopter blades.

Jesus. They were gonna take him away. Away to . . . where? A military base? Like in Area 51 or something? Experiment on him? A guy dressed in black hopped down from the helicopter bay.

Oh, no. Nonononono.

Panic flooded him. He ripped open the last of the restraints and jumped down from the gurney. He was conscious of gloved hands trying to shove him back, but he popped free of the wires and tubes in his arm, stumbling and bleeding.

A man in green scrubs tried to grab him. Cal howled. The guy was much stronger than he was, and tackled him to the ground hard enough to drive Cal's breath from him.

This was it. Tears leaked from Cal's eyes, blurring his vision. He was caught, and he was doomed. He could lie here and wait for them to wrap him up in a nice package to be delivered to the Men in Black, or . . .

. . . or he could fight.

Cal wriggled up his right hand, coated in silver. He reached up to claw at the guy's face, hoping to startle him into letting up . . .

. . . but the mercury had a mind of its own. It leapt from his fingers, reaching toward the nurse's face. His face twisted in horror, and he opened his mouth to shout. Like a snake slithering through a forest floor, the mercury slid into his mouth. It poured into the man, overflowing from his lips. He gagged, flung his head from side to side.

Cal's eyes narrowed. He could feel his fingers crawling into the guy's mouth, choking him. His throat bulged and swelled, like he'd swallowed a brick.

For the first time in his life, Cal felt powerful. It sang in him, like a soaring song at a concert with a ton of bass, swelling his chest and quickening his pulse. He felt . . .

"Gahhh!"

A column of water hit him, shoving the hapless nurse away. Cal flopped on the pavement, spying a couple of security guards wrestling with a fire hose. The hose writhed and seethed uncontrollably in their grip, shooting at the helicopter blades and flinging water in a torrential arc across the pavement. One of the helicopter rotors was hit—it began to thump, unbalanced. The stream knocked the man in black from the helicopter off his feet and tangled him around the landing gear. The helicopter was pushed back six feet, scraping on its skids, wobbling.

Now was his chance. Cal scrambled to his feet and ran. Disoriented, he sprinted away from the helicopter, stumbling through the asphalt parking lot. To the south of the helipad, the dark parking lot stretched, half-full of cars. He crouched as he ran, trying to find cover. Shouts echoed behind him, and flashlight beams bounced into the darkness.

Cal ducked and rolled beneath a van. He held his breath as feet pounded past him. His fingers flexed on the ground. He stared down at them. They were no longer silver—just flesh-colored and bleeding from a torn-out IV on his right arm. The blood was red, which was encouraging.

He crawled beneath the next car, through an oil puddle and antifreeze. It sounded like the voices were receding. They'd gone toward the road, where blue and red cop car flashers were approaching.

Shit.

He kept crawling on his elbows and forearms on the pavement, determined to get as far away from the cops as he could. He whimpered as the large tires of a van pulled up beside him. *More cops!*

Maybe. Maybe not. He could make out a bit of green paint at the edges of the mud flaps. He inched over to the van and peered up. The side of the van was marked SPECIALTY LINENS AND UNIFORMS.

He could hear the driver through the open window, sitting in the driver's seat and talking on his cell phone: " . . . yeah, I'll be a bit. Holdup on the road, but I should be at the nursing home soon . . ."

Cal scrambled out from under the car he was using for cover and wormed around to the back of the van, careful to stay out of the driver's line of sight in the side mirrors. He reached up, a prayer on his lips, hoping to hell that the back latch of the van was unlocked . . .

Yes! He opened the door and slipped inside. He shut the door firmly behind him and collapsed in a heap on the metal floor, heart pounding.

It smelled like piss. He wrinkled his nose and looked over his shoulder. It was dark, too dark to see. But he could reach out and feel the wheels and frames of linen carts around him. On hands and knees, he crawled as far as he could to the front of the van, wedging himself between a cart and the wall. He winced as the truck lurched forward, praying that the cops wouldn't have their shit together enough to start a checkpoint to search for him.

The engine of the van ground forward, and he felt it pick up speed. His heart lifted, and he could very nearly imagine freedom coming closer as the tires crossed the pavement and bounced over three speed bumps that rattled carts and clothes hangers around him. The truck made two right-hand turns, then accelerated into the night.

Cal took a deep breath, scraping his throat. He put his head on his arms and fought the urge to sob in relief and terror. His body screamed in pain, and he had no idea what to do. The cops might take him away somewhere awful if he let them. He had nowhere to go.

A dribble of fluid escaped his nose, and he knocked it away with his knuckle. He didn't want to know if it was snot or mercury.

He had to get it together. Somehow.

As his eyes adjusted to the darkness, he spied something glowing on the wall, like letters. He pushed the cart hiding him aside and crawled to it. The word FIRE was wrapped in Day-Glo letters around a fire extinguisher on an alcove in the wall between the cart area and the walled-off driver in the front. Cal groped around the fire extinguisher and came up with a flashlight. The batteries were half-dead, but it worked if he whacked it hard enough.

He swept it around the interior of the van. Four large linen carts of dirty laundry took up the majority of the floor space, and there were some garbage bags with biohazard stickers slung against the walls. A rack against the right side held plastic dry-cleaning bags. Cal shined the light on scraps of paper taped to the necks. Some were going to a nursing home, others to a restaurant. Feeling the draft on his bare ass, Cal ripped open the plastic to find something to wear.

He succeeded in finding a grey shirt with the name CLAYTON embroidered on the chest pocket, a pair of black pants, and a brand new Carhartt jacket. He figured that would be slightly less obvious than the parcel of pastel-colored scrubs that were due for the nursing home. He had no idea who Clayton was. Maybe a mechanic, maybe a security guard. Could be a professional bowler. But Cal was eager to get out of his drafty calico gown and into something that approximated street clothing. The best he could do for shoes was a pair of flip-flops that looked like they were worn by jail inmates.

As Cal changed, he glanced down at his arms. They were still bleeding from where he'd ripped out the IV lines. He tried to staunch the blood as best he could with a nicely folded stack of hotel towels. At least, he told himself, the blood was red.

For now.

What was happening to him? His hands shook as he raked them through his hair. If Stroud were alive, he could have asked the stringy old alchemist. But he didn't know anyone else with that kind of mojo. A hospital wasn't going to solve his problem. They'd poke him and prod him and slice him up to put under a microscope. But he was sure that they'd just turn him over to the Man in Black he'd seen with the helicopter.

After a half hour, the van slowed, as if coming to a stop sign or stoplight. Cal crept to the back door, cracked it a hair, and peered out.

"Damn," he breathed. "All roads lead to Rome. Or some such bullshit."

The van was idling at the one red stoplight in Temperance, on the main street. From his vantage point, Cal could see the hardware store, the gas station, and the post office standing across from each other, all buttoned up for the night. But Cal knew better. There was one place that would be open this late, where he might be able to rustle up a proper ride.

Cal sidled out the back of the delivery van and dropped to the pavement. His feet hit the broken concrete with a jarring that he felt in the back of his teeth, nearly losing the plastic flip-flop on his right foot. In a belch of sooty exhaust, the uniform truck chugged away.

Cal straightened up painfully and walked across the street to the Compostela, his flip-flops smacking on the pavement behind him.

In its earlier incarnation, when Temperance was founded, the Compostela had been a church. It still retained some of that Gothic charm during the day: peaked windows, stained glass, its stately façade. At night, it was just damn forbidding. The stained glass was lit from within, giving the appearance of strange fires burning behind red and yellow glass.

It was a busy night for the Compostela. At least a dozen beat-up old cars and trucks were ranged along the street and the nearby alley. Cal tried the doors of all of them. Two car doors opened, but he struck out on finding any keys in the dash, under the floor mats, or behind the visors.

Damn. But he came up with about ten dollars in change and half a donut. He pocketed the change and greedily devoured the donut.

He skulked to the front door of the bar, head lowered. His pulse pounded in his throat. Maybe he could get in on a card game and get lucky, maybe lift a wallet or steal some scratch from a table. Maybe he'd run into someone he knew who would be able to hide him or help him. Maybe.

Cal pushed through the doors into the dimness of the bar. Church pews had been converted into booths arranged along the walls, with tables in the middle. Cards fluttered and pool cues clicked against ivory. Cal shuffled to the back of the bar, the former apse, now occupied by a long bar hewn from a single massive tree. He squirmed up on a stool at the corner and scanned the crowd.

At this hour, the bar was full of gamblers, drunks, and the forever dissolute. A man with an obvious tan mark around his left ring finger, but no ring, sobbed into his hat down the bar. Some younger men took turns drinking from a pitcher of beer, dribbling alcohol on the floor. A couple of the card games weren't going well, and two players had just folded at a table with a volley of swearing and threats.

Sweat prickling on his forehead, Cal watched. He rubbed at his brow with his sleeve. It was dark enough that he couldn't tell if it was sweat or metal. Maybe no one else could tell, either. He dipped his fingers into a bowl of peanuts and ate them all in one gulp, licking the salt from his fingers.

The bartender appeared before him, a tall, thin, blond guy with a glass. The glass was full of water. Cal snatched it and drained it greedily.

"You're not looking good, man." The bartender's gaze seemed to dismantle him, piece by piece.

Cal peered over the rim at him. "I'm not good," he confessed. "I'm pretty fucked up." He wobbled on his barstool.

The bartender nodded. "Are you looking to leave town?"

"I think . . ." Cal began, but his attention was arrested by a commotion at the front door.

The door opened, and a group of women filed in. They definitely weren't locals—they were dressed neck to toe in motorcycle leathers dusted in a grey, ashy grime that didn't correspond to any dirt that Cal knew around here.

Still, they were hot. In an Amazon, don't-fuck-with-me-I'll-cut-your-balls-off sort of way. They were tall and short, different bodies and skin, but all of 'em looked totally badass. Cal couldn't decide if he had the beginnings of a hard-on or if he should just cross his legs. He decided to cross his legs.

The bartender stiffened. Cal watched him reach beneath the bar. From his vantage point, Cal spied a shotgun behind a stack of bar mop towels.

"Who are they?" Cal asked.

The bartender didn't take his eyes away. "Trouble."

Awesome. Cal slugged down the rest of his water and planned his escape.

But the women were fascinating to watch. Whispers followed them as they clomped in on their grubby boots, heading to empty tables in the back.

"Hey, sweetheart . . ." one of the patrons in a booth slurred and spread his legs suggestively. "You ride?"

The woman in the lead, a striking brunette, fixed him with a withering gaze. He shrank back, as if he'd been burned. His companions chortled.

"Talk about resting bitch face."

One of his braver companions reached out for the woman as she passed, making a ham-handed grope for her ass.

The bartender swore under his breath.

The blond woman behind the brunette caught a finger on the offending hand and bent it back at an unnatural angle. He yelped.

"Back off."

The women filed in a line to the back of the bar. They seemed to take up a lot more space than they should, shadows curling around them and amplifying something weirdly slithery and loose in their posture.

Two of the women seated themselves at the empty spots at the poker tables, gesturing for cards with fingerless gloves. They plunked down cash that looked real enough. The dealers shrugged and dealt them in. Stranger money was just as good as local money.

The tall brunette, the one who seemed to be the leader, walked up to the bar beside Cal.

"Some beers, please," she asked the bartender.

She gazed into his eyes. There was something odd about how she did it, unblinking.

"None of that in here. No magic tricks, or you're out."

She lifted an eyebrow. "You're perceptive."

"It's my job. If you're in here, you play fair. And that goes for your girls."

"All right."

The bartender wiped his hands with a towel stacked beside the shotgun. He nodded and reached for glasses.

She turned to Cal, and he looked away. But he felt those kohl-smudged green eyes on him, taking inventory. He hadn't felt that kind of gravity in anyone's gaze since . . . since Stroud.

He glanced down at his hands on the bar. Silvery liquid mingled with the condensation from his glass on the lacquered top of the bar. He put his hands in his lap, smearing the liquid on the bar top away with his elbows. Furtively, he glanced back, and knew that she saw. Her eyes dilated, and she gestured to his hands with her chin.

"Did you do that to yourself?" Her voice was soft, kindly.

The question took him off guard. He stammered. "I. Uh. Not really. I don't . . ."

She reached out for him. Her hands were covered in ink. He ducked and flinched. But she reached out to cup his face in her hands, the way a mother would hold a child.

Her green eyes glowed at him. "I can help you."

His lip quivered. He wanted someone to say that, and to mean it. Her hands were cold but soothing, like a cool washcloth on his face. It felt hypnotic. He felt soft and buzzy, the way one felt with a fresh shower, a full belly, and clean sheets.

A hand slapped down on the bar behind her, attached to a six-foot, flannel-covered man.

"Hey, those broads with you are cheating at the poker table . . ."

She released Cal and turned in one swift movement, planting an elbow in the man's gut. As he doubled over, her riding boot snapped up and cracked him in the head. The guy slid to the floor of the bar.

Cal shrank back against the bar. All around him, the fight was on. The women had surrounded one of the poker tables and flipped it, spewing cards and glassware onto the floor. Some guy was getting his ass handed to him by a blonde with a pool cue.

The bartender was having none of it. He'd reached for his shotgun and ratcheted it back.

"Out of here," he shouted.

The woman with the ink wheeled to stare at him. The shotgun was leveled at her chest.

She raised her hands, and it seemed that something passed between them. Understanding, recognition—Cal couldn't tell. But the guy froze. Sweat trickled down the bartender's temple, and it seemed that he was trying awfully hard to pull that trigger, but something stopped him.

The woman reached for the collar of Cal's jacket. He squeaked as she hauled him off the barstool and dragged him out the door, ducking under flying fists and soggy slices of pizza. She hauled him to a line of motorcycles parked across the street that were growling to life. Women jumped on the bikes, turning over the engines.

The woman in black thrust a helmet into Cal's hands. "Put it on."

Cal complied, and he scrambled onto the back of the bike, tucking his feet around chrome and soft-sided canvas luggage. He dimly realized that this was one helluva bike—a Triumph Tiger.

The Triumph roared to life, and Cal wrapped his arms around the woman's waist and clung to her for dear life.

In thunder and wind, they tore down the street into the darkness.

Heading west.

CHAPTER FIVE

MAKING TRACKS

These chicks were weird.

Cal had attended his fair share of half-assed Black Masses and séances. He could only remember maybe two that he hadn't fallen asleep during. Most of those had been run by folks who'd had way too much to drink or people who were selling things like curses that could drop your ex dead in her tracks or spells that could make you an overnight singing sensation. Cal had seen the real deal with Stroud's alchemical lab, with the salamander that lived in the grate and the old books with spidery writing. He knew real magic when he tripped over it.

And he'd fallen in it this time, majorly.

The women had fled into the darkness after the brawl at the Compostela, not stopping until the moon climbed high overhead and Cal's ass was sore from his perch on the motorcycle. He expected chicks on expensive bikes would find a motel or crash at somebody's house, but they turned off the main road and jounced along into the wilderness until the rider of the bike he clung to waved for the group to stop. Cal had had a dirt bike once upon a time, but these gals had the right knobby tires and expensive shocks to handle off-roading with that much chrome and gear.

They stopped in a clearing and shut off the engines. There was no light, no sound but the receding roar of engines in his ears. Cal felt queasy, and nearly fell off the bike. Someone caught him, and he was lowered to the dew-slick ground.

"It's okay." It was a girl, a girl with purple hair. If he were feeling better, he would have thought she was hot and tried to hit on her. Things being as they were, it was all he could do not to hurl in her lap. She must have sensed it, and turned away.

The ground was spinning the way it did when he drank. Overhead, he saw Hercules—he remembered Hercules from science class—spinning around and around in fuzzy streaks. What did Hercules chase in the sky? Was it Draco or Hydra? He couldn't remember. That line of stars over there, maybe . . .

Cool hands pressed against his face, and the stars were blotted out by the woman from the bar. Fire flickered behind her. Her arms were bare, and the tattoos of snakes writhed on her arms. He flinched away, tried to shrink into the ground.

"It's okay." She held him fast. Her hands were cold as water on his face.

"Who are you?" he croaked.

"I'm Bel," she said. "I need you to look at me."

He tried to focus on her eyes, but the snakes . . . oh, God, the snakes were going to get him. The ground swam, green eyes swam above him, and those snakes were on his face, on his throat. He felt the mercury boiling within, crawling under his skin. Jesus Christ, he could feel it churning between his ribs, lashing out . . .

"Get away!" he shouted. The mercury dribbled down his cheeks. He could feel it unwinding in his fingers, reaching out over her wrists.

"Get away, please!" he whimpered. He didn't want to hurt anyone.

"Be still," she said in a serene and even voice. The ink and the mercury and the stars blurred in his vision, and he felt the other women around him, holding him down. Her lips were working around an incantation as her nails chewed into his wrists and her knee jammed into his chest.

"As within, so without. Still."

The mercury reached out, out to slap her across the face, to fling her across the campsite like it had the security guard.

But it fell, fell like water from a garden hose when someone shut off the spigot. It slapped down into his lap and crawled through his pants under his skin. It retreated into his marrow, and it was . . . it was still.

Cal took a shaking breath against her sharp knee.

She got off him, and he felt hands release his shoulders and legs. One of them was the purple-haired girl. She grinned at him.

"What happened?" He only knew that the stars had stopped spinning above him.

Bel knelt beside him, and she brushed sweaty hair from his forehead. It was a tender gesture—the last woman who'd done that for him had been his mother. He blinked up, not understanding, watching the tattoos on her skin move over her muscles.

"The mercury in you is still. For now," she said.

"How did you do that?"

She smiled and pressed her middle finger to his forehead. "I can teach you. Take a deep breath."

He filled his lungs with air. He still felt the liquid metal in a shell around his lungs, but he could actually feel the air in his chest.

"Imagine the metal in your bones, quiet. Feel it sinking toward the back of your spine."

He could feel it, feel it become leaden. His eyes drifted closed.

"Be still."

Cal's consciousness faded.

He was pretty sure that he slept, but he heard snatches of voices, whispers of fire. The girl with the purple hair wrapped him tightly in a blanket near the flames and propped his head up on a saddlebag. He could smell the warm, oiled leather, and it was soothing. Sparks popped and hissed. She poured a dribble of water down his throat. The voices surrounding him were fuzzy and clear. Sometimes, they sounded like chanting. Sometimes, it was simple conversation:

"Priestess . . . will he survive?"

"It's up to him." Bel sat on the ground beside him, sharpening a knife on a flint.

"What will you do with him?"

"He can't be allowed to wander free," Bel answered.

"What is he?" A blond woman squatted beside him, staring into his face. "Is he a warlock? Some kind of sorcerer?"

"I don't think so. I think . . . he is simply unlucky." Bel shrugged.

A smile feathered across Cal's face. That pretty much summed up the entirety of his existence.

Unlucky.

Tracking a magical creature came with its own set of hazards.

A raven perched high in a lodgepole pine, scanning the forest of Yellowstone. Cold dew had condensed on its wings as it waited for sun to illuminate the path before it. In the gold of morning, a serpentine track could be seen in the grass below, a trail of yellowed grass that switched back and forth, heading inexorably west.

The bird cawed softly.

Another bird came to join it, then another. The birds perched on the scruffy pine tree, dozens of them, flocking from miles distant to gossip about what they'd seen. They swarmed the tree, bouncing from branch to branch, as if waiting. Black eyes had gone into the sky and seen their quarry, reporting back in a flurry of feathers.

At the edge of the woods, Gabe squinted into the daylight of the field, shading his eyes from the sun with one hand. His other sleeve hung empty, and his chest and right cheek appeared deeply sunken. Behind him ranged six of the other Hanged Men. They, too, were missing limbs and chunks of flesh. They limped slowly, their clothes hanging at odd angles, like scarecrows after a harsh rain.

Gabe looked up at the tree and nodded. Birds slipped from the branches and slammed into him and the other Hanged Men like black hail, feathers melding into flesh and flannel. He felt the totality of what the birds had seen, felt their light bones meshing with his own. Above, the birds were all gone, save one confused mourning dove who took wing, warbling in terror.

He took a deep breath from whole lungs, flexing his right hand. Glancing back at the rest of his men, he saw that their silhouettes were now complete. Human-looking. Gabe had taken the most passably human of the lot on this mission, hoping to avoid detection from any hikers or passersby. There were far too many people in the park, clogging up the roads and huffing along the trails like winded buffalo. The ranch hands had been successful in avoiding them so far.

They walked through Pelican Valley, along the edge of Raven Creek. It was a place where broad sweeps of grasslands met evergreen forest and swept up to foothills of mountains. Autumn's breath had been felt here——the once-green grass was now golden and brittle, and grazing buffalo were growing thicker, shaggier coats. Pronghorn had begun to move to gentler climes, and the elk were in rutting season, trumpeting to challengers. A grizzly bear crossed the creek with two cubs, slow and sluggish and not seeming to pay the Hanged Men much mind. The lowland had split in a few places, and steam hissed from the cracks in the earth. Gabe had felt the earth tremor here, and the land struck him as unsettled, simmering.

The Hanged Men looked very small in comparison to this vast land. But they had weapons. A knife was holstered in Gabe's belt, a rifle slung over his shoulder. The others held guns beneath their jackets, waiting for the order from him.

He jerked his chin silently at the path in the grassland. *This way.*

The Hanged Men waded into the sun-dappled grass. Gabe narrowed his eyes. He heard no tick of insects or scurry of startled rodents. They were close.

Hearing a sizzling sound, he glanced down. His pant leg had brushed against a few blades of the desiccated grass. The acid had begun chewing into the denim, creeping through the fibers like a cigarette smoldering in a couch. He could feel a stinging where it had soaked into his flesh, like he'd waded into a nest of yellow jackets. This magic was powerful enough to hurt them. The basilisk was close. Very close.

He shrugged the rifle strap off his shoulder and stared through the scope of the rifle at the land before him. The tassels of the grasses moved, pushed by the wind in waves. Gabe squinted at the grass. Some of it moved against the rill of the breeze, moving forward . . .

He gestured to the others. Gun barrels swept the range, sunlight glittering on metal. He disliked this spot in the field. It felt open. Too open.

Gabe's finger twitched on the trigger.

A hissing churn of scales and fangs rose up from the grass. In that instant, he saw his adversary for what it really was, in all its magnificence.

A basilisk. Dark green scales covered a thirty-foot-long body, easily as thick around as a tree trunk. Yellow eyes glared down at him as it reared up, exposing re-curved fangs in a leer, forked tongue flashing between its teeth and hissing. At the crest of its head, scales rose in a crown-like pattern over a plume of yellow feathers, lifting like the hood of a cobra.

Glorious. Likely, this was the only creature like it left in the world, the last dragon. It was said to be born of the blood of the Gorgon Medusa. If it were any other creature, he would have let it be, admiring it from a distance. But he needed this creature, needed its blood for the Lunaria. Not from the left-hand side—that was poison, a gift from the venomous Gorgons. But the right—that was the blood that granted eternal life.

He remembered this from Lascaris's time. The basilisk had been awake then, until Lascaris had put it to sleep. It was now awake— awake and wrathful.

Gabe fired.

The basilisk jerked left with impossible speed as bullets pinged into the grass. A stream of venom spewed from its mouth, like water from a garden hose. Gabe reflexively threw his arm over his face, but he could feel the poison hissing into his hat, his clothes, even eating away at the stock of his gun.

The poison chewed into his skin, fizzling into muscle. He growled and tried to aim his gun, but his trigger finger dissolved against the steel. Around him, he could hear the howls of the Hanged Men, melting like witches in the basilisk's venom.

He made a choice, then, between their unlife and death—to retreat.

Feathers exploded under his shirt, and he poured what remained of his flesh and consciousness into the bodies of ravens. The ravens charged upward into the sky, screaming, to be joined by the birds of the other Hanged Men. Broken feathers drifted down as the birds merged into a retreating flock of ravens, leaving behind empty clothing and melting guns.

Beneath the seething grass, the basilisk hissed as it sank back down to the earth.

Pink morning light streamed through the nursing home window, making a square of perfect sunshine in Joseph Dee's room. Petra sat in a chair beside her father's wheelchair, trying to follow his gaze out the window. She always wondered what he was looking at. The window gave a fantastic view of the Dumpster and the parking lot, but it always seemed that he was looking beyond that, at something she couldn't see. She stared at the Dumpster, but could see nothing more in the open flap than a discarded toilet chair and a bouquet of dead flowers. They might have been the blue monkshood flowers that she'd gathered behind her trailer for her dad last week; she couldn't be sure.

She turned her attention back to her father. He sat in his wheelchair exactly as the nursing home aides had arranged him, wearing a clean, lemon yellow polo shirt and with a blanket over his lap. His buzzed-off grey hair was still damp from a fresh shampooing. He smelled like soap and minty toothpaste. But he just wasn't in there—his hazel eyes were too far distant.

That didn't stop Petra from trying. She turned over his weathered hand in his lap. It was pliable as a sleeping child's. She placed the gold pendant he'd given her as a girl in it.

"Do you remember the day you gave that to me, Dad?" Her fingers traced the design—a lion devouring the sun. "You'd just come back from a trip to Italy, visiting the Domus Galileana and the Città della Scienza. That was when you were a chemistry professor, remember? You were working on some paper on the history of science—that was what Mom said. You sent wonderful postcards of Milan and Naples."

His vacant gaze hovered over the necklace. The chain trickled between his fingers like water.

She continued. "It was summer, and nearly my birthday when you came back. You'd said on the phone that you had brought back something special for me. I was thinking about what it could be . . . I think I'd decided that it had to be a rock of some kind for my collection. You were always bringing me stones. Like that piece of meteorite you found in the woods in Ohio? That was something else.

"So I was thinking that perhaps you were bringing me a pretty piece of quartz crystal or maybe a stone from one of the monuments over there. I wouldn't put it past you to steal a piece of the Tower of Pisa for me." She smiled.

"But you came back with boxes and boxes of books. And this." Her gaze lingered on the stylized pendant. "You said that it was a lion for me, since my birthday is in August. I wanted to name him 'Sol,' after our cat. Remember him? The orange tom?

"Anyway. Mom blew up. At both the pendant and the books. She said that the pendant was too extravagant for a little girl, and she put it away. 'For later.' I finally got it as a college graduation present. But you were long gone by then." She looked away.

"And the books . . . I never understood why she was

upset about that. You always had books. Tons and tons of them. But those books were different. They weren't new. They smelled like mildew, and their old spines were falling apart. I thought that was why Mom didn't like them . . . well, that and they came infested with silverfish. Mom threw a fit about that. You spent a lot of time with them, even when she insisted that they had to go live in the garage. I remember you sitting out there in a lawn chair with the garage door open, squinting at those disintegrating pages and taking notes. After you left, Mom threw them all out in the garbage."

Petra leaned forward, watching his face carefully for any sign of a reaction. "Those books . . . they were about alchemy, weren't they? And when you left . . . you were looking for a secret. Something that would stop the Alzheimer's you knew you had. You came here, and you met an alchemist. Stroud. He said he knew you."

Her dad ran his thumb over the surface of the pendant.

Encouraged, Petra plunged onward. "And this pendant . . . it's an alchemical symbol. The green lion devouring the sun. I looked it up. It has something to do with vitriol devouring matter, purifying it, and leaving gold behind."

She dug into her pocket. "And I found another symbol. Well, Sig found it. But I know that it has to do with alchemy. It can find magic."

She gently removed the pendant and placed the Venificus Locus in his hand, on top of the pendant.

Her father stared at it. His face twisted in an expression of horror.

And he dropped the compass as if it were hot.

It fell to the ground with a clatter, and the pendant rolled away.

"Dad, what is it?" She reached for him. He'd closed his hand into a fist and was shaking. She hugged him, running her fingers over his stubbly scalp.

She bent down to pick up the Locus, to hide it from his view, when her cell phone rang in her hip pocket.

"Hello?" she answered, stuffing the compass into her side pocket.

"Ms. Dee?"

"Yes?"

"This is Dr. Burnard from Park Community Hospital."

"How's Cal?" She sat back down. She'd intended to drive up to the university later today to see how he was doing.

The doctor paused. "There was an incident last night."

Petra squeezed her eyes shut, steeling herself for the news that Cal had died in the night. "Is he . . . ?" She couldn't bring herself to say *dead*.

"En route to the medical airlift, he awoke. He got in an . . . altercation with the staff. I'm not clear on the details." Petra thought she could hear the doctor grinding her teeth over the phone. "But he escaped our custody."

"Escaped?" she echoed. "Why didn't you notify me last night?"

"Our insurance company felt making this known was a liability."

"Great."

"I was hoping that perhaps you'd seen him, that he'd come back to you. He's in serious shape and needs medical treatment, or he's going to die."

Petra leaned forward and rubbed her temple. "No. But I'll start looking for him."

It took much longer to return home than it usually did.

The ravens were injured; they had to stop frequently to rest, shedding feathers as they flew. The birds hopped agitatedly on power lines and tree limbs, grumbling and snapping at each other. Wing feathers and tail feathers were missing, and more than one raven had been partially bleached by the venom, looking like jackdaws as they flew.

They just had to get home, home to the Lunaria.

It was late afternoon before they arrived at the Rutherford Ranch, limping and broken in an opposing wind. The birds made it as far as the barn, where a stiff gust smacked the whole flock of them broadside into the side of the building. They collapsed into black puddles, shadows heaping on themselves, until they could form the heaving shapes of men again. Gabe was missing a leg and half an arm, and the others were no better off. One of the men did not have enough substance left to reform—there were only three birds, rushing against each other as if they expected that they'd melt into a man-shape again. But nothing happened, nothing kept happening, and they were determined to smash themselves to pieces.

A pang in his chest, Gabe carefully picked up those panting birds and placed them in a crate. He'd haul them back to the Lunaria, to the tree. He remembered that man dimly—he was one of the first ones, one of the ones who could pass as human and who could still talk. As if reminding him, one of the ravens began to shout in a hoarse voice:

"Snake! Snake! Snake!"

Feeling the weight of failure upon him, Gabe tried to comfort the hysterical bird by stroking the back of its head. It nipped at him.

"Where have you boys been?"

Gabe turned to see his boss, Sal Rutherford, grinding up to the barn in a golf cart. Rock crunched under the cart's rubber wheels as Sal pulled up beside the edge of the gravel drive. Sal was not in good shape—to Gabe's eye, an eye that had seen Sal since he was a child, the middle-aged cattle baron looked like an old man. His face was swollen and his eyes sallow. He was weak enough now that he could only get around by golf cart or wheelchair. He'd been undergoing chemotherapy for his liver cancer, but Gabe could smell death on him already.

Being weak made him three times as mean. He glared at Gabe, his protruding lower lip demanding an answer.

Gabe lifted his chin, summoning as much dignity as he could muster with one leg, one arm, and a crate of hysterical crows. "We went out. We lost Carver."

"Lost? Where?"

"At the park."

"You boys aren't the type to be going on a leisurely stroll. And there ain't a helluva lot that would cause one of you to get lost or hurt . . ." Sal reached into the box and wrapped his hand around the neck of one of Carver's ravens.

"Snake! Snake! Snake!" its verbal fellow screamed.

Rutherford's eyes narrowed as the bird flailed. "You know what I think? I think you boys were on a mission."

Gabe set the box down clumsily and tried to reach for the bird. Sal put the golf cart into reverse six feet and watched Gabe hop. He shook the bird, whose tongue began to protrude beyond its beak.

"I think . . ." he continued. "That you boys heard the rumor of that damn snake they're talking about on television. And I think that snake got the better of you."

Gabe made another grab for the bird. "And. So?"

"What do you want that snake for?"

Gabe snarled at him. "For you. It can heal you." It was a lie, but Sal was in a desperate place. The rancher had been receiving a steady stream of packages containing crystals, candles, and herbs from dubious Internet suppliers, all promising to heal him. No local shaman would see him, so he sent away for a faith healer from the East Coast. The healer had stormed out of Sal's house, waving his Bible and condemning the rancher to hell.

"Oh, yeah?" Sal lost his concentration. Gabe hopped over to the bird and snatched it away, tucking the exhausted raven into the box on the ground.

Sal began to drum his fingers on the steering wheel. "Is that snake one of Lascaris's experiments? Like you? Is that how it could hurt you?"

Gabe felt less chatty now that the bird was back in his possession. It was true—the Hanged Men were mostly invulnerable to injury—to bullets, to knives, to trauma. To everything but wood. The snake had been different. The snake had been magic. "Maybe. I don't know for certain."

Sal rolled forward. He shoved his cane into Gabe's stomach. "You get that snake for me. If it's got what I need, you get it."

Gabe's mouth twisted. "Yes, Boss."

Satisfied, Sal began to retreat back up the drive with his golf cart. The evil glint in his eye made Gabe certain that Sal would have them do whatever it took to get the basilisk.

"Snake!" insisted the raven.

And Gabe would do his damnedest to save the Lunaria.

More of the Hanged Men trickled in from the

field to help the wounded to the tree. Carver's ravens settled down, perhaps lulled by the gentler motion of being carried by a man with two legs. With help, Gabe climbed into the back of a pickup truck with the other wounded. The truck bounced over ruts and rills in the land, toward the Lunaria.

The Lunaria's brown leaves rattled like rain on tin overhead. Gabe and his men limped down out of the truck, and one of them lifted up the trapdoor at the base of the tree.

With a sigh, he lowered himself into the darkness of the chamber below. Sensing he was injured, the roots of the tree lifted up to help him down. The earthen cellar beneath the tree was lit with dim sunshine twisting through the roots of the tree. In an earlier era, Gabe could have sworn that it burned brighter, almost like the light of day. But now, only a faint, soothing glow emanated from the Lunaria.

Carver's ravens were released. They flitted around the chamber like bats before roosting in the warm roots.

The Lunaria's roots reached down for Gabe, pulling him into its tangled underground nest. Gabe shut his eyes, feeling the energy buzzing through him, reknitting muscle and bone.

He closed his eyes. He never liked to watch this part, the regeneration.

When he closed his eyes, the darkness became a dream. It became a dream composed of fragments, bits of memory welling up and receding without connecting. He heard a deafening noise, an explosion, the one at the Garden that had nearly destroyed him. He saw the face of the woman he'd seen at the hospital. He saw her holding a gun on him. Gabe was afraid of very little in his unlife, but he was afraid of her. Something about her spelled certain death to him, more than Sal or the basilisk or the dying tree. He'd sent a raven to spy on her periodically, to figure out what she was about. It perched in the windows of the Compostela, followed her beat-up truck, even peered at her as she slept through the window of the silver trailer she called home. But the raven had come up with little that was remarkable—she slept and woke and worked and socialized at the nearby reservation. There was no suggestion of magic and mystery about her, even when she sat at the Eye of the World with her friends. She had all the magic of a two-dollar fortune teller.

But he could not escape the weight of those hazel eyes staring over that gun at him.

In his sleep, he shuddered.

He knew that she would be the death of him.

CHAPTER SIX

HAUNTED

All of Cal's old haunts were empty.

Petra drove home, hoping to find Cal peacefully passed out on her doorstep, cuddled around a bottle of vodka, but had no such luck.

Her next thought was to return to the hospital, where he'd last been seen. Maybe he was lurking in the vicinity, or maybe he'd said something cryptic that she could decipher. Maybe someone else had come to visit him, someone she could track down. It seemed like her best bet.

She chewed on Cal's disappearance on the drive over, her gaze lingering on each abandoned trash bag and roadkill, hoping that she wouldn't see Cal dead by the side of the road. She was shocked that he'd found the strength to get out of that isolation tent and make it to the men's room, much less escape from the premises. He looked like he was on death's doorstep. But Stroud had looked like that, too, more than once. Something about the mercury had saved him. It was weird magic, and she didn't understand it.

She had clearly fucked up, taking him to the hospital. Maybe she should have taken him to Frankie, instead. But she had to find Cal, had to figure out what was happening to him, before the kid died.

The hospital parking lot had emptied out from the previous night. There were no signs of the news crew—maybe they'd been booted off the property. She parked in the middle of the parking lot and watched for a moment. No cops.

"Hey, bud," she said to Sig. "Do you wanna go for a walk?"

Sig perked right up, grinning. He tried to scramble over her to get to the door. Petra reached under the seat for a leash and had clipped it to his collar before he noticed what she'd done.

And when he did . . . there was such a look of desolation and abject betrayal on his face. It was as if she'd murdered his last puppy.

"Jeez, Sig. It's a disguise, okay? Pretend you're a working dog."

He stared at her morosely, one gold ear flipped over, his eyebrows twitching in bewilderment.

"C'mon. Humor me."

She popped the door open. He refused to budge from her lap. She picked him up and placed him on the blacktop, where he remained, like a mortally depressed dog with no will to live. She turned to close the door when he took off, ripping the leash from her hand.

"Sig!" she shouted. *That little shit.*

He tore across the parking lot for all he was worth, the blue pennant of the leash flying behind him.

Panic rose in her throat. What if he'd finally had enough of her human bullshit, the rules about where and where not to pee, the baths, shots, and flea dips . . . and he was running away? What if he did and got hit by a car? What if he made it to the wilderness and got snagged on a tree by the leash and hanged himself? What if . . .

"Sig!" she yelled, running after him. She'd throw herself under a bus for him. If something happened to him, she'd never forgive herself.

Sig slowed, but didn't bother to turn around and make eye contact with Petra. He sprinted to the far end of the lot, stopped before a Humvee parked on its own, and circled it with his leash dragging the ground. The Humvee was painted in camo with U.S. government plates—clearly, it wasn't a civilian vehicle. It seemed like it had been parked there since sometime last night, when the lot had been full, and no one had been back out to move it. Maybe it was a coincidence—a case of illness that struck a soldier in an otherwise-uneventful supply convoy through the state. But there was something about it that bugged her. She hadn't noticed it when she had arrived last night with Cal.

She caught up with Sig, snagged the end of the leash, and reeled him in. She threw her arms around him.

"You scared me," she said into his fur.

But she noticed that his ruff was raised, and there was an inaudible growl rumbling under her hands, deep in his chest. He was staring at the Humvee with his upper lip twitching, as if he was tempted to go after one of the tires.

"It's okay." She stroked his forehead, stood, and tightened her grip on his leash.

There was no one in the Humvee. She stepped up on tiptoes to peer in the driver's side door. Nothing out of the ordinary: just a couple of coffee cups and a muddy, utilitarian interior.

When she glanced in the back, she froze. There was a stretcher behind the front seat, from which Velcro restraints dangled. Perhaps not unusual, if the vehicle was driven by a medic, if they had brought someone here for an emergency. But there was a blanket folded in a neat square on the backboard and an oxygen tent perched above it, so crisp that the fold marks were still in the plastic. They hadn't transported someone here;

they were going to pick someone up last night. And they still didn't have that person.

Cal. What if the person they were after was Cal?

Petra stepped back and tugged Sig away. She scanned the parking lot. No one had seen her. Her heart thumped in her chest. What if she wasn't being insanely paranoid . . . what if the hospital had freaked and called not the university, but someone up the food chain in the government, who would be thrilled to get ahold of a boy who was bleeding mercury? The idea of that as a bioweapon was chilling.

Damn it. She should have thought of that last night. She had majorly fucked up. Cal had trusted her, and she might have betrayed his trust in a big way.

"Shit." She pulled Sig away, back toward the hospital.

The entrance looked the same as last night, but she did notice that now there was a guard posted at the door, checking IDs. And there was a portable metal detector set up with two more guys working it. Nice. She emptied her pockets of change and got past on the third try, when it was determined that the studs on the back pockets of her jeans were giving the machine fits. Nothing more exciting than having a guard who looked like he was fifteen pass a wand over her backside a dozen times. He blushed furiously when he patted her down. Sig slunk through the process with his head and tail down, expressing displeasure with every fiber of his being.

The young security guard held his hand up. "No pets, ma'am."

"He's a search dog," Petra insisted. "My friend disappeared from the hospital last night. My dog might be able to figure out which way he went." She said it loudly enough for others in the emergency room to hear. Whispers began to circulate: " . . . *missing patient?*" "*How does someone disappear from the hospital?*"

Sig looked around with interest, inserting his rear foot into his ear in a very professional, search-dog sort of way. He then twisted around to look at his claws, as if he'd mined something very interesting that merited further scrutiny.

The security guard backed down. "He disappeared from the back parking lot, at the helipad." He grabbed his keys and led her outside, around to the back of the hospital. Fairly vibrating with the idea of doing something official, he pointed to large circle painted in orange on the asphalt near the parking lot.

"Is that where the helicopter landed?"

"Yeah. He got loose before they could shovel him in. Probably a good thing that he went apeshit while they were still on the ground. The guys on duty said that he was dripping with mercury and strong the way a guy can be when he's hopped up on meth."

Petra surveyed the area. The asphalt was wet, as if it had been thoroughly decontaminated. If there was any hope of getting Cal's scent, it was dwindling quickly.

She knelt before Sig. "Cal. The kid you hate. He

smells like patchouli and stale energy drinks. Remember him?"

Sig turned his head away and wrinkled his nose. Petra was pretty sure that Sig remembered what Cal smelled like. "Can you find him?"

Sig glanced back over his shoulder.

"Please? For a deli sandwich with salami on top?"

Sig's ears perked up. That got his attention. He took two steps away across the asphalt and lifted his nose.

"Looks like he's got a scent," the security guard observed.

"Or else he's pranking me," Petra muttered under her breath.

Sig took off through the parking lot, snooting around tires and pissing on a fair number of expensive cars. Petra scrambled to keep up, getting more excited as Sig bounced along. Hopefully, Cal was sleeping off his bad trip and would be easily found within a mile or two. Hopefully.

Sig led her away from the parking lot, down a shallow drainage ditch. He circled that twice, peering in. It was empty. He kept going, into some scrub forest, his nose pressed to the ground. He continued for a half mile, crossing back and forth through the scrub. Petra followed him a respectful distance behind, watching where his tail flickered above the weeds. For an instant, he seemed to plunge into the brush, giving an excited yip.

Her heart in her mouth, she raced to catch up to him.

But the coyote had only found an empty fast food bag. His head was deeply installed in the bottom as he made snorkeling noises.

"Some search dog," the security guard said.

"Mmm yeah," Petra agreed. "I think he needs some remedial training. Can I talk to Cal's doctor? It was Dr. Burnard."

"Let me check." He keyed his radio to ask if Dr. Burnard was still on duty. To Petra's disappointment, she wasn't.

"Did any of Cal's friends drop by last night?" Petra asked casually, as they walked back to the lot.

"I don't know, ma'am. I wasn't there. But we've sure gotten a whole bunch of calls about him—from the county sheriff's office, and even some from the military police. Is he AWOL or something?"

Awesome. "I don't think he joined up. But anything's possible," she said mildly. She sure didn't want to get on those guys' radar.

She thanked the guard and stuffed Sig into the truck, gnawing on her lip. Mike used to be an MP with the Army. Maybe he'd have some advice. She fished her cell phone out of the glove box to give him a ring.

"Hello?" It sounded like chaos in the background behind him—children shrieking.

"Hey, Mike. It's Petra. Is this, uh, a bad time? Are you roasting kids on a spit or something?"

An aggrieved sigh crackled over the receiver. "I seem to be chaperoning a kids' party, as the parents are nowhere to be found. My partner and I flipped a coin to see who had to find the parents and who got to stay and babysit the ankle biters." A mighty splash sounded, and Mike barked at someone to "put that down, already, and get away from the water! That is *not* a pool noodle!"

Petra winced. "Sorry. You sound like you've got your hands full."

"I've got time to talk to anyone who's capable of carrying on an adult conversation. What's up?"

"Cal showed up on my doorstep last night, in a bad way. Looked like he'd been drenched in mercury. I took him to the hospital, but he ran away."

"Well . . . that sucks."

"It does. And I'm out looking for him. But something curious happened . . . the military police are looking for him, too. And I have no idea why." It was a half-truth. Mostly.

"Huh." Petra could hear him rubbing his stubble. "Do you think he ran afoul of anybody in the nearby military installations?"

"Don't know. All I know is that he was leaking mercury like it was blood."

"Maybe he got into some kind of a hazmat situation. Let me do some checking around through some back channels and see if I can find anything out."

"Thanks. I appreciate it."

"No worries. I hope the kid isn't in bad trouble, but—*Hey!*" he shouted. "*Get out from under there!*"

"Good luck, Mike," she said as the phone went dead.

To be certain that Cal was well and truly gone, she pulled a pocketknife and the Locus out of the glove box. The Locus had been able to detect Stroud when he was alive. And Cal seemed to have his magic now, whether he wanted it or not. She didn't yet have a good sense of the range of the device . . . that was something she would have wanted to ask Gabe about.

A lump rose in her throat. She would *not* think of Gabe. Gabe didn't need her. Cal did.

She jabbed one of her left fingers with her pocket-knife and dripped some blood in the Locus. The red sank into the metal, without hesitation. She drove around the parking lot and access roads with it in her lap, but there was no change. Clearly, Cal was long gone.

Her next thought was to head over to the Garden, Cal's old home.

"I know that it's just a heap of rubble now," she told Sig on the way over. "But maybe he went back some-place familiar?"

In the passenger's seat of the Bronco, Sig snorted. He'd never been a big fan of Cal, and rested his head in the open window to register his displeasure at wasting time that he could be spending sleeping.

"I know that you don't like the kid. But he *is* just a kid. Cut him some slack."

Sig huffed. But at least he was along for the ride. There was something to be said for that kind of reli-ability in a crime-fighting partner.

The Garden was three hairpin turns off a long, de-serted dirt road. What had once been a two-story white farmhouse was now a charred, rotting heap, punctu-

ated by weeds. The remains of the collapsed chimney
were providing a nesting space for rats, it seemed, and
foot-tall sapling trees were growing up along the foun-
dations. It seemed like nature was hell bent on reclaim-
ing this land from Stroud, as if it could wipe away the
memory of his existence.

Sig trotted up to the trees and began to pee on
them.

Petra waded into the weeds. "Cal?" she called. She
rested one hand on her gun belt. The metal was still
cold to the touch from being stuffed under the seat
of the Bronco. She had hoped that Stroud's followers
had all moved on to greener pastures or wound up in
prison after the DEA raided the place, but she wasn't
sure. Maybe someone was still here. Maybe not. And it
would be a toss-up if they meant her any harm.

The sunlight in this place had always seemed thin
to her. Even in the bright light of day, it trickled sallow
and anemic through the overgrowth. Petra picked her
way around a shattered plastic lawn chair, over bits of
barbed wire, mattress springs, and old tires.

She paused before the shed in which Stroud had held
her prisoner. The door had been taken off its hinges—
perhaps that had been the DEA's doing. When she
peered inside, she saw nothing but broken plastic pots
and busted lawn mowers.

Something moved in the grass, chortling. Sig
pressed his ears forward.

"Cal?" She fumbled with her gun, sucking in her
breath.

But it was only a quail. Sig took off after it like a shot, bounding into the grass.

"Jesus, Sig." She holstered the gun and reached for the Venificus Locus.

She sat down on an upturned bucket. Fishing her pocketknife out of her pants pocket, she stabbed her barely-clotted finger, summoning a nice glob of blood to sacrifice to the Locus. The blood settled into the track and she swished it around, willing it to do something. She stared as the liquid soaked into the compass with a nearly audible slurping sound. The compass wasn't giving anything up.

She whistled for Sig, who came bounding back with his tongue covered in feathers.

"Did you eat that bird?"

Sig cocked his head, as if to say: *Duh.*

"Did you?" she demanded.

One ear flopped over, and he went to go drink out of an abandoned tire that was likely chock-full of wriggling mosquito larvae.

"Get in the car."

Petra called the county jail, with no luck. The county deputies had picked up some minors for underage drinking overnight, but none of them fit Cal's description. The only other arrest had been a sixty-eight-year-old man who was charged with public indecency and the theft of a lawn mower with a subsequent DUI charge involving the lawn mower. After confirming that the culprit was not Frankie, Petra didn't want any more details.

The only other place she could think of to look was the Compostela. Cal had hung around there when Stroud was alive. Perhaps he knew some of the employees. Petra headed back into town, checking her watch to confirm that it was finally open.

Petra parked in front of the bar on the main street of Temperance, told Sig to stay in the truck, and headed inside. The stained glass played bright golden colors on the floor and walls in the setting sunlight. Dust motes were suspended in the air, giving the impression of time suspended in amber.

The bar wasn't in good shape. Long scratches had been dug into the wood floor. Two tables and several chairs were missing from the main floor, stacked in pieces in the corner. A couple of the lights over the bar had been broken.

Petra scanned the booths and headed for the back, to the bar in the apse. A blond man dressed in black was wiping down the counter, not making eye contact.

Petra slid onto a barstool. "Looks like the bar's seen some action?"

The man flicked her a glance with pale blue eyes and kept wiping the epoxied heart of what had once been a giant tree. "Drink and women and gambling. Always leads to fighting. What would you like to drink?"

"I'm wondering if you've seen Cal lately."

The bartender stopped wiping for a moment. "Cal?"

"Yeah. About five-nine, black hair, silver ankh earring. He used to hang out here a lot."

The bartender's mouth twisted. "Ah. That Cal."

"Have you seen him?"

"He was here last night. He wasn't looking too hot when he was here. Little pale, if you know what I mean."

"Was he in the fight?" Her gaze scraped the ruined tin star light dangling above them from one wire.

"That boy's not much of a fighter."

"Do you know Cal well?"

"Well enough."

"Did he say where he was going?" she persisted. She knew that the bartender knew more than he was saying, but the truth had to be dragged out of him.

"No. There was one hell of a fight, and he disappeared afterward with some women on bikes. Haven't seen him."

"Which women?"

"Dunno. Thirteen of 'em, out-of-towners, in a rush to cause trouble." The bartender shrugged.

Petra didn't have anything to lose by fishing. Even with a club. "Cal worked for Stroud. Did you?" Stroud used to own the Compostela. She had no idea who it belonged to, now.

A ghost of a smile flickered across the bartender's lips. "I work for myself. And Stroud is no longer in business, is he?"

"Guess not."

"Yeah. Rumor has it that he got to you and you got to him."

Petra pursed her lips. Maybe this was the way it went— quid pro quo. "Pretty much. Not that I had much to say about it, after Rutherford's men and the DEA showed up."

The bartender reached for a glass, poured a beer from the tap, and pushed it across the slick bar to her.

He fixed her with his cold gaze. "Want some advice?"

Petra's mouth twisted up. "Sure."

"That kid is trouble. It follows him, and it's not gonna let go. Best you leave him alone before it gets ahold of you, too."

Petra looked down at the growth rings of the bar, tracing one with her thumb. "Thanks. For that and the beer." She sure wasn't gonna follow that advice, but it confirmed her gut suspicions about Cal being a perpetual damsel in distress.

The bartender nodded and moved away. Petra gazed at the back of his black shirt. She wasn't sure what to make of him. He wasn't helpful, but didn't seem actively harmful. She'd met very few truly neutral people in her travels. Maybe he was one of them.

A man at the far end of the bar hiccuped and elbowed his bottle of beer over. The bartender's hand flashed out and caught the bottle, setting it upright without the drunk man noticing.

Maybe he was something else.

Petra squinted at the bartender, as if he suddenly could become clear, but he turned his attention to wiping glasses.

She lifted the beer to her lips. She'd never been much of a drinker, and definitely not a fan of beer, but this wasn't bad. It was cidery and sweet. Lightweight. Maybe the bartender saw more than she thought.

"Petra."

She turned at the mention of her name and saw a man in a booth beckoning at her. Frankie. He was half-sprawled in a dark corner, his feet draped over the length of one seat. A candle in a red glass holder flickered dimly at him.

Petra collected her beer, left some money on the bar, and slid into the seat opposite him. "Hey, Frankie. What are you doing here?" She didn't really need to ask. She could smell the booze on him.

Frankie shrugged. "Gotta get out sometime. See the sights. Get some wings." He wiped his fingers on a stack of soiled paper napkins and reached for a chicken wing in a basket. "Have some."

Petra picked around the basket for a wing that hadn't been gnawed. "Thanks." She took a bite and scalded her tongue.

"Jesus, Frankie, that's hot!" She dropped the wing and reached for her beer, drowning the spice in half a glass of cider ale.

Frankie chortled and picked his teeth with a bone. "Good stuff, ain't it? Ghost peppers."

Petra wiped tears away with the back of her hand. "How is it legal to sell that?"

Frankie shrugged. "You gotta toughen up, girl."

"So I'm told." Regaining her composure, Petra wiped the sauce from her hands. "Frankie, if you were trying to find someone, how would you do it?"

"Is this about your dad?"

"Not this time. I'm looking for a teenage boy. In a

lot of trouble. He ran away from the hospital, and I think he's hurt, real bad . . . got into some of that stuff Stroud was into."

Frankie nodded, sucking the sauce from one of the infernal chicken wings. "Ask the chicken."

"What?"

"I'd ask the chicken." Frankie's fingers dipped into the basket of wings, pulling out the bones. He stared at the bits of gristle and fat, sucking pieces from the ends until the bones were as clean as toothpicks. He selected about a dozen of them, seemingly at random, tossing them in the center of the red and white checkered plastic tablecloth.

"Who's the Chicken?" Petra envisioned a tall scrawny guy with a line to the underworld of Temperance. "Is that a prison name or something?" It sure wasn't intimidating, if it was.

Frankie looked at her as if she was plain stupid, and shook his head. He opened the salt shaker and carefully tapped out a circle of salt around the bones on the printed tablecloth.

"Give me your hands."

Petra opened her hands, palms up, and extended them across the table. Frankie picked up the pile of greasy chicken bones and dropped them in her hands.

Petra grimaced. "Ew, Frankie." She turned to find a trash can.

Frankie's sticky fingers landed on her wrists, stilling her. "Think about the boy."

She sighed. She thought about Cal: awkward,

sneaky . . . but still a human being underneath it all. She thought of the mercury leaking from his eyes, knowing that he was going to die if she didn't find him. Splinters of bones dug into her palms.

"Now, throw them." Frankie's slender fingers traced the salt circle on the table.

Petra opened her hands, eager to be rid of the sticky mess. The bones bounced on the vinyl tablecloth. Most of them landed inside the circle, a few outside. They skewed in a completely random pattern. One helluva mess.

Frankie leaned over the table with his hands in his lap, rocking back and forth. His eyes picked out each bone. His lips worked over words, but no sound came out.

Petra leaned in. "What are you doing?"

"Reading the bones. Shut up."

She sat back. She picked up her beer, grimacing at the bone floating on top. She made to fish it out, but Frankie slapped her hand. She put the glass back on the table.

"Hmpf," he said, scanning the table.

He reached for the basket the wings had come in and swept the salt and bones into the wax paper lining, as if they were trash.

"Well?" Petra demanded.

Frankie looked at her, his eyes sorrowful before he spoke: "It's out of your hands. The kid is gone."

CHAPTER SEVEN

THE NEST

In the embrace of the tree, Gabe dreamed.

He dreamed of the basilisk, of the waves it made in the grass as it moved. He dreamed that he was wading in those grasses with a spear, trying to stab it like a fish in shallow water. But he couldn't walk; his feet had dissolved beneath him. He fell to the grass, unable to stand.

In the sunshine, a shadow stood above him. He expected it to belong to the basilisk, come to devour him. He reached for the knife at his belt.

But it wasn't the snake. It was the woman from

the hospital. She stood over him, freckled face dark in shadow, bits of dark blond hair spilling over her shoulders. She held a gun in her right hand, slack, aimed to the ground.

"Who are you?" he asked. He wanted to know; she had haunted his dreams for weeks.

She knelt and reached down for him with her left hand. It was an ordinary hand, empty and nonthreatening, with scars on the wrist. She rested it on his chest, and he felt his heart hammering under his shirt.

"I am your undoing. Your dissolution."

Her fingers dug into his skin, beneath it. He howled as she ripped his heart out.

Gold glittered in her fist as she pulled it away, a golden compass.

His eyes snapped open.

Golden half-darkness surrounded him. The roots of the tree curled around him, holding him in a lover's embrace. His hand slapped against his chest for reassurance, his fingers tracing his sternum. He was whole. He wiggled his fingers and toes, and counted ten of each. The Lunaria had been able to restore his body.

But still not undamaged. He probed the raveled edges of his memories. He knew that woman. Somehow. She stood out in his memory, nearly as much as the fuzzy presence of his wife, Jelena. Jelena was long dust. But this woman was alive. Did she know what he was? Was that how she could hurt him? Did she somehow know the secret of the Hanged Men? Was that what the holes in his memory were trying to tell him? She had to be mortal, though—she had scars. They weren't the noose scars that the Hanged Men covered under their collars.

He shook his head. No matter. Puzzles were for another time. He had work to do.

The Lunaria released him reluctantly, as if surrendering something precious to the world. The light surrounding the tree flickered, and Gabe felt its weakness. The roots set him gently on the floor, one curling around the scar ringing his neck.

"I will restore you," he promised as he dressed.

He searched for Carver's ravens. He'd returned them to the Lunaria's embrace, hoping that this small bit of energy would be absorbed and help feed the tree. Restoring Carver from three such small pieces was impossible, but returning him to the tree was the right thing to do . . .

. . . or not. There was no sign of the ravens.

He hunted among the fruit of the Lunaria, the other Hanged Men slumbering in the glow of artificial sunshine. And he spied something strange, a spot where the Lunaria's rhizomes had woven back into themselves, making a nest about the size of a hawk's. Gabe peered inside.

A severed head lay within. Carver's blank face stared back at him, his eyes black and with feathers sticking out of his scalp. Roots dug deep into his neck, curling through his mouth and over his lower lip.

"Carver," Gabe said.

The head's eyes glistened in the light as they moved right and left. Something was in there. Something that could not survive on its own.

Gabe reached inside the nest.

"Snake!" the head shrieked. "Snake!"

Gabe wrapped one hand around the back of the head and the other thumb around Carver's lip. He pulled the head free of the roots, turning it sharply, like plucking a pumpkin from a tough vine. Luminescent blood splashed back on him.

"Snake!"

A fragment of memory came back to him—he saw himself in the roots of the tree, with the woman from his dreams standing before him. She reached inside the tangle of roots for him, and he heard ravens scream.

He stepped backward, the head dangling in his hands. For a moment, he saw something gold and shiny in the fuzzy mess of his memory, but the image faded.

Gabe reverently set the head down on the floor of the chamber.

"I'm sorry," he said to it.

With a deep breath, he lifted his boot and stomped down as hard as he could.

Petra was two hours late for work the next morning.

She'd wanted to get to work at Yellowstone early. For the past couple of weeks, she'd been busily taking mineral samples from the emerging geothermal features in Pelican Valley, and she wanted to keep on schedule. Her position was a contract position, and she was conscious that she could be let go if she failed to perform to expectations. She had no boss on-site, and her performance was measured strictly by her output. But there was no hope of getting a jump start on things today.

She ground her teeth as she joined a long line of cars at the east gate. This time of year, in early fall, lines should have been dwindling from their summer traffic jams, at least half the levels of traffic from August. No such luck. She drained her coffee and groaned about the lack of a ladies' room and the Bronco's lack of air conditioning. Sig morosely hung his head out the Bronco's window, glaring at the campers, pickup trucks, and shiny luxury vehicles. They were trapped in traffic behind a 1970s-era van painted with wizards and dragons. "Steve's Creature Van" was painted in airbrushed script on the back, above a rendering of what she supposed was the Loch Ness Monster, swimming through a green lake of slime with a naked damsel in its jaws.

By the time she'd made it to the Tower Falls Ranger Station, the antifreeze was ticking away under the hood of the Bronco, and Sig had fallen asleep on the seat, belly-up. The parking lot was full, and she had to make three circuits before giving up and parking on a wedge of grass under a tree. She had barely enough room to pop her door open against the tree, and plodded sullenly to the station. Sig followed, vigorously sniffing the vehicles in the parking lot as he went.

Predictably, there was also a line to the ladies' room. Petra sighed and fidgeted until finally ducking into the empty men's room. Feeling rebellious, she took extra time washing her hands and splashing water on her face when she was through. There had never been a ladies' room on the oil rig in her previous job. Plumbing was plumbing.

The door opened. She jumped to see Mike in the doorway, and splashed water on the front of her shirt.

"Uh, hey. Line at the ladies' was . . ." She hooked a thumb at the hallway.

"There's no talking in the men's room," Mike said, frowning sternly. "It's a rule."

"Well, there aren't supposed to be women in the men's room, either."

He lifted his hand. "I should probably cite you. For something. But don't sweat it. You got some folks waiting for you."

She blinked, reaching for the hand dryer. "People?" There was never anyone waiting for her. As a geologist, she worked alone, drilling out samples and clomping through weeds. "Did they find Cal?"

"No word yet on Cal. My sources are being pretty quiet. And I don't like that. Feels too much like secret squirrel business." He frowned, eyes narrowing. "Take that for whatever it's worth."

"Thanks. I really appreciate it. I know that something bad's happened to him. I just want to help, you know?"

"Yeah. I know. Give it some time. I'll keep shaking the tree and see if anything comes loose. And I'll get my local network in gear looking for him. There's an APB out for him, but there's more that will be done for a missing kid if someone behind the blue line raises a big enough stink."

A boy of about nine walked into the men's room. He looked at Mike, then Petra, then backpedaled to double-check the sign on the door.

"I'm, uh, gonna leave now." Petra headed for the door.

"Probably for the best."

Petra walked past the queue to the ladies' room. She got a couple of glowering looks, but a few teenage girls broke free to go to the men's room. She chortled to herself, hoping that Mike had picked a stall instead of a urinal.

She made her way behind the information counter, to the offices in the back of the vintage log structure. It always smelled a bit like dust to her, but that was the nature of the beast. Sig had already beat her there, and was standing glumly beside the watercooler. She filled a cup for him and let him lap from it.

"Ms. Dee?"

She glanced up to see a man in khakis and a polo shirt staring down at her. He was thin and wiry, balding and tan.

"Yes?" She straightened. Sig leaned around her knees to stare at him.

"I'm Phil Gustavson, and this is Meg Howard." He inclined his head to a brunette woman behind him. "We're biologists with the National Park Service."

"Hi." Petra wiped her hand on the side of her pants and offered it to shake. She glanced down at her coyote. "This is Sig."

The woman crouched down to look at Sig, offering her hand to sniff. Sig turned his head away, wary. "Nice coyote. Did you rescue him as a pup?"

"Nah. He just turned up a couple of months ago and wouldn't leave. Don't worry. He's had shots."

"Neat. I've never seen a tame adult that wasn't reared by people."

"He's a good boy." She reached down, her fingers lingering in the soft, golden fur around his ears. "What brings you guys to Yellowstone?"

Phil looked over his shoulder, toward the crowded lobby. "Can we talk in private?"

"Sure." Petra straightened and led them back to the tiny conference room she'd taken over. It was stacked high along the walls with file boxes, and her microscope and gear were spread over half the table. There was enough room remaining to open three folding chairs, and Petra settled in to listen. Sig slid under the table, and Meg closed the door.

"We're here for the same reason that those guys are here." Phil gestured to the people outside.

"What's that?" She decided to be deliberately obtuse.

"The snake." Meg pulled a file folder out of her backpack, and slid it across the table toward Petra.

"The snake from the news?" Petra lifted an eyebrow. They couldn't be serious.

"That snake." Phil crossed his arms over his chest. He didn't look happy.

Petra opened the file folder. It contained stills of the video she'd seen from the newscast, overdrawn with measurements and indicators of scale over color enhancements. "You think this is real?"

"Depends on what you mean by 'real,'" Meg said. She laced her long, callused fingers together. "I'm not buying that it's a dragon or a naga or some other mythological critter. What was that other thing we saw on the Internet, Phil?"

"Some guy thinks he can prove that it's Quetzalcoatl." Phil rolled his eyes.

"Awesome. What do you think it is?"

"Not sure. It doesn't look like anything we've seen before."

Phil interrupted. "We thought it might be something as simple as a dumped anaconda, and worried about it becoming an invasive species, but . . ."

" . . . but then we did some measuring and looked more carefully. We're more concerned that it could be something new. A new species, entirely." Meg leaned forward, and excitement was palpable in her brown eyes.

"Wow." Petra leaned back in her chair. "But, um . . .

did Mike tell you about the campers who were killed? And the people who wound up in the hospital?"

"Yes. And that's why we're talking to you. We got your samples at the federal lab. They generated a lot of discussion."

"Oh?" Her eyebrow quirked up.

"The stuff you sent in was all over the place. Some phospholipase enzymes, neurotoxins. Metalloproteases that cause hemorrhaging. Arsenic trioxide—which is, weirdly enough, an impurity in gold ore. And a ton of acetic acid. Not normal." Meg's eyebrows had crawled nearly up into her hairline.

"We're working on a theory . . . ." Phil steepled his fingers before him, and Petra had the impression of an academic in an office, surrounded with paper, who had just gotten the chance to play in the field for the first time in twenty years. "We're thinking that there might be something about Yellowstone's geology that caused a unique creature to evolve."

"That's kind of, um, *X-Files*." If anyone mentioned aliens, Petra was ready to bolt.

"You saw the scene of the incident with the campers. You know what's normal for Yellowstone's geological hazards, and what's not. We want to look for the creature, and we want you to come with us to consult."

Petra blinked. "Let me get this straight . . . you want to me to help you guys chase a giant snake?"

"Pretty much," Meg admitted. "Yellowstone isn't our bailiwick, and the park rangers have their hands full corralling the amateur monster hunters."

"But think of it," Phil said. "*Serpens Gustavson Howard Dee.*"

Petra made a face. She wasn't much into chasing immortality with scientific names. But the idea . . . the idea of the unknown creature intrigued her. Irresistible curiosity tickled the back of her brain.

"We're mostly concerned with protecting the public." Meg made an immediate ambition course correction. "We need to catch this thing before it hurts anyone else."

Petra looked down at Sig. He rested his head on her foot.

"What do you think, Sig? Do you want to chase monsters?" Her stomach churned. She *should* be looking for Cal. But Mike was on the case. And Frankie said he was gone . . .

Sig's ear flipped over, and his gold eyes regarded her solemnly.

She couldn't forget the body of the little girl at the campsite, killed in her sleep. She blew out her breath. "So. When do we leave?"

"Tomorrow morning. Bright and early."

After getting all the sign-offs she needed to delay her other work, Petra wound her way out of the park to get a jump start on provisioning. She spent another two hours in traffic getting out to the main road, and she took the back roads to Temperance.

The idea of following the snake made her, at turns, queasy and exhilarated. To see something like that in person would be nothing short of amazing. But she'd seen what the snake had done to the campers. Petra had always tried to follow the rules where wild animals were concerned—she stayed the required twenty-five feet away from bison and all the other critters in the park. She didn't leave food in her truck to tempt bears, and she always took her trash with her. With the exception of Sig, she wasn't interested in creating a situation in which personal space needed to be negotiated.

"What do you pack to hunt a giant snake?" she wondered as she drifted through the aisles of Bear's Gas 'n Go, Temperance's gas station and deli. Sig had ditched her back at the deli counter, where Bear was feeding him slices of pepperoni in violation of every health code known to man.

"I dunno," Bear said. "But giant snakes are excellent for business."

"No kidding. How'd you get all this swag, this fast?"

"One-day shipping from the Internet. If you want it bad enough to pay for it, anything can be on your doorstep in a day."

Shelves had been cleared in many places, sold out of toilet paper and potato chips. One of the reels of lottery tickets was even gone. Bear had jumped on the snake bandwagon with both feet—he had a display of primary-color plush snakes parked in the window, plastic writhing pythons perched on an end cap, and snake-shaped pens in a mug at the checkout. Couldn't blame the man for trying to make a buck off the gullible.

"I suggest staying the hell away from it. If it really

exists," he amended, scratching his salt and pepper beard.

"I kinda signed on for an expedition." Thinking of the dead campers, she was beginning to feel twinges of regret.

Bear chortled. "Well, your odds are probably better than those of the rest of the monster hunters. For one, you're sober."

"Yeah." She wasn't going to mention the Venificus Locus. "I was wondering if . . . you might be able to watch Sig for me while I'm gone? No worries if you can't . . ." She could always drop him off at Maria's, but she knew that Sig adored Bear's cooking.

Bear patted Sig's head. "Of course, I'll watch the little guy. But . . . is this that serious?"

She made a face. "Yeah. Unfortunately."

"So what they said on the news is true." His face darkened, and his gaze lingered on the brightly-colored snake paraphernalia.

"And more." Petra crouched down before Sig. "And I don't want this fella to get hurt."

"He can stay with me until you get back. And I'll make sandwiches for you to take with."

Bear disappeared behind the counter, and Petra looked Sig square in the eye.

"You have to stay with Bear for a couple of days, okay? It's not safe." She didn't want to imagine Sig as a mottled corpse—he was the dearest creature on Earth to her. She had to protect him. She'd lost everything:

her father, Des, and Gabe. And now, Cal. She couldn't
bear to lose him, too. She felt her eyes tearing up.

Sig held her gaze for a long, solemn moment. Then,
he leaned forward and licked her nose.

She laughed out loud.

Still, when she left the store with a sack balanced on
her hip, she looked back. Sig stood inside the door with
his paws on the glass, watching her as she put the bag
in the Bronco and climbed inside. She felt like she was
leaving a dog behind at the animal shelter.

He'll be okay, she told herself as she stabbed the key
in the ignition. *He has Bear. And all the lunch meat he can
eat.*

She cranked the engine over and put the truck in
gear. She backed out of the parking spot and into the
street . . .

. . . when the cow bells at the door jangled and a grey
blur launched through the open passenger window.
Sig sprawled across the bench seat, scrambling for pur-
chase in a flurry of fur and toenails.

"Sig!" she shouted.

Bear was puffing across the parking lot. "Sorry! He
opened the door on his own and . . ." Bear rested his
hands on the open window and stared at Sig, who had
settled down on the passenger seat. ". . . I guess he's
going with you."

CHAPTER EIGHT

BAD COMPANY

"**W**here are we going?"

The young man, Cal, sat beside the remains of the fire as the women raked it out. He blinked in the sunshine, radiating confusion about how he got here and what was next, as the bags were being packed, tires checked, and the canteens passed around. Bel didn't bother to tell him that he'd slept for a solid twenty-four hours. Hypnosis did that, sometimes, to her subjects. Bel had been eager to break camp, but she knew that she couldn't rush the process.

"I mean, I am going with you, aren't I?" There was a mixture of hope and dread in his voice.

"Yes," Bel said. "You're coming with us." She said it gently, but she thought that Cal guessed that he really had no choice in it.

"How did . . . how did you do what you did last night?" He rubbed the back of his neck. He had some color and looked mostly human, now. Maybe he had a hypnosis hangover, but it certainly beat what he'd gotten into before.

"I know magic. And you don't." She sat down beside him, cross-legged, with her hands in her lap. "Your reptile brain can control a whole lot more in your body than your autonomic nervous system."

"Yeah. I don't know anything. The guy that this came from . . ." He looked at the palm of his hand, as if scrutinizing it for traces of the element. "He knew it. The Alchemist."

He told her, in halting terms, that he'd been the footman of a drug lord, how he'd come across the mercury when the alchemist had died. She brushed the back of his neck with her hand, and she could feel the mercury still there, but sluggish. It wasn't trying to assert dominance. She'd cowed it into submission last night. She'd have to do it again. He wasn't strong enough to do it himself.

And she wondered about that. The mercury was an intriguing thing, when it leapt out of him to attack her. It seemed as if it almost had its own volition, not simply reflecting Cal's own fear as a self-defense mechanism. It had been in him for some time, had gained traction. The boy's will was weak. His own kundalini energy stayed tightly balled up at the base of his spine, parked in his root chakra like a frightened rodent in a burrow. But perhaps he could be taught to dominate the mercury. Or perhaps she could take it from him and install it in a more worthy vessel. She hadn't yet decided if it was too powerful to waste energy in taming, or if it would be more useful to her wild, in this body or another. The boy could live or he could die, depending, and make a fine sacrifice to the Great Serpent. Time would tell.

" . . . so it was an accident," he said, fidgeting. "Yeah. It sounds nuts."

She shrugged. "No. It doesn't. Trust me, the things I've seen would make this look like a Halloween prank."

"So . . . Are you guys . . . gals . . . a gang or something?"

She laughed. "Not a gang. We are sisters."

His gaze roved over the women, who clearly did not physically resemble each other.

"Spiritual sisters," she said.

"Oh," he said. But she could tell that he didn't really understand.

"We should get going." She stood up, brushing off her pants.

"So . . . where are we going?"

"We are going to find the Great Serpent," she said.

"What's the Great Serpent?" His brow knitted.

"The Great Serpent is the wellspring of power in the world. It's the beginning and the end of time, the source of creativity, rebirth, and protection. She is the Great Mother of Many Names."

He dodged her gaze and picked at a thread on his sleeve. "Um. Like . . . a real snake?"

She laughed. His naïveté was actually quite charming. "Yes. A real snake."

He reluctantly followed her to her bike. She found a helmet for him, and they zinged through the woods. Dust kicked up as they crossed the backcountry for nearly three miles before meeting the road again, to even black pavement that rode much easier for a newbie like Cal.

They stopped around midday for food, at a chuck wagon caravan set up at the base of a mountain, a place for tourists with eyes bigger than their stomachs. Cal fell into his plate as if he hadn't eaten in a week, going back for seconds and thirds.

Tria watched him on his fourth trip back to the chuck line tent, where cast iron pots of stew, potatoes, and beans hung over hot coals. They sat at a creaky picnic table, a breeze chewing at their paper towel napkins.

"I don't trust him," Tria muttered around a mouthful of prime rib.

"No?" Bel chewed an apple thoughtfully.

"I don't believe that story he told. About the alchemist." She dipped another piece of meat into hollandaise sauce.

"He's got something in him," Bel said. "Something pretty powerful."

"Yes, but . . ." Tria shook her head in frustration. "He's sneaky."

"We don't have to trust him," Bel told her. "But he needs us to survive. That's enough, as far as his loyalty goes."

"What if he talks? What if he tells people about . . . about us?" Tria waved her hand at the group, ranged over the scattered picnic tables.

Bel could feel her disapproval about telling him about the Sisters of Serpens. She rested her chin on her hand, fixed Tria with a look. "Who would believe him?"

Tria deflated, picked quietly at her food with her fork.

Cal, oblivious, returned to the table to tuck into a plate full of baked potatoes and prime rib.

Bel watched him closely. He didn't have the awareness of a master magician. She was convinced that whatever accident had befallen him, it was not of his own doing. She was certain that he had not told her the whole truth, but that would come later. If it was even relevant at all. She'd been practicing magic since she was a little girl, when she'd been bitten by a rattlesnake. Bel had nearly died, had lain in the forest for two days before her father had found her. In that time of paralysis, of lying in a ditch, looking upward at the sun and moon and feeling the worms and ants move beneath her, she realized what a gift it had been. The Great Mother had blessed her with the gift of life and the gifts of the snake.

She turned her face to the breeze and listened. She could feel the Great Serpent moving, just beyond the edge of the horizon. Sometimes, she covered ground, sliding through the undergrowth like steam. Sometimes, she slept, finding a warm spot where the afternoon sun beat down on rocks, luxuriating in that heat. She was ancient—Bel could sense the Serpent's memory deep in her bones. The Great Serpent Mother been sleeping, and something had awakened her. Bel couldn't know what it was—her own ego would like to believe that the snake had awakened just for her and the Sisters of Serpens.

But she knew that was unlikely. A power that massive awoke and slept by her own rhythms, by geologic time and the movement of stars ticking along in the spheres of the heavens. But she was here. In Bel's lifetime. That was all that mattered.

And she would get the Great Serpent's attention, prove herself a worthy follower. She knew that she and the Sisters would be blessed. Once the Serpent saw their devotion, she would share her power with her followers. The Great Serpent Mother would need followers to guard her secret sleeping spots and to bring her sacrifices. They would be useful. Useful, and rewarded.

When Cal had finished stuffing himself like a

tick, the Sisters cleared their dishes and headed to the bikes. They'd parked on a gravel flat spot bordering some woods, down the hill and beyond the sight of the chuck wagon camp. Bel hadn't been in the mood to be chatty with the locals about the bikes, and the walk after riding was always welcome. Cal lurched along, blinking.

"How do you feel?" Bel asked him.

"Better." He gave her a wan smile. "That was really good. Thanks."

"You're welcome . . ." She broke off, as some motion at the edge of the woods caught her eye. Behind the line of the Sisters' bikes, she could make out three young men, howling and laughing at something on the ground.

Her eyes narrowed. She broke away from Cal and strode up to them, her boots crunching harshly in the pea gravel.

The men were in their twenties, with their T-shirt-covered backs turned to her.

"What are you doing?" she demanded. Men in packs were rarely up to anything good.

The men turned, laughing. One of them held a stick, on the end of which dangled a dead snake.

"Check out what Rob found on the road!"

It was a beautiful snake—a rattler, with a pale belly and diamonds working up and down its four-foot long back.

Bel could feel her teeth gritting, her eyes narrowing. "Did you kill that snake?"

"Yeah!" The one named Rob twirled the snake on the stick, like a little girl with a streamer at the end of a baton. She could see that the snake had been pierced behind its jaws, the mouth split open with the tiniest runnel of red. "It's gonna make one helluva belt!"

This was a test from the Great Serpent to prove her loyalty. She could feel it.

"That's unfortunate," she observed.

The Sisters of Serpens did not fuck around.

The Sisters flocked from behind Bel to the men with the snake. It was like one time Cal remembered from his childhood summers, when there had been a heavy rain that drove the earthworms up out of the ground. When the rain stopped, there were night crawlers on the road in front of Cal's house. A murder of crows had descended from the sodden sky and fought over the night crawlers. The worms had been pulled apart, helpless against the onslaught of all those black beaks and furious claws.

The women swept over the young men. Shocked, the man with the snake dropped it and tried to run. So did one of his friends, who disappeared into the tree line with two of the Sisters in pursuit. The third tried to fight. He took a swing at one of the women.

But there were more of them. And they had knives, glinting in the dull sunlight.

"What are you doing?" Cal blurted.

Bel stood with her arms crossed, watching. "I see

their souls. And their souls deserve a reckoning for such an act."

"The snake?" Cal squeaked. He'd never hurt an animal in his life, aside from any creatures that wound up on his plate. When he lived at the Garden, he'd release daddy longlegs outside, even though they'd only get chased down by the chickens. Dumb bugs. But this seemed sort of . . . excessive.

"The snake. And everything else they've done." Bel's hollow voice drew chills down his neck. That green gaze looked like it could pierce the fabric of these meatsuits that humans wore, and for a moment, he believed that she could actually see into men's souls.

But . . . oh, my God.

Two of the women had pounded the fighter's face into a rock. He was bloody and unconscious, leaking red from his nose and swollen eyes.

Others held Rob the Snake-Slayer down on the grass. Bel strode to him, walked over him. She picked up the stick with the impaled snake. She tenderly separated the snake from the stick, curling its limp form in her arms as if it were a beloved pet.

She knelt over him. "You will pay for this."

Rob was writhing and grunting. But they were too far from the view of the chuck wagon for help to come. He had to know it.

"It's a snake!" he yelled. "It's just a fucking snake!"

Bel gently placed the snake in the grass. She reached to her belt, pulled out a silver knife with a blade the length of her hand. Deliberately, she crossed to the tree line, and cut down a small sapling with it. She stripped the branches from the trunk quickly, easily, and crossed back to Rob.

She stood before him, holding the branch like a spear. Its sharpened edge pointed to his throat.

Spittle flew from Rob's mouth, tears from his eyes. "It was just a fucking snake! What's wrong with you?"

Bel thrust the spear down under his chin, up into his mouth, and out through the back of his head. Blood gushed. Cal watched, horrified, as the muscles in her shoulders worked. She'd skewered him on the ground, like a bug on a pin.

The women released him. But he was held by the neck by that stake. He reached up to try to dislodge it, but couldn't. His fingers scrabbled on the shaft of the spear as he gurgled.

Cal edged away slowly, one foot after another. Maybe if he didn't make a sound, they wouldn't notice. Maybe they wouldn't see him as he turned and ran . . .

He plunged into the forest, his breath ragged in his throat. His flip-flops made smack-smacking sounds as he ran, and he kicked them off. The bristle of thorns and pine needles on his feet, anything, was preferable to being discovered.

They fucking killed that guy.

He lifted his arms, thwarting the lash of branches as he fled, gasping. He knew, instinctively, that he had to get away from Bel and her crazies. Bel might have a bit of magic that could save him, but even Stroud hadn't been that mercurially brutal.

His head pounded, and the forest spun around him. He ran blindly, bouncing off trees and whimpering, zinging through dappled shadow.

And he felt the mercury twitching in him.

Not now, he thought. *Not now.*

He heard a man's scream elsewhere in the forest, somewhere off to his left. They'd caught the other guy—no way they would leave witnesses.

Cal lurched forward, but the mercury twisted in his gut, doubling him over. It lunged upward in his esophagus like the worst case of acid reflux known to man. Silver liquid dribbled from his lip. He shuffled forward, but the cramps ratcheted through his body. It felt like his stomach was being perforated.

He heard footsteps in the leaves behind him.

He spun, trying to escape. But the dark figures of Bel's women surrounded him. He ducked right, then skidded left on the wet leaves, zagging over a shallow gully, into mud on his hands and knees.

"Cal." Bel's voice, as calm as if she was reading from the newspaper on a Sunday afternoon.

He twisted back at her. "You killed that guy! You just . . ."

"He needed to die." She lifted her chin at him. There was only a wet glisten on her leather jacket to give any evidence of what she'd done. "You don't need to."

"Get away from me!" he howled.

The mercury flared within him. He felt it dripping from his hand and he held it out, a shaking threat.

Bel took two steps toward him. "Cal. You can't run."

The mercury reached out for her, then deflected, like steel filings at the wrong pole of a magnet.

He scrambled up the bank, sprinted a half-dozen paces before he fell in a patch of thin grass. The mercury howled within him, churning through his lungs.

"You can't run, Cal." Bel knelt before him. "Without my help, the mercury in you will devour you. You'll die."

Cal sobbed and hiccupped. Mercury trickled down his nose in a long string. He could feel his heart being squeezed and crumpled, like a paper cup in a fist.

Bel reached out for him, touched his brow with her thumb.

The force of Bel's magic stole through him, like the chill clearness of a half pint of vodka. A buzzing suffused his limbs, damping down the mercury. It uncoiled around his lungs and limbs, and he could feel it retreating back into his spine, his vertebrae crackling as it drained back into his spinal fluid. His face pressed against leaf mold, he struggled to breathe.

"Stay with me, Cal." Her cool hand was on the back of his neck. He remembered when his mother would hold a washcloth on the back of his neck when he threw up as a little boy. That was a good memory, tangled in memories of her beating the shit out of him. He felt that way about Bel—he was terrified of her, but those small kindnesses brought him to his knees.

"Bring him."

Two of the Sisters lifted him to his feet. They draped his arms over their shoulders and carried him through the forest. Cal's head lolled back on his shoulders, and he blinked upward at the light playing through the leaves. His toes barely brushed the cold leaves and ground. He idly wondered if his feet were bleeding red or silver.

"You're gonna be okay," the one with the purple hair whispered into his ear. "You'll see."

When they came to the edge of the parking area, only the Sisters' bikes were there. There was no sign of the men, not even a stain on the grass to suggest they'd been there. Cal began to wonder if he'd hallucinated the whole thing.

The women placed him on the gravel, and he sat there, stunned and thoughts rumbling.

The blond one, Tria, knelt before him. She was holding a pair of men's boots. She pulled out his rubbery legs and began to tie the boots on his scratched and bleeding feet. At least they bled red. That was something.

"Where did those boots come from?" Cal whispered.

She looked up at him impishly, under a fringe of black eyelashes.

He recoiled, turning away.

And he saw the only sign of what had transpired here—the snake.

The snake had been hung on a tree, draped over

arms of the tree that reached out parallel to the ground, like a cross. It had been carefully hung over the branches like a stole.

At the foot of the tree, Bel knelt in prayer.

Cal hiccupped and passed out.

CHAPTER NINE

DOWNSTREAM

"Ready to hit the trail?"

Petra shifted from foot to foot in the overcrowded parking lot of the ranger station, uncertain. She'd packed a backpack containing most of her gear, a hazmat suit with a minirespirator, a gas detector, a fistful of sample bottles, a steel flint, a first-aid kit, a couple of plastic tarps, a change of clothes, food and water for herself and Sig, and some miscellaneous odds and ends from Bear's store. Her sleeping bag was tied to the bottom—this time of year, the days could be in the fifties, but the nights routinely dipped below freezing, and she would take no chances. She wore a knee-length vintage leather coat she'd picked up at the pawn shop in the summer and cargo pants stuffed with her cell phone, a solar charger, sunscreen, the Venificus Locus, and ammunition for the guns she wore concealed in her gun belt under her coat. Her battered canvas safari cap perched on top of her head, and she wore her old boots. They were broken in, and she knew they wouldn't give her blisters.

She thought she'd overpacked, but now she felt severely underdressed.

Phil and Meg had arrived with massive aluminum-framed backpacks that were larger than they were. Petra was pretty sure that each one weighed fifty pounds, minimum. They'd shown up in matching camo jumpsuits and coats that looked like they'd been military-issue, except that there were no names embroidered on the left breast pockets. Each of them carried hikers' poles that looked like ski poles.

"Um. Hey," Petra said, looking down at her scuffed boots.

Their boots were Gore-Tex with gaiters up to the knee. New. Maybe they didn't get out much and just went overboard with shopping.

"Is that all you're bringing?" Meg asked.

Petra slung her back over her shoulder. "I've got enough to get by for three days. Is that enough?"

Phil and Meg swapped glances. "Sure. We can radio to the rangers if we need more stuff. They should be able to airdrop supplies to us if we come up short."

Petra nodded, and Sig pressed close to her knees. She flipped open a coat pocket. "And, hey, I brought bear spray."

She meant it as a joke, but they looked uncomfortable. She wondered if perhaps they'd forgotten bear spray. Pelican Valley was notorious for grizzlies. They generally minded their own business, but they were walking around with bags full of food, and that was hard for a hungry bear to resist.

Mike tooled up in a Forestry Service Jeep. "Hey, campers."

He looked like shit, but she wasn't going to tell him that. Dark bags clung to his eyes. It didn't look like he'd shaved, which was an admission that shit was seriously out of control for him.

She climbed in the backseat with Phil and Sig, while Meg called shotgun. The gear got piled in the back, and Sig set about inspecting it. Phil gave him a sidelong glance.

"I'm gonna let you guys off about four klicks away from the location of the campsite Petra and I checked out the other day," Mike told them as he pulled the Jeep out onto the two-lane road. "I've got your permits in the dash, in case you run across other rangers. Nobody's supposed to go off the marked trail in that part of the park."

"You're not coming with?" Petra pushed Sig's cold nose off her neck. That had been the original plan, pending a quagmire of sign-offs from Mike's chain of command.

"I'd love to go chase monsters with you guys, but I've got enough of a circus on my hands. I'm gonna be the only one at the Tower Falls Ranger Station after noon."

"Bummer," Petra said. "I know that you really wanted to meet the critter in person."

"I'll be on the radio, though. We kept the site out of the media as best we could, so you guys should be alone. For a while, at least." He whistled the title theme to the *X-Files*.

"Tell us the truth. It's the sweet overtime you're getting," Petra teased him.

"Oh, yeah. All that sweet time-and-a-half OT spent telling people that we do not issue hunting permits for giant snakes. With all due respect to the esteemed scientists present . . . bite me," he said sourly. "I spent the largest part of yesterday looking for some dude who fell off a cliff, reportedly because he was walking backward with his selfie on a stick."

"It's a selfie stick," Meg supplied.

"What's a selfie stick?" Petra had never heard of one. "Is it like cheesecake on a stick?"

"Yum," Phil murmured. "Fair food." He offered Petra an awkward fist bump.

"You stick your camera on the end of one and your self-portraits are more wide-angle. Also, they're great for getting your camera around nooks and crannies. I packed one!" Meg announced brightly.

I bet, Petra thought. "Did you find your hiker?" she asked Mike.

"I did. He was lucky enough only to have broken about half of the bones in his body."

In the opposite direction, a load of teenagers in a pickup truck whooped and hollered. They were clearly speeding, and no one in the truck bed was wearing a seat belt.

"Excuse me," Mike said.

The Jeep spun a tight U-turn on the blacktop, sending bags and the coyote shifting to the right. Petra held on to the seat in front of her and Sig's collar, relieved not to wind up in Phil's lap by virtue of her seat belt.

"What the heck?" Phil muttered.

"Mike's a rules kind of guy," Petra said.

Mike floored it and caught up with the pickup truck. He motioned for them to pull over, and the truck reluctantly stopped at a scenic turnoff.

"Be back in a sec." Mike popped open his door and approached the pickup.

Petra reached in the back to straighten out the gear. She was startled to be shoved aside by Phil.

"I got this," he said.

"Okay." She slid back into her seat. Clearly, the guy didn't like anybody touching his stuff.

Mike, ever the rules-stickler, scribbled out a raft of citations. The unhappy teens were stuck at the side of the road, waiting for their parents to come pick them up, when he returned behind the wheel.

"It's been that kind of week," he muttered.

"So the scene is clear—the spot where you found the dead campers?" Meg asked.

Petra piped up. "It should be reasonably safe. I wouldn't roll around in the grass, but it's rained since then, and the air samples I took were clear."

"Did you bring dog booties for Sig?" Mike asked.

"Funny you should ask," Petra said. "I have plastic bags and zip ties. Since this is a classy operation."

They wound south, past the spectacular Tower Falls and the Upper and Lower Falls and over the Fishing Bridge that spanned the Yellowstone River. Mike gave the scientists the tourist spiel:

"This part of the park is off the beaten trail, a bit. There's a loop trail, and tourists are supposed to stick to it. It's not unusual to see elk standing in the creek for a great photo op, but it's also bear country. There's not supposed to be any camping around here at all, and folks are required to clear off the trail by dusk—you guys are the exception. We still spend a lot of time chasing down folks who ignore the rules and pitch tents, anyway. Had one grizzly last year invade a campsite and get stuck in a steel fire ring while looking for stale marshmallows. That was fun to resolve."

"The campers you found dead . . . they weren't following the rules?" Meg inquired.

"Nope. No permit. Neither were the morons who saw the snake on the news. You can tell people what to do, and for very good reasons, but there's a certain percentage that think you're just kidding and that they're smarter than the rules."

"Any other wildlife that we should be aware of?" Phil asked.

"Just the usual assortment of coyotes, fishing birds, and some wolves. You might run into a wolf pack, if they're in transit from here to the Lamar Valley. Those guys will leave you alone, though."

"They're part of the wolf reintroduction at Yellowstone?"

"Yeah. This group is called Mollie's Pack. Neat animals, if you get to see them."

"You mentioned some unusual geological activity in this area."

"There has been," Petra piped up. "There used to be a lot of defunct thermal features, and it was pretty quiet in this area for many years. But in the past few weeks, many of them have become active again, and new ones have formed. I've cataloged twelve new fumaroles, sixteen mudpots, and even a new hot spring."

"So these are different from the paint pots and mudpots in the other parts of the park?"

"There are probably more than ten thousand geothermal features in Yellowstone. The vast majority of the features I deal with are small and somewhat disappointing to tourists after they've seen Mammoth Hot Springs and Old Faithful."

"Bigger is better."

"Eh. Bigger just means it's been more thoroughly studied. I like to look at things that are weird. To see a feature that nobody's ever seen before is just really neat stuff."

Mike pulled off to a forestry road near the scene of the campsite, and the Jeep's underbelly scraped over tree roots and rocks for more than an hour. When he could go no farther, he put the Jeep in PARK and came to the tailgate to help them with their things.

Meg and Phil lugged their packs out immediately and began logging their notes into handheld tablets. Phil was already taking air readings, wandering toward the edge of the forest.

Mike leaned on the tailgate and spoke to Petra in a low voice that didn't carry. "Here." He handed her a small black device, about the size of a retail theft tag.

"What's this?"

"GPS tracker. Put it in your pocket."

"But I have a GPS device. And a phone, and a walkie in case we get within range of anybody at the Pelican Springs patrol cabin, and . . ."

"Your cell reception is gonna suck in the valley." He spoke with his back to the biologists. "I put one on each of those guys, and I'm telling you to take one and hide it on your person. If I knew that you were bringing Sig, I'd have brought one for his collar."

She lifted an eyebrow. "You planted bugs on Meg and Phil?"

"In the aluminum casings of their backpacks. They might find them if they discern a rattle."

"That doesn't sound like standard-issue ranger gear."

"It's not."

"No matter how extensive your personal network is, there can't possibly be enough cell towers around to triangulate anything."

"Doesn't need cell towers. Those babies run on satellite."

"And might I ask why you decided to drop major coin on gadgets to keep tabs on us?" She slipped her tracker in the front pocket of her pants, and crossed her arms over her chest.

"Well. Not to be a total pessimist, but the mission might be a bust, and I might need to go find your bodies."

"That's sweet. But you could just tell us. All of us."

He frowned. "I don't trust those guys."

"What do you mean?" Her brow furrowed.

"I checked with a friend of mine who's still in the military. Just to know what they were up to. I was talking to him anyway about Cal, and I figured . . . what the hell."

"That's . . . invasive."

"Do you want to know what he found or not?"

She shifted her weight from foot to foot. "Yeah. I want to know."

"He found nothing. On either one of them."

"That's good, right?"

"That's good, for a ghost."

"A ghost," she repeated.

"Yeah. One of two possibilities. Either those two grew up as choirboys . . . er, girls, or whatever. No speeding tickets, no insurance claims, no fingerprints on file, anywhere. Or they're something else."

"Like what?"

"Could be military, operating way above my friend's clearance level. Could be corporate spies."

"Awesome." She rolled her eyes.

"Look, it might be nothing. But I wanted you to know, in case you wanted to back out."

"Thanks." She punched his sleeve and hoisted her backpack. "But I'm down for the ride."

"Look, I would go, but . . ." His eyes drifted back and forth from the biologists to the road.

"You're the only one at the station. I get that. Drunk teenagers need you to stop them before they fall out of trucks and split their brains open on the pavement." She grinned. "Ya gotta protect and serve."

"It's kind of one of those 'needs of the many versus needs of the few' things." He put his hands in his pockets and looked guilty. "I have to do it."

"Mike." She put her hand on his shoulder. "You're a cop. That's your thing. See you back at the station in a couple of days."

"Sure."

She whistled for Sig, and followed the biologists up the trail.

When she looked back, she could see Mike standing beside the Jeep, looking back after them. He stayed there until she couldn't see him anymore.

Gabe had sorely misjudged the basilisk before. He would not do so again.

Unwilling to sacrifice whatever bit of unlife remained in the Hanged Men, he had decided to search for it on his own this time. If he failed, it would be entirely his own failure, and hopefully the Lunaria would die quietly and take the rest of the Hanged Men with it. He hoped that they would simply fall asleep one evening in its glowing embrace and not rise the following morning—the peaceful death that they all deserved.

He had taken one of Sal's horses, a sorrel with a bit too much wild for Sal himself to handle. But Rust was sure-footed and had good instincts. Most importantly, he tolerated the Hanged Men. When Sal had been thrown years ago and ordered Rust shot, Gabe had quietly moved the horse to the back field with the other work horses. Sal was unobservant enough not to be able to tell a sorrel from a chestnut, and Rust had spent his days beyond the reach of Sal's scrutiny.

Rust was curious enough about Gabe's mission: his rider was covered neck to feet in an oilskin coat he'd rubbed down with linseed oil and lead salt. It might buy him a little time from the snake—enough time to get close. Tied to the saddle on one side was Gabe's rifle, outfitted with a new scope, and on his hip hung a loaded revolver. On the other side of the saddle was a bundle of spears made from dropped branches of the Lunaria. If the basilisk could hurt the Hanged Men, maybe there was enough magic still in the tree to take some blood from it.

Gabe and Rust took the back way to Yellowstone, through the pine forests. Quaking yellow aspen were beginning to drop their leaves, masking the little-used trails. The park was crowded with tourists, and Gabe wanted no part of them.

Gabe sent out a solitary raven to scout the skies above. It had rained recently, rinsing the stink of acid away, and the raven had a difficult time picking up the trail. He kept the bird close, scouting among the tree-tops for signs of the basilisk's passing.

He knew that the basilisk had to be one of Lascaris's old experiments, though his exact memory of his time with Lascaris was spotty. The basilisk had awoken somehow, crawled out of some nook or cranny. Maybe some of the recent seismic activity had awakened it. Maybe it was the other way around. In alchemy, the crucified serpent symbolized the removing of poison and the precipitation of mercury. The ouroboros, the snake devouring its tail, was a sign of regeneration. He remembered that much. He hoped that he could bring the good out of the ouroboros, the elixir of life, to save the tree and continue to work the magic of the Hanged Men's regeneration.

He reined Rust in at the top of a ridge. Something moved in the valley below, where a creek slipped among large sandstone rocks. A pale shape drifted in the water, beyond the tree line.

The raven lit on his shoulder and slid underneath the collar of his oilskin coat, fluttering against the pulse in his neck. Gabe lowered his hat and nudged Rust forward, down to the creek.

Rust paused halfway down. His nostrils flared, and

his ears swiveled back. He sensed something, something wrong. He dug in and would go no farther.

Gabe could respect that. He could smell it, too: the faint residue of poison. He slid down out of the saddle, looping the reins through a tree branch. That would be enough tension to keep Rust here for a time, but if he didn't return, the horse would be able to disentangle himself and escape. Gabe lifted his rifle in the crook of his right elbow and slung the bundle of spears over his left shoulder.

Noiselessly, Gabe descended to the creek, to the flash of brightness he saw drifting there.

A pale silhouette had gotten hung up on some rocks. A body.

Gabe advanced into the creek warily. Cold water lapped up his boots, and his coat fanned behind him.

The body of a girl bobbed against the rocks. Long blond hair with pink streaks was twisted in pine needles and twigs. Her fingers were open, splayed, and her jeans and white hoodie were stained with mud. Her eyes, like the eyes of the victims at the morgue, were blood red, and her skin was turning violet and mottled. Her bee-stung lips were slack, and an oak leaf was caught in her earring. Gabe didn't need to touch her to know she was dead. The acid vapor had been mostly washed from her, but the soft smell of decay had taken hold. She'd been in shade and cold water for some time, but the rotting had begun.

She looked like a younger version of Jelena, his wife from more than a hundred fifty years ago. He could still see her delicate features etched behind his eyelids if he closed them. She could be Jelena's younger sister from that time, or perhaps her descendant in the present.

Likely, this was the girl who had vanished with the group of young people days ago. In this isolated part of the park, it could be a very long time until she was found. Maybe heavy rains would dislodge her from this bit of the shallows, maybe a visitor would find her at the campground miles downstream. But it would likely be a long time, if she stayed here.

Gabe reached out and grasped her arm. He gently tugged her free of the rocks and debris. She came loose, and he pushed her down the river.

She drifted, feet first, down the creek, into the singing chorus of late-season frogs and cicadas.

It was all he could do. Hopefully, someone would find her and give her the peace of a proper grave.

CHAPTER TEN

VENOM

"What do you think a snake that size eats?"

Petra genuinely wanted to know, and it seemed like as good a question as any to pose to the biologists.

"Anything it wants," Meg offered. "Depending on whether it eats its prey whole, it could be coyote, beaver, deer . . ."

Sig cast her a dirty look. He wasn't a happy camper, as is. Petra hung with him at the edge of the campsite where the family had died, her fingers tangled in his leash. To protect him, she'd zip-tied the plastic baggies on his feet, and he was focused on chewing them off.

He had shown absolutely no interest in going near the yellowed grasses—in fact, he'd wrinkled his nose and turned away.

But Meg and Phil were fascinated. They'd donned their plastic suits and were fingering everything in sight. Phil was shooting pictures with a digital camera, and Meg was taking measurements in the grass. The scene had been cleared, only surrounded by yellow caution tape. The tent and the campers' belongings had been removed. It had rained, and it was likely that any damaging substances had been rinsed away. It looked like a lawn on which a plastic swimming pool had been parked for a whole summer—sallow and thin.

While Meg and Phil fussed over the area, she turned her back and wandered a bit away with Sig. Sig seemed content to stick close by her heel, and she was grateful for that. She took him off the leash and dug into her pocket for the Venificus Locus and her knife. With her back turned, she poked her little finger and dropped some blood into the channel around the rim. The blood slipped into the compass and remained still.

She let out a deep breath. Good. The snake wasn't anywhere in the vicinity. Maybe the poison was entirely gone, too.

"This trail . . ." Phil photographed the track of brittle grass going off to the west. "This thing could be massive."

Petra pocketed the compass and joined the biologists. They followed the trail as far as it went, but lost it in the rocky land beyond, as Petra had before.

Petra spread out a topographical map of the area on the ground. "We're here." She marked a spot on the map with a pencil. "The group that videotaped the snake reported encountering it . . . here." She made another mark. "That's a good bit of ground covered, about two miles through grassland."

"Well, we need to decide if it behaves like any other snake," Meg mused, looking at the horizon.

"Do you think it's nocturnal or diurnal?" Petra asked.

"Most snakes aren't strictly one or the other," Phil said. "They generally follow the habits of their preferred prey."

"Do we think that humans are the preferred prey?"

Phil's mouth twisted. "It didn't eat the campers, right? So . . . I'm guessing that was just a fear response, a defense mechanism when it came across them."

"But it's got to be pretty aggressive, then. Those campers weren't posing a threat. Two of them were asleep, and the other was just sitting," Petra observed.

"Maybe it's attracted to the noise," Meg suggested. "The group partying by the river were probably making some racket."

"But does it even know what its prey is? If it's the only one, or the only one of a very few, it might still be figuring that out." Phil rubbed his chin.

Petra stared at the map. "Well, both those locations were near geothermally active areas." She showed them the campsite and the spot near the river. "There are mudpots near both of these sites. New ones. There's been seismic activity in the valley that's been opening up even more. I've been exploring them as they come up, mapping them out." She pointed to her pencil marks and notes scribbled on the map.

"That's just . . . weird," Phil said.

"Eh. Yellowstone is always weird. Not everything is as predictable as Old Faithful. Geothermal features can wither away without explanation, and new ones form all the time. But this spate has been unusual. I mean, we get over one hundred tremors a day. Most of that is minor, but the ones lately have been much larger. We're lucky that the disturbances are here, in the backcountry, with fewer people around."

"So, maybe the snake wants warmth, and doesn't like to be disturbed," Meg mused.

"In which case . . . what exactly are we gonna do if we confront this beastie?" Petra felt like it was a little too late to be asking the question.

"Observe. Photograph. But definitely not confront," Phil said. "If we see it, we'll call the Department of the Interior. We'll have actual proof then that it exists, that we're not a couple of crackpots." Phil gave a wan smile.

"And what are they going to do with it?"

"We'll get more personnel on the ground to secure the perimeter and minimize the risk to civilians. We want them to capture it," Meg said earnestly.

"Gotcha." Petra's finger traced the map. "The next nearest geothermal spot is here."

"Let's try there. Maybe we can pick up the trail."

They headed into the gold grass, the long tassels

brushing Petra's pants as she walked. The grass was tall enough that Sig disappeared beneath it. This broad path in the valley had been scraped clean by a glacier, and it was a pleasant walk. She whistled for him to stay close, and he obliged by drifting between her and Phil.

Petra stared at Phil's pack. That still seemed like an awfully lot of gear for simple observation. She sympathized with the desire to observe the creature from a safe distance, but . . . she sure hoped that they'd brought some guns.

They'd walked for nearly an hour through the grasslands when something caught her eye. A vehicle was parked at the bottom of a dry stream gully. It looked familiar.

With a shout to the biologists, she waded through the grass to the truck. It was an old, beat-up pickup truck, with faded red paint and a skin of rust spots. It hadn't seen wax in years. A residue of straw was in the bed of the truck, still sodden from the rain. The rains had rinsed the mud from the fenders, and a rodent was making a nest in the wheel well. It had been here a few days.

Petra tried the doors. They were locked.

"Does it belong to anyone you know?" Meg asked.

She glanced at Sig. "Yeah. Some guys who work at one of the ranches around here." The Hanged Men. This truck had come from Sal's ranch. She was sure of it.

"Doesn't look like anybody's been here lately."

"I hope not."

She scanned the sky for ravens as they continued. She spied redwing blackbirds, a tanager, and a tree full of wrens patrolled by a red-tailed hawk. No ravens.

But the Hanged Men had been here. They might still be here. They had to be looking for the snake. And perhaps Gabe would be with them. Her stomach churned at the thought. Gabe was lost to her, mindlessly following Sal's orders. Without that spark of life in him, he was little more than Sal's puppet. So that meant Sal wanted something from the snake, that it had something even more insidious to do with the dark magic and alchemy that infested this land. And that meant nothing good.

"Look at this."

Meg was a hundred feet to the south, poking at something with her walking stick. Petra and Phil circled the area, peering at what she'd found.

The ground was scorched, burned black. A puddle of what looked like metal had melted into the ground.

"Is that a meteor?"

"That's not a meteor." Petra pulled on her gloves and worked at it with a trowel. It turned over, and she could see the outline of a trigger in it, tool marks. "It *was* a gun."

"This looks like leather . . . shoe leather." Phil picked up a melted bit of brown pulp with a stick, from which dangled a metal eye and a shoelace.

"Looks like someone else met the snake."

Petra poked in the weeds with the trowel. She heard Sig whine, paces away. She climbed to her feet.

"Sig?"

She saw the tip of his tail moving in the grass.

"Whatcha got, boy?"

She parted the grass to find Sig staring at a hat.

It was a white cowboy hat, spattered with acid holes. Part of the brim had melted. The hat was familiar—it was the one she'd last seen Gabe wearing, when she'd confronted him on the street in Temperance. He'd looked right through her with empty amber eyes.

"Gabe found the snake," she whispered to Sig. "And it . . . it killed him."

There was truly nothing left.

She radioed the location of the truck and the ruined gun and shoe leather in to Mike. Maybe Sal Rutherford would care that one—or more—of his men were missing. Maybe he wouldn't. But it was worth raising as much hell as she could.

It's just a shell, she tried to tell herself as she plodded along in the wake of the biologists, numb. The personality, the man she'd known as Gabe was gone. She tried to tell herself that he was a walking automaton, and that being dissolved in acid likely made as much difference to him as whether it was going to rain that day or not. But that wasn't fair—he was alive. Unalive. He'd survived the explosion at Stroud's Garden. And maybe he would have gone on to create his own memories and his own life, ones that just didn't include her. Believing that he'd died entirely at the Garden—that was the unfair part of her thinking, ego-driven, and she tried to challenge it. That had just been the part that she knew, that knew her. But it just summoned tears to her eyes, and she rubbed at them with the palm of her hand when no one was looking.

But Sig saw. He walked close to her, his tail thumping against the backs of her knees as she trudged along.

The sun had lowered toward the horizon by the time they approached the next mudpot, tucked in a thicket of forest. According to Petra's survey, this one was larger than the others. Maybe it would be more attractive to the snake. It was difficult to see, with the sun streaming across the land. Petra lowered her hat on her head and unbuttoned her coat, deriving some comfort from the idea that her guns were within reach.

She surreptitiously consulted the Locus. It suggested that they push forth to the mudpot. She had no idea of the range of the device, but the knowledge that the snake was close made her uneasy.

"That's interesting." Phil pointed to a slash through the pine trees, curled bark as high as his waist. The green pine needles had begun to yellow, as if something caustic was chewing deeply in the sap.

"It's fresh." Meg stared at sap dripping onto the ground, where it fizzled in resinous puddles that speckled the ground. And the smell was unmistakable—it reeked of sulfur, even upwind of it.

"Okay. Let's call your buddies with the federal government." Petra's first instinct was to back away and let someone with helicopters and firepower swoop in for the glory.

"I want to see it." Phil's eyes shone in fascination, and he stepped into the stand of pine trees.

Meg had lowered her backpack to the ground. "Phil, wait." She'd unzipped it and was donning her gear. Which seemed like a really good idea right about now.

Petra set down her own pack. She crouched over her gear and quickly consulted the Locus. Her fingers were getting sore from stabbing, but forewarned was forearmed. The blood in the Locus swished around agitatedly, lurching east, then west. Magic was close at hand. The fluid separated into two drops, one to the right, and the other to the left.

Shit. There were two of them, and they were circling the expedition party. Two fucking snakes.

"Look out."

She drew a gun and swept it in a circle, through the blinding sun. Sig pressed against her leg, growling, the fur on his back lifting.

A shape rose with the sun at its back, casting a long shadow over her.

They were so incredibly fucked.

Gabe had tracked the snake over the grassland of the valley. The snake had become less obvious in the trail it left behind. He followed bits of blackened grass and curled leaves with broken veins, sidestepping Rust around hazards. The horse, wary, was still bribable with wild crabapples, and consented to move forward.

Gabe had partitioned a bit of his left shoulder into raven form. From the sky, he could detect the patterns the snake made in the grass, broad sidewinder stripes that were too subtle to see from the ground.

But he'd gathered the raven back into himself on the final approach, dismounting from Rust and clutching his spears and guns. He thought he would lie in wait with his rifle, wait for it to move, and take it out from a distance. But there was a commotion at the edge of the field, where it met a stand of trees in the last flicker of brilliant sunset. He lifted his pistol and advanced, pulling the hammer back and ready to shoot. He could taste the magic, feel the serpentine alchemy of it unwinding just behind his field of vision.

A figure stood up in the field, in the glorious sunshine. It wasn't the snake—it was *her*. It was the woman from the hospital, the woman he'd been spying on with his ravens, the woman who'd been haunting his dreams. She blinked at him, tendrils of her hair leaking from her hat and her coyote crouching and snarling at her feet.

She stood before him and leveled a gun at his chest.

It was just like his dream. Just like it. He could feel that ache in his chest, and he knew what it meant: She was going to kill him.

"Gabe," she whispered at him, in sunshine.

He pulled the hammer of his pistol back.

"Gabe." Her face broke into a smile. "You're alive."

His brow knitted. She was happy to see him. His grip on his gun tightened. It made no sense; she wanted him dead. She'd ripped the heart right out of his chest.

She lowered her pistol. At her feet, the coyote wound up to pounce. And he saw her left hand . . . in it was a golden compass. That thing . . . he flashed on it, picturing her pulling it from his chest when he'd hung in the Lunaria's embrace. He'd screamed, screamed with the voice of a raven.

"Gabe."

The coyote at her side snarled. She blocked him with her leg. "Gabe, I know that you don't know me. Not anymore. But I'm glad . . . I'm glad you're alive." Her voice dropped, and it seemed that she had resigned herself to something.

She was a threat. Every cell in his body screamed it at him, in the voice of a raven.

But something in him remembered. He remembered her standing in the chamber below the Lunaria, holding the gun on him. It had been . . . to take him out of his misery. He had been broken. She should have done it, but she hadn't been able to bring herself to shoot. She'd done as she had now—she'd lowered the gun.

"You're alive." She said it again, as if really trying to convince herself.

He stepped closer to her, so close that his gun was inches from her face. She closed her eyes, and the breeze moved a strand of hair over her freckled cheek.

He reached out, brushed it aside. His hand slipped down to her warm, sunburned cheek.

And he remembered.

She'd saved his life. He remembered her hauling his broken body from Sal's barn. He remembered seeing her sliced-open arms at Stroud's Alchemical Garden. He remembered that she knew the secret of the Hanged Men, that he had led her through the warren of tunnels beneath Sal's ranch. He'd shown her the Star Chamber. He remembered the way her mouth tasted, like the sea.

"Petra."

He blinked and lowered the gun.

She opened her eyes, brilliant hazel in that bright light. His fingers brushed the smile creases around her eyes as she looked up at him.

"The Locus. I love it best when it leads me to you." Her smile froze. "Wait. Are you alone? The Locus said there were two . . ."

A scream rang out, and she jumped. Her coyote wheeled in a blur of fur, and Gabe looked over her shoulder. The sun had dipped below the tree line, pulling down shadows.

"Phil!"

A woman in a hazmat suit stood at the edge of the darkening pine forest. Her back was turned to them, and she was struggling with a backpack.

"The snake." Petra turned, aiming her guns at the darkness.

Gabe advanced toward the woman, the gun before him as he reached for a spear with his free hand. This was going really bad, really fast. He hadn't figured on collateral damage. He hadn't figured on Petra.

She ran beside him, plunging into the pine woods, with the coyote a blur on her heels. The sun had dipped behind the trees, casting them in shadow.

"Where's Phil?" she demanded of the woman in the hazmat suit.

"He was just here!" The woman in the suit wrestled a yellow plastic gun out of the bag. It was longer than her arm and covered with warning stickers. "He fell, and I lost sight of him!"

"What the hell is that?" Petra demanded.

"Stun gun."

"Christ."

Gabe peered into the woods. Shadow passed over his face, and his boots pressed quietly into the soft earth. The pine needles had smothered the undergrowth here—there was no brush to speak of. He assumed that the man was wearing the same bright white suit as the woman, and he scanned the shadows. Nothing moved.

"Phil?" the woman called.

Overhead, something rustled.

A blur of white plastic dropped down on them. It was apparently Phil—or what was left of him. He dangled lifelessly, like a limp sock on a clothesline, from the mouth of the basilisk. It curled around the trunk of the pine tree, trying to wolf down one of Phil's legs.

"Shit. I guess we know what it eats now." Petra aimed up at the snake and fired. The muzzle flash lit up the half-darkness. The basilisk lashed back into the canopy, where it glowered with yellow eyes.

"No!" The woman in the suit shoved her back. "Don't kill it!" She raised the yellow plastic gun and fired into the dark. Two darts zipped into the canopy, toward the creature's eyes.

Electricity crackled, and the snake shrieked. The dart lines got tangled in the pine branches, and the woman in the suit wrestled with the gun.

The basilisk turned tail and flipped through the trees, flinging itself from tree trunk to trunk, tail churning like a whip. The supple pines bent, as if under the force of a gale force wind.

Gabe sprinted, trying to catch up with it. He unslung his rifle, taking a shot. He didn't care if the serpent lived or died. He just needed its blood.

Branches broke. The snake crashed through the canopy, catching itself on the bottommost branches. It opened its jaws and hissed at Gabe. Its feather crest stood up, slitted eyes dilated. Venom spewed from its mouth.

Gabe rolled to the right, reaching for one of his spears. The snake landed on the forest floor with a soft *thump* and writhed after him. Gabe hurled the spear near the fast-moving snake's right side. It bounced and skipped along its scaly surface, not making direct contact.

"Get away from him."

Petra stood yards away from him as she shouted at the snake, pistols lifted. She shot at the basilisk, muzzles flashing in the gloom. The sun had dipped behind the mountains beyond the forest, and they were losing any advantage of light.

The snake dove into the thick bed of pine needles, freakishly fast, and turned.

"Run!" Gabe yelled at Petra.

The snake hissed, and a thin white vapor leaked from its mouth, like dry ice.

Petra saw it and stumbled back. She turned to run to the safety upwind in the grassland, where the coyote barked furiously.

Gabe fired at the snake. Getting the blood was meaningless, now. The basilisk retreated, sliding behind a rotted log and into deeper shadow as it circled back toward the woman in the plastic suit, who was now on all fours, retching into the pine needles.

Petra ran, got about twenty-five feet toward the meadow.

Gabe watched as she stopped, wobbled on her feet . . .

. . . and collapsed to the ground in a heap, her hat falling off her head like a feather from a shot bird.

Gabe scrambled to his feet. He charged to Petra, scooped her up, and ran for the field, upwind of the snake's poison.

He looked back once, to see the snake striking at the woman on the ground. She couldn't even draw enough breath to shriek. She was done for.

The coyote ran to meet Gabe, yipping and jumping. "Petra." Gabe shook her.

Her head lolled back in the crook of his elbow. In the twilight, he could see that her eyes were half-open, but bright red broken blood vessels had overtaken her left eye. A spidery violet bruise was forming beneath the freckles of her right cheek.

The basilisk had gotten to her.

He whistled for Rust. The horse hadn't skidded completely to a stop before he had one foot in the stirrup. He swung into the saddle with his burden and jammed his heels into Rust's sides, wheeling away.

There was only one thing that could stop magic, and that was more magic.

He galloped away across the meadow as the moon rose, the coyote a gold sun trailing behind him.

Cool night air swept through the grasslands as he rode. The bullfrogs and the last of the late-season cicadas sang, giving the impression of a land seething with life.

He'd been stupid. He hadn't thought there was a possibility of collateral damage from confronting the basilisk in a remote area, but *she'd* been there. And she had the ability to dissolve his best-laid plans.

"What were you doing there?" he asked.

Her head bounced against his shoulder, and she didn't answer him.

She was a scientist. Of course, she would have been interested in this marvel. And she had the Venificus Locus. He remembered it now, the feeling of it growing over in his chest in the Lunaria. If anyone would have been able to find this creature, it would have been her.

He should have known.

But he hadn't—he could still feel the black spot around his memory, gingerly poking at it as it filled in with color. He hadn't known. The Lunaria hadn't been able to restore everything to his flesh and his consciousness, but some part of that memory had been locked away. Not destroyed, just partitioned.

And now that it was open, despair welled up in him. If he'd known . . .

The moon had risen to its zenith overhead, draining the color from the landscape. The grass and roads were silver ribbons in the dark, churning in the cold wind that had kicked up. He plunged through that colorless land, over roads and creeks, running the most direct path to any help.

Petra was still breathing by the time he reached the Lunaria.

He dismounted and propped her up against the base of the tree. She sat there with her chin on her chest, limp as a rag doll, as he pulled open the door in the sod to the chamber below.

The coyote came trotting up, sides heaving, his tongue lolling from his teeth. He remembered the coyote now . . . his name was Sig. The coyote walked up to Petra and washed her face with his tongue. Gabe thought he saw a finger twitch, but it might have just been a trick of the light, cast by the moon tangled in the Lunaria's branches.

"Give her here, Sig." He lifted her, but the coyote held on to her coattail. Maybe the coyote knew something of what he planned. Sig tugged and pulled, lips pulled back, eyes shining gold.

Winning the tug of war when the hem of Petra's coat gave way, Gabe stumbled away from Sig to the mouth of the portal. He jumped down to the floor of the chamber in one motion, landing in a square of moonlight with the edges softened by disturbed dust. Shadows hung around him. One or two gold eyes opened, disturbed in their slumber.

He took two steps into the darkness. The Lunaria's roots reached out for him, inviting him to sleep with the others. But the roots paused as they explored the burden in his arms. A root brushed her forehead, curious.

A thump and a yelp sounded behind him. Gabe turned to see the damn coyote staggering upright in the moonlight. Sig growled at Gabe, a deep bass note in the darkness chewed out by white teeth.

The Lunaria reached out for Petra with a tendril wrapping around her wrist, dangling in space.

Gabe stepped back, pulling her arm away from its grip. "No. You can't have her."

It was tempting, to give her to the tree. But the tree didn't have enough power to undo this, not the right kind of magic. It would try, it would dig deep into her.

It would remake what it found there, regenerate all it could.

But Petra needed an entirely different alchemical process that the tree could not provide. Not a regeneration, but a purification.

The coyote lunged at him, tearing into his sleeve. The teeth tore into his arm, harmlessly. There was no blood, no pain. He shook the coyote off and turned to the tunnels worming deeper into the earth.

Sig followed him with a low, thunderous growl emanating from the bottom of his chest. When Gabe glanced back, he could see the shining eyes a few yards away, tracking him. There was nothing to be done for it. The coyote wouldn't trust him, and Gabe wasn't entirely certain that he knew what he was doing.

"You think that I mean to work some darker magic than the tree on her," he said to the coyote.

The growl increased to a snarl. Sig was a good guardian.

"You aren't wrong. But it's the last chance."

A hospital would be unable to cure her in time—they wouldn't even be able to identify the elements of the basilisk's venom soon enough to concoct an antidote. Gabe suspected that, given enough time, some brilliant mind like hers would be able to distill an antivenom through exotic snake venom. Science did, after all, have a certain kind of persistence that ultimately could succeed, given enough brute force and sheer bullheadedness. But by then, she'd be a puddle of liquefied goo at the end of a respirator hose, and there wouldn't be enough left of her to pour into a jar. Dread and certainty of that outcome welled in his chest.

The tunnel opened up into a chamber of sparkling darkness. This was Lascaris's Star Chamber—the Stella Camera. Lined in crystalline salts, moonlight from the open well above shattered into shivering reflections. At the bottom of the chamber, a lake of black water reflected the sky above, still and heavy as an obsidian mirror.

Sig whined, looking up at the moon and down at the water.

Gabe knelt at the water's edge and shifted Petra in his arms. Her pulse thumped weakly in her throat.

"Petra, can you hear me?"

She made no indication that she did. He stripped off her coat.

"The Stella Camera is a place of purification, a place of distillation. If there's any magic that can stop the poison, this is it."

He lifted her body and waded into the water. His coat floated behind him like black wings. The salts were heavy enough in this water that a body could float on it. It was warm from the underground spring feeding it from below, like bathwater.

The water soaked Petra's clothes and hair, pulling it out of its pins like seaweed. When he was waist deep, he let go. She floated in the black pool, suspended. She had been here before, had loved it. Maybe she would remember.

He wasn't sure what he expected to happen. He

suspected that the basilisk was an embodiment of the second phase of alchemy, the dissolution process. The Stella Camera was a place that Lascaris had constructed to work the distillation process, to purify the soul. Was there enough magic left in it to drain the poison from Petra? Or was it like the Lunaria, weakened and faded beyond any use?

Her body drifted a bit away from him in the water. He reached out to take her pulse. In despair, he could feel that it hadn't changed.

Perhaps . . . perhaps it was like the Lunaria, in that it would take time to work. Lascaris had used it once against poison, Gabe remembered, when a rival had slipped him strychnine. Lascaris had convulsed in the pool for hours before emerging, exhausted, but wrathful. On assignment from the Pinkerton Agency to spy on Lascaris, Gabe had watched. He had not intervened, as he had not yet been given an order to execute Lascaris. And truth be told . . . Gabe was curious about what Lascaris knew. As an investigator of the occult, Gabe had seen a great many things, but Lascaris was unique. And the alchemist had been tougher than he'd thought. Lascaris slept for three days, then murdered the culprit. The memory gave Gabe hope.

He touched her wet cheek with the back of his fingers. He bent and kissed her cold lips. They tasted of the soft salt of the pool and a tang of acid, bright as lemons.

"I will be back."

He turned and waded back to the shore. The coyote watched him with narrowed eyes.

"Stay here and watch her," Gabe said.

The coyote's suspicious gaze followed him as he walked from the chamber. He stared out at his mistress floating in the black pond and lay down like a dog at the foot of a bed.

"Good dog."

Gabe strode into the darkness.

If the Stella Camera couldn't help, there was only one thing that he was certain would: the blood of the right side of the basilisk.

And he would wake all the Hanged Men to get it.

CHAPTER ELEVEN

UNDERTOW

Everything hurt.

Even places without nerves ached. Her toenails hurt, the joints in her body, the lining of her lungs . . . even the hair on her head ached like a bad case of road rash soaked in hydrogen peroxide.

She'd tried to hold her breath when she ran from the snake, running as fast as she'd ever run in her life, but she'd tripped on a rock and taken in a small, involuntary breath. That tiny bit of air burned, rushing into her lungs like fire. And then there was darkness.

She felt heavy in this darkness, like a stone at the

bottom of the sea. She could hear the trickle of deep water filtering through stone and the echo of that drip. There was no wind, no sounds of animals or birds—just that hollow sound of water's persistence.

Shivering, Petra opened her eyes. She was lying on cold ground, her fingers wound in Sig's fur. He turned and licked her cheek with his warm tongue. He made a face and rubbed his tongue on the roof of his mouth, as if she tasted bad.

She struggled to sit and gather her bearings. It was dark all around her, dark in the way that only the world underground can be dark. A diffuse light emanated from a cavern roof overhead, shining with dim phosphorescence in stringy clusters. It reminded her of the Waitomo Glowworm Caves in New Zealand, starry filaments of chandeliers gleaming with a blue sheen above her.

As her eyes adjusted, she could make out what looked like streets—bricked streets worming away in the dark, coming together from five directions to form a single point. She ran her fingers over the brick. It felt old, centuries-old cracked clay, and it seemed that each one was carved with symbols. Her fingers felt oddly sticky, and they seemed to smear into the brick.

She bent closer to get a look. Her gold pendant spilled from her collar, scraping the brick. She squinted at triangles and stars—some of them she recognized from her research as alchemical symbols for earth, air, fire, and water. But the rest of the script was foreign to her.

"You shouldn't be here."

A voice echoed from over her right shoulder, and she jumped.

A man in a white cloak stood over her, carrying a lantern. He unshielded the lantern, letting its golden light spill over Petra and the bricks. He removed his hood, and Petra found herself staring into a familiar lined face.

"Dad?"

He knelt beside her, and she flung her arms around his neck. "I've been looking for you!"

He embraced her with bony fingers, then held her at arm's length, frowning. His hazel eyes were clear and present, not cloudy and distant as they were in the nursing home. His buzzed-off hair had grown past his shoulders and was tied back in a knot. He was not who he had been in the physical world, but he seemed so much more extant in this black here and now.

"Is that why you're here—looking for me?" He looked at her as if she'd done something monumentally stupid, like that time she'd blown up the back side of the carport playing with her chemistry set when she was eleven.

"I . . ." she looked around at the converging dark paths. "I think I might have fucked up."

"Yes. I think you might have fucked up, too."

Sig sat on his rump, tongue lolling from his mouth. It seemed that he agreed.

Her dad reached out to pet Sig, and Sig allowed it,

making an awful face of contentment as her father rubbed his golden ear.

"Where are we?" she asked.

"We're at the Umbilicus Mundus—the navel of the world. It's the gate to the underworld."

"The underworld?"

"This is where all roads meet. You must have really been fucking up topside to get here."

She made a face at her father. "It wasn't on purpose!" She winced at the sound of her voice. It sounded like she was thirteen again.

"Clearly not." Her father untied his cloak and wrapped it around her shoulders.

"Dad!" She flinched back.

Her father's head and hands were flesh, but the rest of him wasn't . . . he was bone. Pure white bone, bleached as if he'd been a corpse lying in the sun for hundreds of years.

Sig squinted at him and cocked his head.

"Yes, I'm naked." He sighed.

"Ew. That's just . . . bizarre." She didn't want to think about what it meant for her, psychologically, that she was clearly hallucinating her father as a skeleton. It disconcerted her almost as much as falling back into speaking to him as if he was her parent and she were a cranky teenager.

"I don't always get to pick the form I get in the underworld. Not that you're doing much better." He gestured at her.

She looked down and bit back a retort. She was

covered in goo. Black goo, like crude oil. When she rubbed her hands together, it seemed like her hands were smaller than before, as if some of her flesh had rubbed away with it.

"Oh. Yeah. Maybe not."

"You're stuck in an alchemical process. Dissolution. What happened to you?" He took her hand in his and squinted, poking at the ooze. "Are you following in your old man's footsteps and fucking around with the wrong alchemy texts? Which ones? Not Melchoir. Tell me you're not reading Melchoir. He was full of so much shit . . ."

"No. No, I am not fucking around with any alchemy texts!" Petra rubbed the bridge of her nose with her free hand, only to feel her fingertips pushing into the cartilage. She pulled her fingers away, and they come back with a string of tar. She tried to flip it off, but it wouldn't detach from her middle finger. "I was chasing a snake and inhaled some of its breath. Which, apparently, is pretty toxic."

"A snake?" Her father sat upright, bones rattling. "What kind of snake?"

"A huge snake. About thirty feet long. Green, with a yellow crest . . ."

"And yellow eyes! Yes, yes!" Her father became excited. He picked up a pebble and began to draw on the brick. He drew a fair likeness of the snake in white, with its feathered crest and slitted eyes. "You met the basilisk."

"Don't look so enthused."

"The basilisk is amazing. Well . . ." He looked her over again. "Well, she's amazing from a distance. At least a quarter-mile upwind. With binoculars."

She lifted her gooey hands in surrender. "Lesson learned."

"The basilisk represents transformation and dissolution. She's poison, but she's also the key to eternal life. Blood from the right side of the basilisk yields eternal life, and the left side is Medusa's blood, certain death."

"Mmmkay. So is it—she—is one of Lascaris's leftovers?"

"Probably. I did a fair amount of looking for her back in the day. But I suspected she was buried too deep for me to reach her, sleeping."

"She's a subterranean creature?"

"That's my guess."

"I wonder if the earthquakes woke her up. We've had some weird seismic activity lately."

"Could be. Or she might have woken up on her own to lay eggs."

She stared at her father. "Are you shitting me? There's more than one?"

He shrugged, a motion that made his humerus clatter against his scapula. "Why not?"

"Awesome." She rested her head in her hands, forgetting that she was apparently made of goo in this spiritual plane. She made a face and pulled her sticky hands away. Sig made no move to wash her face again. She wasn't sure what to do with her hands, and they dripped on the symbols of the brick.

"What is this stuff?" she asked.

"The bricks tell the story of the Emerald Tablet, the first alchemical text. It was rumored to have been a gift to humanity from Thoth himself. In painstaking detail, it goes through all seven alchemical processes: calcination, dissolution, separation, conjugation, fermentation, distillation, and coagulation. I've been working on translating them from the source material, trying to learn the processes firsthand." His fingers brushed the brick with a bit of possessiveness.

"But that's really the least of your worries." Her father pointed to her. "You've got to solve *that* problem before you chase down any more snakes or further your alchemical education."

"No kidding." She let her hands dangle in her lap. "What do I do?"

"Not sure," her dad admitted.

"What do you mean, you're not sure?"

"I don't know *everything*." He crossed his arm bones across his ribs with a grating sound. Sig had sneaked up beside him and took a test bite of his fibula.

"Sig, that's rude," Petra said. Not that Miss Manners had written a newspaper column on it, but she was quite sure that was rude, on any plane of existence.

"Listen to me." Her father took her gluey hands in his. "All I can do is share what I know about alchemy, and you'll have to make your own decisions. I screwed up, not too far from where you are now. I don't want you to get stuck here. Like me."

"What do you mean, you screwed up?"

"I got stuck in my own phase. The separation stage, the third stage of alchemy. I was trying to isolate the Alzheimer's, to get it out of my brain. Things went wrong, and . . . this is the only way that I can keep my wits. Here." His hand sketched the underworld.

"I'm sorry, Dad."

"I know. And I'm sorry, too . . . for everything that happened when I left. But listen . . . we don't have time for that now. You have to use what I did as knowledge to help you move on. You've got to get through dissolution and into separation. That's the next stage."

"So." She took a deep breath and looked around her, at the bricks and the roads into darkness. "I can't stay here."

"No. You've got to pick a road. Find a symbol that speaks to you. Bring it back here. That's your best hope."

"Is that what you did? In this place?"

He nodded. His smile was wan. "And I picked wrong."

She climbed to her feet. "Are you coming with me?"

"I can't. I can't influence your decision. Just . . ." He shook his head. "I took bad advice, and I got stuck."

"Stroud. He gave you the bad advice."

"Yes. And I'm ashamed of that. Just . . . just follow your heart, kiddo." His hazel eyes shone.

Petra kissed him on the receding hairline above

his forehead, the way she had so many times before in the nursing home. This time, she left behind a tar-like smudge. He handed her his lantern.

Squaring her shoulders, she faced the paths.

Sig stood beside her, wagging his tail, nose working at the dank smells in the darkness.

She peered at each path. She didn't have an intuitive bone in her body. She had no idea how to follow her heart. The darkness was impenetrable, and no path looked any better than any other.

She dug into her pocket for the Venificus Locus.

"That's cheating," her dad said. "The underworld is about weighing your heart, not the logical stuff."

"I don't care if it's cheating, Dad. I want out."

She found the Locus and held it up to the bluish light. The goo on her hands slipped into the channel around the grooves, clogging it.

"Damn."

"Told you."

She resisted the urge to stick her tongue out at him.

The right-hand path was closest. That was as good as any. She struck off down the tunnel.

Behind her, her father made a *harrumphing* sound.

The lantern cast a golden light along the walls of the tunnel. It reminded her a bit of the tunnels beneath the Lunaria in the Hanged Men's subterranean domain. The floor of the tunnel was smooth underfoot, as if it had been trod by many feet before her. Maybe that was a good sign.

Or not.

The tunnel opened into a round chamber. She lifted her lantern high as she spotted a glimmer of something in the center of the floor.

It was a cluster of rock quartz about as big as her skull. A lovely specimen. She knelt and lifted the lantern high over it. Shadows shifted in the flickering light within the facets of the quartz. It had surprising clarity for a cluster, with well-formed symmetrical facets and beautiful ghost inclusions within.

This must be it. She was a geologist—surely there must be a metaphorical rock in the center of her chest.

She reached down for it, but a voice stopped her.

"I wouldn't do that."

She glanced up, as a figure detached from the shadows gathered around the ceiling. It fluttered down by her feet.

She blinked. It was a great blue heron. But it was talking to her in a familiar voice: Frankie's voice.

"Frankie?"

"Don't look so shocked." The heron cocked his head and looked at her. Sig sidled around to take an experimental nip, and the heron slapped him with a massive grey-blue wing.

"Is this how you get around in the spirit world?"

The heron ruffled his feathers. "Sometimes. It gets me where I need to go. At least, it gets me around a lot faster than the toad suit does."

Petra rubbed her sticky fingers against her temple.

The spirit world was giving her one helluva headache. Her brain did not process symbolism well. "What are you doing here?"

"I'm here to tell you that things aren't always as they seem."

"Oh. So quoth the talking heron. Are you sober in the spirit world?"

The heron shook his feathers. His wingspan was impressive, nearly five feet across, and he wasn't even really stretching. "I'm *always* sober in the spirit world," he sneered.

"My dad says that I need to take this rock and bring it to the center of the underworld, the umbilicus."

The heron snaked his head down and stared at the quartz. "Look carefully." His dark eyes were reflected hundreds of times in the backlit quartz.

Petra got down on hands and knees and squinted at it. She looked deeply within, saw the normal ghosts and reflections moving in it. It seemed stable. Real. She reached for it . . .

"Look underneath," the heron insisted.

She peered at the base of the cluster, where it sat on the floor. Something was moving around it, not just a trick of the light.

She scuttled back. A snake had curled around the base of the rock and was regarding her with luminous eyes. It hissed, opening a hood.

Oh, fuck. It wasn't just a snake, a cute one, like a garter snake or a DeKay's snake. It was a cobra. She slowly backed away on her hands and feet, crablike.

If she'd snatched that rock up, the snake would surely have struck her.

The heron walked up to the stone, looking right and left at the reflections of the asp in the quartz. The giant bird ducked right, snatched up the snake in its beak, and swallowed it. It was a bizarre process . . . the snake's tail flipped and lashed at the edge of the heron's mouth, and the heron struggled to swallow it. It was visible, undulating and alive, as it descended down the heron's thin throat. Petra watched in fascination until the swallow was complete, and the snake had disappeared somewhere deep within the heron's gullet.

"Tasty." The heron nodded at himself, then at the quartz. "Are you sure you still want that?"

"Mmmm yeah . . . maybe not."

"Good choice. Gotta get back topside. Maria's making spaghetti for dinner. Which will be weird, after snake, but . . ." The heron burped and took wing into the shadows above.

"Thanks, Frankie!" she called.

She looked at the quartz cluster at her feet, then traded glances with Sig.

"I think I'll pass."

Sig was the first to turn and leave.

The second tunnel she picked was much the same as the first, except she could hear air moving through it—there had to be an opening to the surface world here, somewhere. She lifted the lantern as high as she could, but couldn't discern exactly where the sound was coming from. It sounded like an exhalation over a bottle, and she could feel the change in barometric pressure. She popped her ears three times before she reached a cylindrical chamber at the end. It was empty, except for a peacock feather lying on the stone floor.

That looked like something suitably magical that the Umbilicus would approve of.

She reached for the feather, but a breeze pushed it away.

She held her lantern aloft. She couldn't see the ceiling of this chamber, but the sound of the exhalation had increased above her.

No matter. She set the lantern down and went to pick up the feather.

The feather scuttled up, away, as the wind rose.

"Damn it." Petra tried to catch it by cupping her hands, but the air pushed it away. It was like trying to catch a plastic bag in a rainstorm. She lunged over her head to try to snag it, leaping like a circus performer. If she could just get one sticky finger on it, she'd have it caught.

But the soughing wind sucked it up, out of reach, over her head and into the darkness above. Petra waited, thinking: *What comes up must come down.*

But it didn't. It had been carried away, likely sucked to the surface or jammed into a crevice somewhere.

She put her hands on her hips. "Well, fuck." She was reminded of a myth she'd read about in school about the Egyptian goddess of justice, Ma'at, who weighed the hearts of the dead against a feather. If the heart was lighter than the feather, the soul would ascend to the sky and not get gobbled by the crocodile-headed god, Sobek.

She had apparently failed this test.

She squinted upward. There was air there. Maybe a way out. Who said she had to play by the stupid rules, anyway? Her dad. But clearly, he didn't have a handle on the underworld, anyway.

She found a bit of a ledge and put her foot on it. That seemed easy enough. She found a handhold and started to haul herself up the wall, hand over hand.

Sig barked at her.

"Yes, I know that this is cheating. But nobody asked me if I wanted to play."

She jammed her hand into a fissure in the rock, hauled herself up, and planted her feet in footholds. She was doing a good job, she thought—ten feet from the ground, now. Maybe . . .

A gust of wind hit her, and she pressed herself to the wall. She thought it would pass, but it didn't. It just got stronger, pushing her from her footholds. Surely she was sticky enough to cling to the wall, to wait it out?

But, no. The wind intensified, and she was forced to back down. She slid the last three feet to the floor, leaving an oily smear on the wall.

The wind dropped back, and she made a face at it.

Damn. She guessed she'd have to play by the rules and find something else to bring back to the umbilicus. Three more tries.

The third path felt warmer, as if there might be an inviting fire at the end of the path. This path was lined with coal and soot. It reminded her of the one time she'd been in a crematorium, the way the heat shimmered in the air. She sure hoped her new sticky form wasn't flammable.

A red glow emanated at the end of the tunnel. On a slab of stone lay a sword, just pulled from a blacksmith's forge glowing in the wall. The sword was bright orange, not yet thrust into a bucket to cool it.

A sword. Perhaps that was the tool she needed to separate herself from the spirit world, to move forward. That would be the most tangible way to do it. But how to grasp it without getting burned?

A figure in black, wearing a blacksmith's apron, turned.

Her breath snagged in her throat, and Sig growled. It was Stroud, the Alchemist of Temperance.

"Shit," she hissed.

CHAPTER TWELVE

ONCE UPON A TIME IN THE UNDERWORLD

The Sisters of Serpens were going to kill him. Cal was convinced of it. Or worse. They could come up with much worse things to do to him. They seemed to have no issues with killing, and they liked to be creative about it. That was a bad combination, in Cal's experience.

Cal clung to the back of Bel's motorcycle like a flea on a wolf. Wind tore through his hair, and he buried his face against her back. He didn't want to look. He didn't want to see the trees zinging past at crazy speeds and close angles—this off-roading was worse than the land speeder chases in *The Return of the Jedi*. Cal had had a dirt bike once upon a time, and he thought that he was kind of cool because of it. Now, he realized that he'd been riding like someone who actually treasured his existence. A June bug hit him in the throat, and it felt like he'd been shot. Branches and leaves whipped past his face and slashed through his clothes.

Well, they weren't the clothes that he'd ripped off from the uniform truck. They'd re-dressed him in one of the dead guy's clothes. He was wearing the dead dude's boots and his leather jacket that smelled like bad aftershave, and Cal wanted to vomit. He was acutely aware that the clothes' original owner and his friends were currently crumpled up like broken dolls in the Sisters' luggage.

If that didn't make him want to barf, the ride sure did. But Cal wasn't sure what would happen if he hurled the entirety of his four-course chuck wagon meal down Bel's neck. If he did that, he was pretty darn sure that the hour of his demise would hasten to . . . *immediately*.

Not that any of this shit mattered. Bel had made it clear that he was on her magical leash. If he was beyond the reach of her pacifying power, this hypnosis, whatever the fuck she did to him, he was as good as dead.

Bel seemed to be guiding them by her own woo-woo internal compass. She would stop without warning, sit on the ground and meditate for what felt like hours, then get back up again to lead. She sure acted like she knew where they were going, and where they were going had run out of road. She led them into the wilderness, across dry creek gullies, through valleys, and among the pine trees of the deep forest of the backcountry. The park was crawling with rangers; more than once, she'd double back and take a different route to avoid the law. When they stopped to rest or eat, she'd be watching the horizon with a thousand-yard stare. Wherever they were going to meet the snake, only she knew.

Bel finally stopped at the edges of a forest, dismounting, and seeming as if she were listening to some supersonic sound that only bats and certain comic book heroes could hear. Probably just her and Aquaman. Cal was relieved to stop; the inside of his thighs and his ass ached from being on the bike, and he was grateful to have the chance to stop and stretch and settle his stomach.

"She's close," she murmured, her gaze distant.

Fuck. Cal squinched his eyes shut. "Is it like . . . a big snake? Like the anacondas on the Nature Channel?"

"Yes, Cal," she said with infinite patience, as if he were in kindergarten. "She's a very big snake."

He wondered what very big snakes typically ate, but decided that he didn't really want to know. He kept close to the bike.

Bel walked into the woods, her hands open at her sides, holding no weapons.

Maybe it wouldn't go well for Bel. And that was the

only possible way that Cal could imagine that things could go worse for him.

He sat on the ground, slapping at mosquitoes, as he waited with a handful of the others. The Sisters had built a fire, anticipating Bel's return. Edging close to the flames, he tried to force some warmth into his body. He had nothing to distract him but the dead guy's wallet, which had kindly been left behind in his jacket pocket. The guy's name, according to his driver's license, was Lewis Wayne Stewart. He was twenty years old and was from Idaho. Lewis had about five hundred dollars cash on him. Likely, he and his friends had been on vacation when they'd hit the wrong place at the wrong time.

He looked for a cell phone, but didn't find one. There was no reason to believe that the Sisters hadn't gone through Lewis's stuff before they turned it over to him. Maybe they thought he could use the driver's license as a base for a fake ID, but the whole thing was really squicking him out. Cal had no intention of taking on the name of a murdered dude. And he wanted out of this guy's clothes as soon as possible. It was all just bad karma.

"Are you doing all right?"

The girl with the purple hair sat down beside him and offered him her canteen.

"Thanks." He took a long draught and handed it back to her.

"Do you want a candy bar?" She fished a couple of chocolate bars out of her jacket pocket. They were the kind you got for two bucks when you donated to some kid's sports team.

Cal still felt queasy, but he didn't want to offend any of the Sisters. "Thanks." He fiddled with the wrapper and watched her sidelong as she nibbled her bar. "I, uh, usually don't take candy from strangers."

She extended her hand to him, which was covered in a fingerless glove crocheted from silver yarn. "I'm Dallas."

"I'm Cal. Is, uh, Dallas where you're from? Or is that your real name?" Cal didn't want to insult her by asking: *Is that your stripper name or something?*

"It's the place that I met Bel. Everyone changes her name when she becomes a Sister."

"So it's kind of like being a nun?"

"Kind of." She looked younger than the other women. Maybe it was the pale lavender hair. She had dark eyes and tawny skin. If he had met her on the street or in the Compostela, Cal would have been too bashful to speak to her—she was really hot. But it wasn't like he could do anything about that.

"How did you, uh, join up? Is it like joining the military or something?"

"Bel says that everyone comes to the Sisters on their own path. I had run away from my parents. My stepdad was kind of an ass."

"I can relate."

"Dallas was the nearest big city, and I figured that if I could survive my mom beating the shit out of me as much as she did, I could make it there. It didn't work out so well." She looked at the chipped blue fingernail polish on her hands.

"Yeah. When I left my family, I tried to go to Billings. It wasn't so good." Cal wrapped his arms around his knees.

"I wound up with a pimp who took all my money. I didn't have enough left over to eat and buy basic stuff. Like food and soap and things. It was pretty bad. One night, I saw Bel and the Sisters driving down the street. I thought they looked strong. Powerful. I really admired that." She picked at a loose bit of yarn on her glove. "They parked their bikes and went to a diner to get some food. I was watching them. One of my regulars tried to steal a bike. I went into the diner and stopped by her table. My heart was going ninety miles an hour, and my knees were knocking. I told her that this guy was trying to steal the bike and pointed him out through the window."

"Wow. That was really brave." Cal understood that life. If she snitched on a regular, and the regular told her pimp—that was at least a hospital-worthy beating, and could have wound up with her dead in a ditch, depending on the pimp's mood.

"I just wanted to do the right thing," she said. "For once."

"I get that."

"It was probably the one best thing I've ever done. Bel thanked me. She sent the Sisters out to watch the bikes, and she fed me. She asked me where I was from and where I was going. And she told me that I was coming with her, that she'd never leave me behind. And I've been with Bel ever since." She smiled. "I've always had a full belly and never had to turn a single trick. So . . . I feel safe."

Cal felt queasy. The Sisters were capable of unmistakable brutality. But also a weird kind of compassion. He didn't know what end of the spectrum he fell on, but he figured that being alive put him on Bel's good side. For now.

Dallas stretched out beside him on the ground, offering him part of a blanket. Shyly, Cal accepted it. They stared up at the stars, and he began to feel a little more normal. He began to relax, and dozed. Every light sound disturbed him, whether it was a crackle of fire or a voice at too high of a pitch. He curled up in a ball and wanted to melt into the earth.

"What's the most terrible thing you've ever done?"

Cal turned over, startled. Dallas was lying on her back and with her fingers behind her head. She wasn't looking at him, just up at the darkness.

"Wow. Most . . . terrible?"

"Yeah. What's the one thing you've done that you can't forgive yourself for?"

Cal was silent, but Dallas went on: "The worst thing that I ever did was providing an alibi for my pimp. I knew that he had something to do with murdering one of the girls. She was around one day, acting squirrelly, then she wasn't. We all knew that she was stealing from him. And I guess he found out. My pimp told me that I had to say I was with him when the cops came around. And I did." Her lip quivered. "I betrayed her because I was scared. I know that he did something to her."

"But if you'd told, he would have killed you, too."

"Maybe. Maybe I coulda gotten police protection or something. I know that I can't bring her back, but at least her mother would have known what happened." Her voice dropped. "But I was too scared."

"It wasn't on you," Cal said. He wormed a bit closer to her under the blanket so that their shoulders touched. "It wasn't your fault."

"Bel says that we all have darknesses thrust upon us. Many of those things are things that we have good intentions about. But we have to embrace our shadows."

"And you're having a hard time with it?" *Nothing like murder to cause you to have a crisis of conscience.*

"No. Not with any of the work I've done with Bel. Just what came before."

There was a silence then, settling over the blanket.

It was a long time before Cal spoke: "I've done a whole lot of things. Really shitty things. But the worst thing that I ever did was covering for a friend. She'd been driving drunk and hit the guardrail on the freeway. Totaled the car, but neither one of us was hurt real bad or anything. I told the cops I was driving, because I was sober. So I got a ticket, and she got nothing. Later that weekend, she drove drunk again, wrapped her dad's car around a telephone pole, and died. If I had told the truth to the cops, she would have been in jail and not out driving that night. So . . . yeah." He blinked. "I know that I'm responsible for her death. But I can't tell anybody."

"You just did." She reached under the blanket and squeezed his hand.

He blew out his breath. "Well, you're kinder than most."

"Bel can take that memory away from you, if you want."

"What do you mean?"

"Through a course of hypnosis, she can close it right off from the rest of your brain."

"She can?" Cal didn't like the idea of anyone putting their fingers in his head with a giant Sharpie and redacting things out.

"Sure. She took out years of memory from Irina." She gestured with her chin to a tall, willowy woman gathering firewood. "Irina was sold as a child bride. She has peace now."

Cal stared at the woman. A flower was braided in her hair behind her ear. There was an aura of serenity about her.

"So . . . why don't you have Bel take that memory of Dallas from you?"

"I will. I'm not ready yet. I still feel like there's something I need to do about that experience . . . maybe call up the detective on the case and give an anonymous tip. Once I work up the nerve to do that, then, yeah . . . I want Bel to close that door for me. We don't have to carry our sins with us forever, you know. It's okay to let go when it's time."

Cal mulled that. Bel could wipe out memories. What could she take from him? Could she take any of those dozens and dozens of miserable experiences from him that made him the raging wuss he was today? Could she make him a blank slate? Would he even want that?

And he realized the extent of her power over the Sisters. She had the power to bend their wills and memories, to calm the beasts within. She was much more dangerous than Stroud had been. All Stroud had to control his garden flowers was drugs. Bel had much, much more: She had the power of reshaping how they experienced their lives, from the inside out. She could take away pain and grant absolution. She could channel violence and command loyalty. She was the most dangerous person he'd ever known.

He pulled the blanket up to his chin and pretended to sleep.

The rest of the Sisters had returned by the time the moon had sunk overhead. Tria was in front of the processional of women, grinning. There were flowers wound in her hair and the hair of the other women—it was like they had just come from some kind of hippie love festival. Maybe this was their version of a victory march. He expected to see Bel with a snake draped over her shoulders like a boa, petting it and whispering at it. He craned his neck to see around the sparks and fire.

Fire glinted on scales and milky eyes.

Cal squealed and scuttled back.

But it was Bel. Bel was wearing the skin of a giant snake. Her gaze was distant, as if in a deep trance. The head of the snake fit over her head like a suit of armor, with the cloudy eye membranes perched on top. The silvery skin behind the head, translucent as mica, was about four feet wide. It flowed down her back like a wedding veil, where it dragged on the ground for yards.

"They killed the snake," he gasped

"No," Dallas said, laughing. "They found its shed skin. It's a gift to the Priestess. It means that we have been accepted by the Great Serpent."

Cal had no idea of how she was possibly able to make that kind of logical leap, but she grasped his hands and pulled him to his feet. "Rejoice with the Serpent!"

Someone pulled out a drum, and the Sisters began to dance around the fire. Cal waddled clumsily among them. Some knew the cha-cha, three were working on a line dance, and there was more than one belly dancer in the group. Bel was one of the belly dancers. As she moved, the fire played through the translucent snakeskin, giving it fire and volition of its own. Other women picked up the tail, and Cal had a weird memory of being in a school parade once upon a time.

Once upon a time ... when the world wasn't fucked.

Once upon a time when his chances of survival were greater than a mosquito in a bat cave.

Dallas grabbed his sleeve and drew him into the inner circle of the dance, showered in sparks and glitters of silver jewelry.

Once upon a time was over, so he might as well dance.

It was getting awfully crowded on the trail of the basilisk.

Gabe swore as he scanned the horizon. He'd brought as many of the Hanged Men as he could wake (and they had been more sluggish than usual; he blamed the winding-down of the Lunaria for that). They'd ridden on horseback to the remote location where he'd last seen the creature; he'd hoped that the snake would remain to feed upon Petra's traveling companions. In a perfect world, the snake would be full and lumpy and sluggish . . . and easy to shoot.

But the field and the edge of the woods were crawling with ranger vehicles. The raven that he'd sent out to spy on them showed him that yellow tape was tangled in the bark of the pine trees, and radios crackled over the flash of red and blue light in the darkness. Men and women came in a steady stream, their hands covered in gloves and faces by gas masks. Some wore the same type of plastic suit that Petra's traveling companions had been wearing.

"Damn." Petra and her companions must have filed some kind of itinerary and missed a check-in.

"What now?" One of the Hanged Men, Mitchell, was alert enough to ask as he fidgeted with the reins. Mitchell was nearly as old as Gabe, and was one of the ones who still remembered how to speak.

Gabe was silent for a moment, thinking how best to manage this without being seen by the rangers. If the Hanged Men were discovered for what they were, then this mission was pointless. They had to stay hidden.

He checked to make sure that his pistol was loaded. "We make some noise. Just don't shoot anybody."

They left the horses at the sheltered edge of the clearing. Half of Gabe's men fanned south with Mitchell, around the cordoned-off scene, while Gabe took the remaining handful north, creeping through the crickets and the grasses to outflank them.

Minutes later, gunshots sounded from the south.

The rangers shouted and swept spotlights into the darkness. A vehicle moved, shining headlights to the source of the distraction. Shadows ran away from the scene.

And Gabe and his men rushed in. They sprinted into the pine forest, ducking under the yellow tape. He hoped that if the basilisk had been driven off, then at least it had left a trail. Gabe's men needed little light to see, but the moon was strong and clear, streaming through the branches above.

The basilisk had left something behind. A half-chewed, plastic-wrapped body lay on the ground, like leftovers on a picnic table. There was no sign of the one that had been dangling in the tree. Maybe the rangers had taken it down, or perhaps the snake was digesting it. Gabe sidestepped the blackened bits of pine needles and the yellow bark burned by acid.

He scanned the dark for any evidence of a trail.

The rangers had left fluorescent plastic markers where bullet casings had fallen, scattered on the ground. One of the markers had been placed beside a pine tree— and it was stained with something other than acid. He could make out a crimson smear on the soft bark. It wasn't Gabe's blood—Gabe's blood turned a phosphorescent gold, like a firefly, after dark. Petra hadn't been bleeding, and the members of her traveling party were too far away for the blood to be splashed and smeared by the snake here. This had to be from the snake— likely grazed by a stray bullet. But there was no telling which side of the snake it had come from.

Gabe took out his knife and scraped the bark from the tree.

"Drop it and put your hands up!"

Gabe glanced up. A man in hip-wader boots, a forest ranger uniform, and plastic gloves was aiming his service gun and a flashlight at him. The guy looked familiar—he had seen him with Petra before. The name HOLLANDER was embroidered across his chest pocket.

Gabe's fingers tightened around the piece of bark and the knife in his hand. He wasn't giving it up.

"I said, drop the weapon. And that evidence, too."

"I can't." Gabe stood.

The rest of the Hanged Men slipped around the trees, guns lifted. Gabe waved them back. In the moonlight, Gabe guessed that Hollander could only see silhouettes and perhaps the glint of moon on metal, but nothing more.

But Ranger Hollander turned, aiming his gun at

the Hanged Men. "Drop it, gentlemen. You're tampering with a crime scene."

Gabe didn't want to have this confrontation. He stepped back. "I don't want any trouble."

"Then quit screwing around with my crime scene and drop the weapons."

More rangers were closing in—flashlights bounced over the trees and swept over Gabe's knees.

"Gun! Gun!" someone shouted.

And someone opened fire.

Gabe felt a bullet collide with his shoulder. The bullet wasn't magical. It wasn't wood. It passed through the material of his shirt, skipped along his skin, and deflected into the pine needles.

There was no point to this confrontation. Against mortal men with ordinary weapons, the Hanged Men would be immediately victorious. But the murder of rangers in a park would call more trouble down on his head than even the snake could manage.

Among the bright muzzle flashes and crazed sweeps of flashlight, Gabe and his men retreated, melting into the darkness. The rangers tried to pursue, but Gabe and his men didn't need their light so see by, and they slunk away.

He had what he needed.

As he snagged his horse and rode away with the others, he was reminded that there were no such things as easy choices.

When Gabe was living, things had been easy. Choices were black and white then, living and dead, night and day. Since he'd been dead, everything had washed out to a curious shade of grey, and there were never any good answers.

He returned to the Lunaria with the blood of the basilisk—what little there was. The Hanged Men followed him, waiting silently for him to offer the blood to the Lunaria. The blood would either save them or kill them, depending on which side it had come from. He held their unlives in their hands, with this small piece of bark stained with magical blood.

Their judgment weighed on him, thick as shadows. But the decision had already been made: Life over unlife.

Without comment, he let himself into the chamber below the Lunaria. As he descended, he felt the roots of the tree inquiring, tugging at his shirt. The tree could taste the magic, just as much as he and the rest of the men could. None of them could tell whether it was a destructive or a creative power—only the magnitude of it. It was thick magic, this little sliver, and the Lunaria was curious.

Gabe twisted away from the tree's probing and headed down the tunnel to the Stella Camera. If he had more of it, he'd consider using Sal as a guinea pig. He'd steep it into a tea and feed it to him, see if he recovered or withered before proceeding. But Petra had no time. Sal and the Lunaria had more, whether it was weeks or months.

And she was alive. That was worth preserving.

The moon had sunk beyond the opening of the well, and the Star Chamber was soaked in darkness. With his preternatural vision, he could see Petra's silhouette off in the center of the pool, like a leaf on a puddle.

The coyote had fallen asleep on the shore. He didn't open an eye as Gabe's feet crunched in the salts on the edge of the water.

Gabe stripped off his oilskin, gripped the piece of bark in his teeth, and waded in. He swam out to the dark shape on the water, letting the heavy salt support him as he reached her.

He hoped that she was still alive, that he hadn't been too late. Her flesh was the color of a dark bruise, and the skin on her throat had an alarming stickiness about it. But her chest rose and fell shallowly, the gold pendant on her collarbone shining softly in the dim.

Gabe gently opened her mouth, slid the piece of bark under her tongue. He closed her jaw tenderly.

And there was nothing left to do now, nothing but wait.

Stroud was here.

Petra reached for the sword. But the red-hot metal scalded her hand, sizzling the black tar on her palm. She gasped and clutched her hand, stepping back. Sig flung himself between Petra and Stroud, barking furiously.

"Hello, Petra," Stroud said smoothly. A cold smile crackled over his craggy face. "You didn't last long in the material world."

"It figures you'd be down here. In hell."

"And doing my damnedest to figure a way out."

Petra backed toward the opening of the tunnel. She reached down for Sig to pull him away. Stroud might be alive in the spirit world, but maybe she could outrun him.

Stroud lunged for the sword. His hand glinted silver, like he was wearing an oven mitt. She'd seen that trick before. He snatched up the freshly-forged sword and advanced on her.

"Maybe I could trade you for a way out. Your spirit might be worth something to . . . something. Despite your current state of . . . well, disarray." He looked her over head to toe, at the black gunk covering her.

Sig was having none of it. He pounced on Stroud, flinging him to the floor. Metal hit the ground with a ring—Petra couldn't be certain if it was his fist or the sword that hit first. Unwilling to abandon Sig and flee, she rushed behind the stone slab to find Sig standing on Stroud's chest and snarling. She stomped and kicked at the sword, succeeding in knocking it away from his fist . . .

. . . but her boot got stuck in Stroud's mercury hand.

Stroud howled. Petra figured that anything that caused Stroud pain was a good thing. She ground down harder with her heel, and the slick metal smeared under her foot. Like dragging her foot out of a fresh cow patty, she struggled to free her boot. Stumbling back, she was shocked to see Stroud writhing around his hand, which was stuck to the stone floor like a smeared bug on a windshield.

"Sig!" she shouted.

Sig backed away from the melting Stroud. They retreated back down the corridor to the intersection point among the roads.

Her father was still there, sitting at the center, tracing the symbols on the brick like a child doodling in a coloring book.

"Dad," she panted. "Stroud is . . ." She hooked a thumb back over her shoulder.

"Yeah. He's been around. You might want to avoid him." He made a face, the same one he used to make when his in-laws were in town.

"Dad!"

"He's not going anywhere." He looked up at the ceiling and squinted. "But you're running out of time. Unless you want to spend an eternity trapped here with him and your dear old dad . . . you'd best get a move on."

She threw up her slimy hands in disgust and picked another tunnel.

In this one, she could strongly hear the sound of water. Perhaps there was an underground river? She minced through ankle-deep puddles to move forward, and was conscious of the sound of water ringing through the fissures in the rock above her. Water sluiced in sheets along the walls, and she was mindful not to touch them and wash away what remained of her oozy skin.

The tunnel dead-ended in a wall of water, a small cataract. A low pedestal hewn of basalt stood in a puddle, and on the pedestal perched a glass chalice. Within the glass chalice, a goldfish swam.

"This is it," she told herself. Her father had told her to follow her heart. "Water is all about the heart and emotions and that touchy-feely stuff, right, Sig? This is all symbolic. I suck at this symbolism stuff, but this *has* to be it."

Sig cocked one ear, seeming to agree with her train of thought.

She set the lantern down. Crouching, she reached out over the puddle to pick up the chalice. It felt cool and shone clear as crystal. She was careful not to spill any water or disturb the fish, holding the chalice in her filthy cupped hands. The fish swam in a clockwise direction, slowly. It was kind of hypnotic, really, the way the glass reflected light on its gold skin. It looked a lot like the fish she'd won at a carnival as a little girl. That fish had lived for over ten years in a bowl on her dresser, surviving three moves and numerous toys dropped in the water. What had she named that fish? Jaws? Remembering gave her a warm fuzzy feeling that she hadn't experienced in a long time.

A coyote face took up her field of vision. He pressed his muzzle into the chalice and devoured the fish.

"Sig!"

She jerked the chalice back, sloshing water. He just leaned in and began to slurp noisily out of the chalice.

"Jesus, Sig." Defeated, she set the chalice down on the floor of the cave. Sig grunted his approval and licked it clean.

"Well, I hope that was awesome for you." She sat down on her ass, dejected. She was certain that the chalice had been her key out of the underworld. "That was really an asshole move, my friend. *You* may not be stuck in the spirit world, but I don't want to be."

Sig snorted and trotted from the cavern.

"I sure hope eating that fish did something for *your* spiritual development."

After a few moments, she climbed to her feet to follow him, feeling more than a little pissed off by how the universe had been treating her, lately. The idea that she was personifying the universe as something that was singling her out for extra-special negative treatment disturbed her, too. It showed her how truly out of touch her rational thought processes were becoming.

Maybe there wouldn't be something that wouldn't kill her in the last tunnel. Maybe it wouldn't be poisonous, or burning or . . . Stroud. Yeah, that would be good.

The last road led to a drier chamber. On the bare floor sat a birdcage that contained a single black raven. The raven stared at her with black eyes.

"Oh."

She looked down at Sig, who was looking all smug. "I'm sorry, dude."

Sig *harrumphed*. He wasn't going to let her forget this.

Gently, she picked up the birdcage. It was an old, chipped wire cage, the kind of thing you'd see in a catalog that sold shabby chic furniture and things covered in chalkboard paint. But the bird inside was very much alive, cocking its head and watching her as if she were something shiny.

"Let's give this a shot."

She carried the birdcage back out to her father, set it on the floor between them. She felt a bit proud at having successfully brought back *something*, and she stood over it with her arms crossed.

"Well, that's interesting," he said, peering at the birdcage.

"What's interesting about it? Other than the fact that I managed not to break it, and Sig didn't eat it?"

"The raven's symbolic of the fermentation stage of alchemy, the fifth stage. That's the stage where everything rots."

"Okay. Is that good or bad, given our current predicament?"

Petra's dad wiggled his finger between the bars of the cage. The bird pecked at him. "Not sure. It's a more advanced stage than where you are now. So, it could be good. Or it could mean that you're well on your way to getting oozier. Come here."

She stood before him, expecting some kind of magical ritual or at least a knighting of some kind.

"Stick out your tongue," he ordered.

She did as she was told.

"Not like that. Say '*ahhhh*.'"

"Ahhhhhhhh."

He peered into her mouth, at her tongue, and shook his head.

"What?" she demanded.

"There's not enough. So little against so much poison."

"Awesome." Petra made a face. "Well, I ran out of roads. This is it."

Her father nodded and placed the cage in the center of the crossroads, where the bricks had come together in a circle.

"Good luck, my dear," her father said, his eyes crinkling.

"Wait." She grabbed his wrist, trying to ignore the disconcertingly-bony ulna under her fingers. "You're not coming with me?"

"I doubt there's enough magical juice in that cage to get both you and your coyote back intact. Hitchhikers would reduce your chances of success." He lifted his hand to touch her sticky cheek. "There will be another way for me. Another time."

The cage began to rattle, like a teakettle on a stove. The bird fluttered inside, agitated, as the cage turned in circles of its own accord. The door of the cage sprang open, and the bird flew out.

"Oh, shit!" Petra cried, reaching out to catch it.

But the raven had split into two birds, bleaching from inky-black to white.

She glanced back, saw her father smile.

"Excellent, my dear. Most excellent."

She'd never seen him look this proud of her before, and she was confused. She hadn't done anything, yet . . .

Light filled the chamber, bright as sun on ice. And it all faded to white—her father, the cage, the cavern—it all disappeared.

CHAPTER THIRTEEN

SACRIFICE

When Petra opened her eyes, black sky stretched above her in a skylight cut in the earth. She could make out a handful of stars overhead, and a pale violet glow to the east.

She was cold, cold and heavy, and there was something stuck to her tongue that tasted like pine sap. She gagged, spat it out, and took a deep breath. Water lapped up around her chin.

A furious crashing and rain of water collapsed into her. Sig. He slathered her face with his tongue, dogpaddling into her chest hard enough that her head nearly went under.

Hands gripped her collar and she gasped, slapping the water with her arms to regain her equilibrium.

And she found herself staring into familiar amber eyes, bright as coals.

"Gabe?" she sputtered. "Where are we?"

He smiled, scraping her wet hair back from her face. Jesus, it had been ages since she'd seen him smile. His arm supported her shoulders as they trod water, and he pointed up. "The Stella Camera."

Her brow wrinkled. "Why are we here? What happened to the snake?"

"The basilisk is still free in Yellowstone."

"And Phil and Meg?" she dreaded the answer. "Are they okay?"

Gabe shook his head. "They didn't survive."

She shivered, hard enough to shake water from her hair into Sig's face. Sig circled them in the black water, yipping and making low conversational *mrrps*.

"Tell me what happened."

"First, I need to see if the poison has worked through."

Gabe swam them to shore, towing Petra in the crook of his elbow, Sig in the lead like a happy little flagship. Petra felt leaden and puffy at the same time, as if she'd taken one hell of a beating, and the swelling had started to rise. She stumbled up on the bank, and Gabe picked her up and carried her to a semicircle of rocks at the edge of the cave. Fire sputtered inside a galvanized steel bucket. Sig shook himself off in a shower of salt water that fizzled against the flames.

Petra gratefully extended her shaking hands to the warmth. She looked down at them as if they were a stranger's hands. Underneath the freckles, her skin was pale as curdled milk, and the blue of her veins pulsed oddly beneath, as if they were trying to push something away.

Gabe took her face in his hands. At first, she thought he meant to kiss her, and she lowered her eyes. But he turned her face right and left, tracing his fingers over the veins of her neck.

"Look up." She did, and he peered intently into her eyes. "Look down."

Her gaze fell to the salt crystal ground. He lifted each eyelid with his thumb.

"What are you looking for?"

"Signs that the venom has been defeated." He lifted her hair off the back of her neck, resting his fingers there while his thumb took her pulse. "The basilisk's breath is legendary poison."

"That must have been what killed those campers at Pelican Creek." She envisioned that violet mottled skin of the little girl, the red, bloodshot eyes of her father.

"Yes."

He knew. He *had* been spying on her. "So that was you . . . your raven there?"

"Yes. Open your mouth."

She stuck her tongue out at him. He was exasperating, and he deserved it. The gesture seemed lost on him, or else he was ignoring it, while he examined her as if she were a piece of horseflesh at auction. He nodded, and she closed her mouth.

"Give me your feet."

She struggled to sling her soggy feet in his direction, but numbness made her clumsy, and her boot laces flapped against the fire bucket with a bell-like ring that made her wince.

Gabe took her feet and put them in his lap. He unlaced the boots and stripped off her socks. Petra stared at her feet. They looked like they'd gotten a good case of frostbite, black and bluish. She wiggled her toes, experimentally, just to see if she could. That much was a relief.

She shrieked and nearly kicked Gabe in the face when he drew his thumbnail down the arch of each foot to check her nerve reflexes.

"That's an improvement over where you were," he said dryly.

She resisted the urge to stick her tongue out at him again, and pulled her legs back with her hands beneath her knees.

"I brought you some clothes," Gabe said. He reached behind the bucket and handed her a canvas pack.

"Thank you." She worked at the drawstring of the back with dead fingers, took two tries on the laces before he took it from her and opened it. She stared down at the glittering salt, embarrassed. She felt as helpless as a child.

Gabe reached for her again, and she thought he

meant to check her pulse again. Instead, his fingers worked the buttons of her shirt.

"I can . . ." she began.

"Hush."

She closed her eyes and let him pluck open the buttons of her shirt. He undressed her as tenderly as a lover would, his fingers hesitating over a broken vein or a bruise on her shoulder or calf. She was exhausted and tired of fighting. He dressed her in a soft flannel shirt that she guessed belonged to him, a pair of broken-in jeans, and socks that felt like wool.

He wrapped a blanket around her shoulders, tucking it under her chin. Sig snuggled up against her thigh and put his wet head in her lap.

"Thank you," she said, keeping her eyes shut.

"You're welcome."

His voice sounded more distant. She opened her eyes.

He was dressing in the half-darkness beyond the rocks. In glimmers of the firelight, she could make out the line of his shoulder and his thigh.

She looked away, aching and confused. In her lap, Sig grinned and shook, as if laughing hysterically at God-knew-what. She frowned at the coyote. If he had any bit of Coyote, the one with a capital "C" within him, he was certainly no stranger to the confusion of human and inhuman flesh.

Gabe returned to sit beside her at the fire, dressed in dry clothes. He offered her a canteen of water. She drank greedily, and it felt soothing on her swollen throat. It tasted vaguely of iron, not salt, and she was grateful for it. Water trickled down her chin, but she didn't care.

"So . . . what happened?" she asked softly, when she finally stopped for a breath, clumsily wiping her cheek with the back of her hand. "How did you happen to be right there, at that time?" She wanted to add: *Did your spying raven find me? How long have you been following me? That's completely creeper, especially for a guy who can't acknowledge my presence on the street.* But she bit it all off and waited for him to tell her.

Gabe stared at the fire and put a chunk of wood in the bucket. "We were following the basilisk. I kept . . . I kept seeing you on the trail." He shook his head. "I couldn't remember who you were. I had the image in my head of you, you holding a gun on me. I kept seeing—the Venificus Locus. And I had the feeling of it being pulled from me . . ." His fingers pressed his heart, where she had taken it from him.

"Below the Lunaria. I thought you were dead. You were hanging there . . . in pieces." She shuddered.

He pulled away from her a few inches. "I wasn't . . . completely reintegrated. And I wouldn't have been able to, if you hadn't pulled the Locus out. Still probably am not. The tree is dying. That's why we're pursuing the basilisk."

She wasn't going to let him retreat back into himself. She grabbed his wrist, clumsily, with her hand. He seemed to hesitate, then covered it with his hand.

"The basilisk has venom, but it also has the power of

eternal life," he continued. "Lascaris conjured it, back when his hold on Temperance was beginning to falter. He went to the spirit world, trapped it, and brought it back here to serve as his guardian. At that time, he had come under attack by some powerful interests of the town who suspected him of dabbling more in magic than business."

"And was that part of your work—as a Pinkerton agent sent to investigate him?" He had spoken of this before, and she wondered if he still remembered as much.

"I was more covert in my dealings with him. I worked myself into his social circle, and we became . . . well acquainted."

"You were his friend."

Gabe was silent for some time before he spoke again. "I was fascinated with him. He had a gift for connecting the impossible with the possible. He was so much more than the charlatans I'd seen before, the table-tippers and the channelers of the dead. I did my best to disprove his work in my own mind, but I could not. He did amazing things, and I let myself be pulled into his orbit. He came to trust me, over time, and revealed many of his miracles to me."

Petra shuddered. "Strange company you kept."

"You were not the only one to think so. He also came under the scrutiny of the Church. A new priest had been sent to Temperance after the old one had died. Father Brennan was rumored to have studied as an exorcist, so you imagine that he might be . . . somewhat overly sensitive to such things. And Lascaris was never the type to successfully hold himself up as a morally righteous man. If you recall, Stroud traced his lineage back to a liaison with Lascaris and the town madam."

"So he was easy pickings?"

"For a priest with a great deal of charisma, who could strike the fear of God into his congregation? He was certainly a target of interest. Father Brennan's sermons became heavy on the ills of womanizing and merits of stoning sorcerers." He shrugged. "I forget most of it; I was barely able to sit still for half a sermon in that time."

"But Lascaris was convinced he had enemies. And he was not wrong. Aside from the skeptical investors I represented and the priest working on his own, there were some members of community who had witnessed strange things around his house. There was talk of ghost lights traveling up and down the roads, of women who he'd called on who had vanished. One of them was found later in a valley, with a cabbage where her head should have been."

"That's . . . kinky?"

"I never did figure that one out," he admitted. "Nor did I determine exactly why he had a patch of pumpkins that bled when they were cut. I suspected that he was growing a homunculus, but . . . with him, one never knew."

"Halloween at his house must have been something else."

"Many of the rumors that surrounded him were

just idle gossip and ignorance. But Lascaris got poisoned taking Communion, and was concerned enough to call upon a guardian afterward. That little incident took a great deal of his energy to resolve—he stayed here, at the Stella Camera, for many days, to purge it from his system."

"Which is why you brought me here."

Gabe nodded. In the telling of the story, she had pressed her head against his shoulder, and she could hear the buzz that passed for a pulse in his chest. His right hand tucked the blanket more tightly under her chin. "Yours was a much more serious poisoning than the ordinary strychnine Lascaris had been dealt by the priest. But I hoped that it would work against the basilisk's poison."

"The basilisk. It's a lot tougher than I imagined for a spirit-world creature." But it was here, and that gave her some distant hope that perhaps her father could eventually be drawn back.

"Lascaris brought it through with a great deal of trouble. Anything that moves from the spirit world into ours must have a vessel to contain it. It can be as simple as a mirror, or as complicated as a fresh corpse. For this creature, Lascaris began with an ordinary rattlesnake. But the creature's spirit was too large for such a small body. And it changed, evolved into what you saw today."

"So, it *is* a snake?"

"It started out in this world in that shell, but it was never a simple snake. The basilisk and its ilk were said to have sprung from the blood of Medusa when Perseus decapitated her. I have no idea how far Lascaris had to travel into the spirit world to find such a creature in the first place. I saw it once at his house, sunning itself on his roof. Lascaris had a hard time convincing it to crawl down his chimney, away from casual passersby."

Petra didn't want to imagine that creature curled up underneath the Airstream. Her trailer was perched on the land where Lascaris's house had once stood. She hoped that it didn't have a sentimental attachment to its old home.

"Lascaris ultimately found it to be too difficult to control. They had a standoff one summer, at Turbid Lake. The earth shook, and the creeks ran backward for many hours, until Lascaris emerged alone from his ordeal three days later. He went into seclusion for a month. I don't know if he was in mourning for the creature, or regenerating his energy." He trailed off, his amber gaze settling on the dark glass of the salt pond.

"And you pursue it now because it can save the tree?" She imagined the snake slithering around in these tunnels, and shivered.

"The blood from the right side of the snake has the power of eternal life. And the left is poison of Medusa's blood, living death."

"You want the blood for the tree."

"I think it can restore it, just like it restored you."

She blinked at him, remembering the taste of pine sap and copper on her tongue. She knew Gabe not to be especially prone to acts of altruism. He'd gone after the snake at great risk.

"You got the blood . . . and you gave it to me?"

He nodded and looked at her with his level amber gaze. "You're more important."

"Gabe, I'm not . . ." There was nothing miraculous about her, not like the Hanged Men. She wasn't magical or undead or a living avatar of the power of alchemy. She was ordinary, and she had no understanding of why he would risk such a thing—his world and the other men in it—for her.

He reached for her cheek, and his touch on her jaw was like a feather.

A smile played on his lips. "Well, to be fair, I didn't know what side of the basilisk the blood had come from."

"Gabe, shut up."

"You're worth it."

He cupped her face in his hands and kissed her. He tasted like sunshine with a rim of something metallic, something utterly fascinating. It warmed her, trickling down her throat to her chest, full of promise and a stillness of the certainty of time.

She was so close.

Bel could feel it.

The knowledge hummed within her, singing along her spine and gathering behind her eyes like unshed tears. This moment. It was the culmination of everything she'd sought, the long journey and all the blood and all the interminable miles of road. She reached out with her senses, and they brushed up against the Great Mother. She was curled up here, waiting.

Bel stood on the edge of a seething mudpot that had formed by Raven Creek, sinking to her ankles in silt. It burned even through the leather of her boots, pressing around her calves with scalding intensity as it mingled with cold creek water. The mud steamed around her, twisting in pale tendrils around the snakeskin she wore. Her breath made ghosts in the chill predawn air.

Ahead, the mouth of a cave rose from the sea of mud, erupted from deep within the earth. The rock of it was sharp and new. Air, earth, fire, and water had gathered here, in this spot. Hot gases from the underworld sighed with the sound of a dragon inhaling, exhaling . . . And it paused, as if the earth itself were holding its breath, waiting with Bel.

"Great Mother, Medusa. We have come to serve you."

She was conscious of the Sisters of Serpens behind her, gathered at the shore of this sea of earth and steam and bubbling water. She could sense the pulse of their fear, their weakness.

She opened her arms, unfurling her hands in supplication. Her rings glittered in the light, and her heart hammered in anticipation.

Something moved in the mud, back at the mouth of the cave.

"Great Serpent, come to us, your faithful servants."

A pair of yellow eyes glowed in the dark and rushed forward. Bel sucked in her breath. Gasps sounded behind her, and she heard Cal whimper.

The serpent skimmed forward, whipping over the surface of the mud. Her dark green body was easily thirty feet long, with a golden crest of feathers flaring above her eyes. She had taken the form of a basilisk in this plane of reality. The Great Mother reared up before Bel, looming easily four feet above her, in the posture of a cobra, regal and timeless. She was atavistic in her beauty, untouched by the civilizing influences of men. She pulsated pure id, beyond good and evil and any human constraints.

She *was*.

A smile split Bel's face, and her heart sang. "Great Mother, you are magnificent. You honor me with your brilliant presence." What had this magnificent serpent seen, in all her time on this Earth and in other planes? What did she know? What had she brought back?

The basilisk lowered her head a foot, inspecting Bel. Her tongue flickered beyond her mouth, and Bel glimpsed her fangs, embedded in a head larger than a pumpkin.

"We have brought you a sacrifice."

Footsteps slogged through mud behind them. The basilisk looked over Bel's shoulder, twitching in alarm.

Bel didn't look back, but lifted her hands to the serpent, cupped as if she were offering it water in a bowl. "Please accept this offering."

The bravest of the Sisters slogged forward, carrying

the large military duffel bags they'd tied to their bikes. They dumped the contents of the bags into the mud at Bel's feet: three bodies, the three young men who had tortured the snake to death. They were curled in on themselves to fit the bags, sawed and twisted and broken. But they were meat.

The Sisters retreated, but Bel remained, rooted in place. This was the most sublime moment of her life. Her body hummed so loudly with magic she was certain that the basilisk could hear it. It sang from her heels to the crown chakra at the top of her head, completing a circuit in the mud and steaming air.

The snake peered at each body in turn, flipping at them with her tail, the way a cook might test pancakes with a spatula to see if they were done.

Bel dared not move. She hoped that the Great Mother Goddess would find these acceptable. If not, she still had Cal. She glanced back at the bank. The boy was held fast in the grip of two of the Sisters. He wasn't going anywhere. She'd cast him to the mud, without any hesitation, if the Mother preferred live food.

The serpent lunged at Bel.

Bel held her ground, expecting in that split second to fulfill her duty to the Great Serpent by becoming breakfast. But the basilisk sunk her teeth into the body floating at Bel's feet, splashing hot mud against Bel's jacket. The basilisk dragged the body away, back to the darkness of the cave. Waves of hot mud lapped at Bel's boots in her wake.

She grinned, elated. The Great Serpent had accepted the sacrifice. The Sisters of Serpens were now her servants, aligned with the will of this irresistible force of nature.

And they would be unstoppable.

CHAPTER FOURTEEN

THINGS WORTH FORGETTING

Petra dozed against Gabe's chest. She'd been conscious of Sig kicking her a few times in his sleep, but Gabe seemed to sleep less fitfully than the coyote did. Pressed against her ear, she listened to the hollow buzzing of his blood, like a radio tuned between stations. It was soothing, in its own odd kind of way. Once in a while, that steady pulse would be punctuated by something that sounded like the flutter of wings.

She wondered how much longer he could last, how much longer the tree could. She felt such sorrow at the idea that he'd sacrificed the tree for her, and a marrow-

deep unworthiness. Yet, she also wondered what that meant for her. She could no longer taste the basilisk's blood on her tongue, and she knew she had gotten barely enough of it to drive off the venom—her father had said so. But she was pretty sure she'd be checking the bathroom mirror to make sure that she wasn't sprouting scales anytime soon.

And she wondered about Gabe. She took him at his word, that his fractured memory had returned, that the regeneration was occurring more slowly. Still, what was to keep him from forgetting her again in a few hours? From dissolving slowly from her sight and her world, like he had before? And what if he couldn't remember the rest of the Hanged Men, forgot himself? Forgot how to pretend to breathe?

She felt him shift a bit beneath her. She turned over, pressed her chin to his collar, and asked, "Could it happen again?"

"Could what?" He kissed her temple.

"Could you lose your memory again?"

His mouth thinned. "I don't know. If the tree dies . . . I would think that we'd all begin our processes of disintegration, somehow."

"We can't let that happen," she vowed. "We have to find the basilisk and get more of its blood."

"'We' are doing no such thing." He tucked a tendril of hair behind her ear. "You are going to go home and recover from the venom. I'm going to gather the rest of the Hanged Men and find the snake."

"Nuh-uh." She pulled the Locus out of her pocket.

"I can track the basilisk better than you can. Ravens or no. And that thing's killing scientists, campers, and probably random picnickers by now. I'm going with you."

He blew out his breath in frustration and stared up at the ceiling.

She settled back on his chest, placing the Locus on his collarbone. "I'm glad that's settled."

"You are impossible."

"But I'm rational. You can't argue with reason."

"I might take issue with that."

Daylight had begun to cast a pink glow inside the Stella Camera. A thin, pearly mist from above had sunk down over the pool, casting a weirdly reflective softness into the room.

A shadow flew in. Petra started, and a raven landed beside them.

It stared at Gabe hard and began to caw an alarm.

"What's wrong?" she asked, scrambling to catch the compass as Gabe sat up.

"Something," Gabe said, reaching for his gear. He turned his head away from her and opened his hand. A mass of feathers arose from his palm, forming a raven of its own. That raven took wing and flew up to the hole in the ceiling with the other.

His gaze was distant, as if following something she couldn't see. Petra started pulling on her waterlogged boots. They were crusty with salt, but hadn't shrunk.

"There are police at Sal's doorstep," Gabe said, frowning. "They're looking for you."

"Why would . . ." Her brow creased. "Oh, shit."

She reached into her pile of wet clothes, into one of the dozen pockets of her cargo pants for the tracker Mike had given her. She held it in her palm. "Mike Hollander gave this to me before we went to track the snake. The water certainly killed it, but it likely tracked my location here."

Wordlessly, Gabe climbed to his feet and gave her a hand up. "We'd better concoct a convincing cover story."

With Sig plodding sleepily in their wake, they wound through the tunnels. Petra lost her sense of direction more than once, but Gabe's sense was unerring. He gripped her sleeve as they walked through the darkness, and she followed the firefly-like brightness of his eyes.

They climbed to sunlight in a pasture, as Gabe pushed open a sod-covered door in the ceiling of a tunnel. Horses grazed in the bright morning, and Sig was enchanted by the sight of them. Once lifted to the surface, he immediately lowered himself to his belly and began to skulk through the grass around the horses.

"Sig, you're going to get kicked," Petra muttered as she and Gabe climbed out.

But the stalkees ignored him. Gabe whistled, and a sorrel horse came to him, his mouth full of grass.

"You remember Rust," he said.

"No?" Petra reached out to touch his speckled nose. Rust let her, chewing thoughtfully.

"He brought us here. He's secretive and fast."

"Very good qualities for a horse in your company."

One of the Hanged Men approached, holding a saddle and bridle. He handed them to Gabe and did not make eye contact with Petra.

She stared down at her sodden boots, feeling guilty as Gabe saddled Rust. And she wondered if the Hanged Men would ever mutiny against Gabe. She had the impression that they needed him to interface with Sal and the outside world, on some level. But she realized that she knew very little about them, as individuals.

"Thank you," she said.

The Hanged Man had turned to go, but he stopped and looked back, startled. He tipped his hat at her and nodded. Maybe they weren't used to being talked to.

"Can you ride?" Gabe asked her.

"I can drive anything with wheels. I don't know anything about horses," she admitted.

"You won't be on him long, and he's a good horse. Pull right or left to turn, and back with the reins to stop. He'll figure that out, so you don't need to think about your feet."

"You're not going up to Sal's house with us?" Her brow creased.

"No. Your friend Hollander and I already had a run-in last night. I'm hoping he didn't see me clearly, but it's not wise to tempt the deductive skills of cops."

"Do I want to know about that?"

"No. It's better if you act surprised—both to see him, and when he tells you about last night."

"I'm sure I will be." She lifted an eyebrow, certain it was one helluva story. "I'll see you at sunset, then?" She patted her pocket to make sure that Gabe hadn't lifted the Locus from her. It wasn't like he could work it, anyway . . . but she didn't trust him not to try to put her on the "fragile items" shelf.

"At sunset."

He reached for her and kissed her soundly. Petra smiled against his lips, feeling the buzz of that dark sunshine against them.

"Up you go," Gabe said, gathering Rust's reins.

Petra stepped into the stirrup and swung her leg over. She called for Sig, and Rust began to walk north, toward Sal's house. She noticed that a raven followed them, circling in broad arcs above.

Sal's sprawling house was at the edge of the property closest to the main road. The Rutherfords had been here since Gabe's time, and the house looked as if it had been the crown of a rustic empire since then. It was a timber lodge, the roof oxidized green from the rain. In its scale and rustic style, it was a house that was meant to be seen.

A green Forestry Service Jeep and a county sheriff's car sat in the driveway. Petra wondered if the deputy had come with Mike, or if Sal had called them. Sal was related to the county sheriff, and the sheriff's deputies were as useless as possible when it came to enforcing laws against Sal. She couldn't imagine Sal taking too kindly to Mike showing up on his doorstep, with or without a warrant.

"Well. Speak of the devil, and she shall appear."

Sal sat on his porch, which had been outfitted with a ramp. He was perched, pale and pasty, in a motorized wheelchair, with one hand on the controls and the other around a mug of coffee. A pair of deputies in uniform sat on Adirondack chairs beside him.

The raven perched on Sal's copper gutter, watching closely.

"Petra!" Mike Hollander fairly sprinted down the ramp to greet her. "We've been looking for you. Your tracker signal stopped somewhere in Sal's back forty." He glanced back and gave Sal a dirty look.

"I told you I had nothing to do with that girl." Sal glowered. He finished his coffee, shook the empty mug, and one of the deputies got up to take it back into the house. He returned in moments with a full cup. Clearly, the deputies were used to hanging about in Sal's kitchen.

Petra clumsily climbed off the horse, not exactly sure which leg came over which side first. Rust huffed and trotted away, not seeming to want to have anything to do with Sal.

"I don't remember much of what happened." That was true, and it was the jumping-off point of the misdirection. "The snake attacked, and Phil and Meg were down. I got hit with some of the vapor . . . I got as far away as I could."

Mike stared at her face as she spoke. She expected that he saw some of the fine lines of the venom still beneath her skin, since dark shadows still crossed the backs of her hands and her arms.

"There was a horse . . . I climbed up on him and passed out. I woke up in Sal's field."

Mike was scrutinizing her, and she could see him itching to ask about the shirt she wore, which was obviously too big for her.

"I guess the horse belonged to one of Sal's employees. And Sal's men were kind enough to offer me some clothes and a place to wash up."

It was true. All of it. But there were enough omissions to satisfy the local police and give Sal cover. Which, by extension, was good for the Hanged Men. But it sure wasn't going to be good enough for Mike.

"See. It's a simple misunderstanding," Sal drawled, as a deputy handed him a fresh cup of coffee.

Mike nodded. "Thanks so much for your time, Mr. Rutherford. We always appreciate it."

"Anytime, young man."

Mike grasped Petra's elbow and headed for the Jeep. Sig was already enthusiastically pissing on Mike's tire, as if he'd been holding it in all night.

"You know, you could have called," Mike said.

"I lost my cell." She gestured at the house. "I was heading back here to see if Sal would let me use his landline." The raven on the gutter cocked his head and watched her as they piled in the Jeep. Sig bounded into the backseat and began to root around in Mike's gear.

Mike started the Jeep and put it in reverse. He

backed out of the driveway and had made it out to the main road before he spoke again.

"I am pissed at you. But also happy to see you."

At least he was in touch with his feelings. "Mike, I'm sorry. I . . . did you find Phil and Meg?"

"When you missed your call-in, I hit the GPS trackers. We found Meg at the edge of the pine forest. She was in the same shape as the campers at the campsite—decomposing, but torn all to hell like a dog's chew toy. We haven't found Phil yet."

"Phil's dead," Petra said, pressing her fingers to her upper lip. "He . . . the snake dragged him up a tree. There wasn't a whole lot of him left."

"We saw a good deal of blood," he said quietly. "I tried to ping his tracker. I got a few blips, but it died for good about a hundred yards from the site. I'm guessing that it got eaten? Or maybe crushed beyond repair."

Petra stared down at her hands, still mottled from the venom. "Look, Mike. I didn't intend for this to go all wrong."

He blew out his breath in frustration. "I'm not mad at you. I just . . . I know I should have been there. And I let all you guys down. It was a shitty idea, and I should have put a stop to it."

"You couldn't have prevented it," Petra said. "And you could have gotten killed."

"Well, I'm sure as hell gonna prevent any more fatalities. The park is closed. The official reason we're putting out is unusual seismic activity. When I called up Meg and Phil's chain of command, it sounded like they're gonna send out the rest of the ghost squad."

"More biologists?"

"Yes and no. Turns out, Phil and Meg were active duty Army. Toxicologists."

"You were right. And that stun gun they had didn't look standard issue."

"Yeah. So you can well imagine that the Feds are mighty pissed. There will be boots on the ground soon, and they'll hunt that snake down." Mike squinted into the sunshine. "They'll want to talk to you, about what you saw."

"Of course."

"And you might want to work on your story. They might not buy the idea of a unicorn coming out to save you."

She grimaced and turned away. It had sounded like an excellent idea at the time, but was sounding lamer and lamer, the more Mike gave her the business about it.

She asked to go home, but he drove her to the hospital. After a thorough argument, she consented to an exam, with the condition that she would call for a ride home when she was through. She argued that there was no point in him waiting in the ER when he'd been up all night with no sleep, and he grudgingly agreed that he had work back at the station. It wasn't like she had wheels or a horse to wander away with. He did, however, distrust her enough to hover over her until she'd been officially admitted with a hospital bracelet. She made him promise to drop Sig off at Maria's house while she was tied up. He agreed, and left her in an exam room, satisfied that she seemed confined in someplace abominably uncomfortable.

"Oh. You again." Dr. Burnard pulled aside the hospital exam curtain to greet Petra.

"Hi." Petra swung her legs on the edge of the bed. "Do you live here?"

"More or less." Dr. Burnard flipped over the notes on her clipboard. "So . . . you managed to get involved with every weird case on my record."

"It's a gift."

Petra gave her an abbreviated and well-edited version of coming into contact with caustic vapors in the course of her duties that might or might not have involved a giant snake. Dr. Burnard examined her skin and eyes, listened to her lungs and heart, and ordered blood drawn.

"Is there any news of Cal?" Petra asked quietly.

Dr. Burnard shook her head. "No. Not a thing. Though there have been a lot of folks who have asked, including Cal's Army recruiter."

"What?"

"Cal's Army recruiter came by to check on him. I told him that Cal would not pass anybody's physical, on any day of the week."

"Cal isn't an Army type of guy."

"Well, he might want to be clearer on that if he ever turns up outside of a body bag. Those guys are persistent."

Petra sat back and mulled that while her blood was being drawn. Did Phil and Meg hear about Cal's case while they were here? Or had the military run across this through the course of their preliminary investigation of the scientists' deaths? It was as she'd suspected: bad news for Cal, and it was bad news for anything supernatural lurking in the shadows of Temperance—including Gabe and the rest of the Hanged Men.

They had to get the basilisk and put it to bed before anyone else got it. Of that much, she was certain.

Petra spent the late morning watching shows on home remodeling on the television in the waiting area. Apparently, no one on cable television ever checked for load-bearing beams, duct work, or electrical wiring before knocking walls down, willy-nilly. She'd been ravenous, and she'd devoured two bowls of cereal, an apple, two cups of coffee, and three cups of Jell-O before Dr. Burnard came back.

"Let's discuss your results." The doctor led her to a private exam room and closed the door.

"Okay." Petra was feeling better; the marks on her skin were fading, the Locus had verified that there was no alchemical funk remaining in her blood, and she was ready to get on with things. She sure as hell didn't want to discuss magic and the blood, breath, or venom of the basilisk.

"You appear to be in a mildly hypercoagulable state. Which is not unexpected—when cobra venom comes into contact with blood, it clots and causes blood to turn into some pretty gelatinous goo."

"That's a scientific term?"

"For our purposes, yeah. So I'd say that you got exposed to something extremely unusual, but you're processing it out well."

"Awesome. Can I go home?"

"Not yet. We have to talk some more about your blood." Dr. Burnard pulled up a chair and sat opposite where Petra perched on the bed. Warning bells went off in Petra's head. That was the kind of thing physicians did when they donned their bedside manner hats, and she didn't like it.

"In your last blood test, I commented on an elevated white cell count."

"Yes, and you told me to follow up with my regular physician."

"I'd like to do a couple more tests now. I'd like to check your lymph nodes."

"Um. Okay."

The doctor checked the lymph nodes in Petra's neck, under her arms, and groin.

"So. What's up?" Petra perched on the edge of the table while the doctor stripped off her gloves.

"I think you came out of the poison thing pretty well. You're breathing nicely, not having any respiratory distress or undue pain. The rest of your numbers are similar to what I saw when you were last here. Your white cell count is a little higher, though."

"You mentioned that it could be an infection or a cold or something."

"Yeah. Your lymph nodes are swollen. You need

to make an appointment to get that checked out. I'll write you a referral."

"Thanks." Petra took the sheaf of paper she was given, and called Maria's house from the nurse's desk. She'd have to figure out how to get a new cell phone. Maybe she could pick up a throwaway phone up at Bear's store.

"Hello?" It was Frankie, voice slurred by sleep or drink; she wasn't sure which.

"Frankie, it's Petra."

"Hey, congrats."

"Huh?"

"You made your way into the spirit world. Nice work. And it seems you got back all right."

"Mostly. I . . . I was wondering if maybe Maria might be around to pick me up? I'm at the hospital." She felt vulnerable now, without Sig and her truck and even her own clothes. The only clothes she had were Gabe's soft but ill-fitting jeans and flannel, unless she felt like parading around in a drafty hospital gown.

"Maria's at work, but I'd be happy to come get you."

"Frankie, no." He was likely drunk. "I'll just call Mike . . ."

"No worries. I'll be there in a jerk."

And he hung up.

Fuck. She was contributing to Frankie's rap sheet.

She waited on a bench outside the hospital, watching people go in and out. Many seemed in much worse shape than she felt, and she tried to cheer herself on: *Gonna get ready to battle the basilisk. The Lunaria will* be safe, and the Hanged Men will be recharged for another hundred and fifty years. Yeah. Everything's gonna be just fiiiiiine.

Frankie drove up to the patient pick up area in Maria's Explorer. Sig sat in the passenger's seat, seemingly taking his job as navigator very seriously. Frankie popped open the passenger's door.

"Climb on in. Sig and I were discussing the merits of potato soup for lunch. Do you like potato soup?"

Petra climbed in. "You know, I would love some potato soup."

"Excellent. We can discuss the mess you've gotten yourself into."

Frankie seemed sober, actually. He didn't drive through any stop signs, go over the speed bumps too fast, or ignore the lights. He stayed in his lane the whole trip back, didn't go over the speed limit, and didn't leave his turn signal on. Petra began to relax. Sig crawled on her lap, and she stroked the coyote's ears as she stared out the window.

"You saw your dad."

"I did."

"And you clearly made a good choice, one that got you back to this place."

"How is it that my father is stuck there, but you can pass back and forth at will?"

Frankie tapped his head. "Years and years of accumulated crazy will do that. And some tequila worms. It's a talent."

"There's got to be a way to get him back."

"You've taken the first step. You've found him. With a proper soul retrieval, he might be able to come back."

"I hope so." She leaned on the window, her gaze miles away.

"You're going to hunt that snake, aren't you?"

"Yes."

"With Sal's vultures."

"With his ravens, yes." Frankie hated the Hanged Men. If he knew how closely she'd been involved with them, he'd take a swing at her.

"Stay away from them. Those boys are inhuman." He chewed his bottom lip, and his chin jutted out. Petra knew they had done terrible things to him, on Sal's orders. There was no making peace between them. "Not that you'll take that advice anytime soon."

Petra said nothing. She could lie to Mike, but there was no use lying to Frankie.

They arrived at Maria's house. Petra had never been so relieved to be there. Frankie invited them in and began to poke at the soup in the Crock-Pot. Sig flopped down in the middle of the colorful carpets of the living room floor, to the chagrin of Pearl, Maria's cat. Pearl climbed up on the top of the couch and stared daggers at him, which he ignored.

The screen door banged open, the bells tied to it jingling. "Hi, there!" Maria's face broke into a grin at seeing Petra. "I had a feeling to come home for lunch. How are you?"

She dropped her briefcase and extended a hug for Petra. Petra took the hug and held on tightly.

"Honey, what's wrong?" Maria sat her down at the kitchen table, rubbing Petra's flannel sleeve. "You look like you went three rounds with Mike Tyson."

"Yeah, that's not . . . I mean . . . There's a lot of stuff going on." Petra took a deep breath and filled Maria in about her search for the giant snake that left bodies in its wake. The words came out in a tumble, and she was certain that she made less sense than Frankie on a bender.

"Okay. Giant snake. You went looking for it. Of course." Maria remained still, blinking, seeming to absorb what Petra had said. She wasn't shrinking back in disbelief, just seemed to be processing the knowledge that a giant magical creature was wreaking havoc in the backcountry. Since Maria hadn't suggested a voluntary psych hold, Petra was assuming that she believed her.

"The snake killed two people in our scientific expedition, but didn't kill me, thanks to some woo-woo that I still don't get. Gabe and I are going after the snake tonight," Petra blurted. "We have to find it before the military guys do . . . the snake's blood is key to the Hanged Men's survival. It's just a fucking mess."

Maria took Petra in her arms. "Oh, honey."

Petra couldn't help it. Confronted with so much sympathy and acceptance, she broke into tears. The one thing she couldn't stand was people being nice to her. Maria held her while Frankie rubbed circles on her back, until she'd cried herself down to dry hiccups.

"Here." Frankie slid a coffee cup with three fingers

of whiskey in it across the table. "You need this more than I do."

She downed the whiskey and the potato soup. Maria called off work for the afternoon, over Petra's objections, saying: "We need to take care of you. We need to prepare you for tonight. I'm going to draw a hot bath for you, stuffed full of herbs and potions to get your circulation going. Then, you're going to take a nap. I will find some women's clothes for you. And, finally, we'll figure out what provisions you're gonna need to fight the snake."

Petra nodded. She was unused to having anyone take care of her, but after last night, she realized that some part of her craved the simple kindnesses that humans gave each other freely, without expectation of return.

In the sun-drenched cottage, Maria and Frankie spoke about her in low, unintelligible tones as Petra soaked in a hot bath stained the color of tea with fistfuls of herbs tied up in cheesecloth. The herbs and the oils soaked the pain from her muscles, and she felt softer, more alive. Maria provided her with a pair of jeans, a clean T-shirt, and socks and underwear. Grateful, Petra dressed and fell asleep in Maria's bedroom, which was decorated with beautiful wallpaper of birds and a mountain of crocheted blankets and hand-pieced quilts. Maria's bed smelled like lavender, and she fell asleep within one or two breaths.

Her dreams were disjointed. Snakes slithered over Phil and Meg, who lay motionless on the ground in

Tyvek suits. She felt Mike's disapproving glare on her, and heard her father humming the theme to *Hawaii 5-0* in the background. She thought she heard Cal's voice somewhere in the dreamscape, but she couldn't find him, no matter how hard she looked in the forest. A raven perched on her shoulder, plucking at her hair with his beak. Bits of chemistry leaked into her dream, formulas of acids and bases and things that fizzled and burned.

When she awoke, afternoon sun streamed in through Maria's lace curtains. Petra rolled over and contemplated going back to sleep. It was tempting to remain here, in this cocoon of calico cotton, for a few more minutes. She felt safe. Which was a rare thing, these days.

But safety was an illusion. She forced herself to roll out of bed and pad out to the living room.

Frankie was stretched out on the couch, and Sig lay on top of him. "Good morning, Sunshine." Sig wagged his tail, pounding the colorful afghans on the back of the couch.

Maria handed Petra a cup of coffee. "Feel better?"

"Yes. Much." She drank the coffee greedily. "Can I borrow a pencil and paper?"

"Sure thing." Maria dug a notebook and a pencil out of the stack of phone books beside the refrigerator. "I called Mike and let him know that you're here. I didn't tell him anything else."

"Thanks. He'd just . . . overreact."

"He does that. But don't worry about him. He's a big boy."

Petra sat down at the kitchen table and began to scribble.

"Whatcha working on?" Frankie asked.

"A grocery list. Of stuff I'll need to fight the basilisk."

CHAPTER FIFTEEN

FIRE

Preparing to fight the basilisk involved a lot of beer and hair spray.

Maria drove Petra, Sig, and Frankie to the hardware store in Temperance. Petra muttered to herself as she traveled up and down the dusty aisles, filling the countertop with a nonsensical collection of items: drain cleaner, copper pipe, a pipe cutter, aluminum dryer vent, aluminum foil tape, PVC pipe and fittings, pipe cement, a handful of bolts, duct tape, a barbecue ignitor, a welder's blanket, gloves, and helmet, tin snips, a hacksaw, drill, and a massive roll of pink fiberglass in-

sulation. The hardware store clerk, to his credit, made
no comment as she checked out. She stopped across
the street to pick up some aluminum foil, hair spray,
a pair of latex dish gloves, a disposable cell phone, and
four six packs of locally-brewed beer in glass bottles
with screw-on caps from Bear's shop.

"That looks like one heck of a party," Bear re-
marked.

"Yeah. It's gonna be." She sighed.

"I should warn you. That beer really sucks." He
held one bottle up to the light. There was sediment
drifting in the sludge.

"It's okay. Really."

"Your bad party is all on you, then."

They hauled all the gear back to Petra's trailer.

"I've never seen hair spray in your possession."
Maria picked up a bottle of Aqua Net from Petra's bags
and stared at it with suspicion.

"First time for everything."

"What can we do to help?"

"Actually, I need those beer bottles emptied . . ."

"Done," Frankie said, hauling the six packs out to
the front step.

Petra spent the next hour sawing at the pipe, gluing
adapters to create an area for the ignitor chamber at
the end of the pipe, and drilling space for the ignitor
in the chamber she created. She got the parts sealed
together in a shape that vaguely resembled a cannon.
Frankie had polished off several bottles of beer by the
time she was ready for a glass bottle.

"What is it?" Maria asked.

"It's a potato cannon!" Frankie exclaimed.

Petra grinned. "You bet. But we're not shooting potatoes today."

She went outside the trailer, popped the bottle into the end of the cannon. It fit snugly, and didn't fall out when she turned the pipe upside down. She sprayed the hair spray into the chamber end of the cannon for a couple of seconds, and screwed the pipe cap on. She aimed the cannon at a clump of sagebrush about fifty yards away, and pulled the ignitor.

The cannon erupted in a flash of fire and launched the bottle in the air. Behind her, Maria and Frankie whooped in victory. The bottle overshot the clump of sage, and she prepped the cannon to try again, holding it at an angle. Frankie was only too happy to oblige by draining the beer bottles for her to try, and she experimented with bottles full of water, figuring out that the device had a decently reliable range of about seventy-five yards. But closer was better.

"So you're going to shoot the snake with beer?" Frankie asked. "That works for me."

"Nah. I've got something more interesting in mind for the snake." She took the cannon back into the trailer, donned the pink latex gloves she'd picked up from Bear's store, and began to measure out the drain cleaner into the empty bottles over the kitchen sink. She sealed them with the screw-on caps, shaking them and holding them upside down to make sure that they wouldn't leak.

Maria opened her windows to let the trailer air out. "Drain cleaner is a nasty surprise."

"The lye in it should neutralize some of the acid. At least, that's what I'm hoping. And the glass bottles should be impervious to both the acid and the lye base."

Maria busied herself with cleaning and loading Petra's guns, sitting on the steps outside the trailer with a gun cleaning kit she'd brought. She'd also brought her shotgun to leave with Petra, properly accessorized with two boxes of shells.

"Just in case it gets closer than cannon range," she said.

"Thanks. I appreciate it."

As the sun lowered on the horizon, Maria made a sandwich run, and the three of them sat at Petra's table, eating sandwiches from Bear's deli. There had been a curious quietude to the afternoon as they made the preparations.

"We could go with you," Maria suggested as she fed pieces of salami to Sig.

"No. You guys should go home. This could go awfully bad, awfully fast." Petra smiled over her sandwich crust. "And besides, I need somebody to run interference with Mike. He's not going to be happy when he figures out that I'm not here."

"He's not your dad. You don't need his permission."

"Yeah, well. I hate lying to him."

"And I wouldn't ordinarily advise it. But . . . this is something that you've got to do. You and Gabe."

Frankie snorted. "You can't trust them. They're

Sal's men. They'll protect their own interests, and they'll protect him."

Petra placed her hand on his. "I know what I'm dealing with, Frankie."

But she sounded a lot more certain than she felt.

Sal's anger was a palpable thing, like a shimmering humidity before a storm broke.

Gabe knew that he was furious when Petra left with Hollander. The deputies departed shortly afterward, and Sal took that opportunity to take some potshots at Gabe's raven with his rifle. Sal's aim was terrible, and the raven escaped unscathed.

Gabe's strategy was avoidance. He had enough to do to prepare to fight the basilisk without worrying about Sal's tantrums. He and the rest of the Hanged Men kept a wide berth, readying their gear, cleaning their guns, and casting glances at the house.

The Hanged Men were not happy with Gabe, either. They spoke little enough at the best of times, but the silence now was deafening. They knew that he'd given the blood of the basilisk to Petra, and not the Lunaria. And certainly not Sal. He'd put them all in jeopardy by placing them in the line of fire once again. It felt like betrayal.

And he wasn't sorry for it. Not for an instant. The memory of Petra had been brought back to him, and he would not lose her again. In all the years that he'd been dead, he'd felt a gradual dulling of sensation, an erosion of emotion as time passed over him. It had worn away the sharp edges of feeling and left a smooth black stone in his chest.

But she made him feel something—more alive. He felt the churning of possibility. His blood quickened, and he had wanted nothing more than to linger with her in the Stella Camera. If there had been no time, no pain, no future of best-laid plans—he would have given anything to stay in that place. He wanted to memorize the pattern of freckles on her body, to feel the warmth of her mouth on his, to taste the salt on her shoulder.

She was ordinary. She was miraculous.

And he would sacrifice anything for her. The simmering resentment of the Hanged Men, Sal's wrath . . . it was all nothing in light of seeing her open her eyes in the dark. If she walked away forever, washed her hands of all the filthy business of the undead, it still would have been worth it for that one night of her dozing against his shoulder. He had not felt this way about any other woman, not even Jelena.

The decision was made, and he would make it work. He'd save the Lunaria, and he'd figure out some way to placate Sal afterward.

But Sal had other ideas.

In the afternoon, Sal's shiny pickup truck came barreling down the drive from the house. It plunged into the fields and jounced over ruts, splashing mud and breaking a fence post. Seeing him from a distance, Gabe first thought that Sal must have finally had a stroke, but his head was upright in the rear window of the truck, and he kept driving. He didn't stop for the Hanged Men, just went barreling past. Driving west.

A chill trickled down Gabe's spine, and he began to run.

The other Hanged Man sensed his disquiet. Ravens exploded overhead, heading to the Lunaria.

But Sal was already there. He had limped outside the truck with a cane and was pouring a can of gasoline over the trunk of the tree. The vapors shimmered in the afternoon sun, a warning of his invisible malice.

The ravens flooded to the tree, screaming.

Sal turned to look at them, murder on his face. He struck a match and tossed it at the roots of the Lunaria.

Flames blossomed, spiraling up the trunk. The birds that meant to roost in the tree flew past, cawing in a deafening cacophony of panic.

"Get some water!" Gabe shouted at the Hanged Men. Most fluttered back to the barn as birds to find feed buckets and anything that would hold water from the faraway siphon. The few that remained as men took off their coats to try to beat out the fire.

But it was going to be too late. That much was clear. The flames licked up the brittle tree, chewing through the leaves and branches. The fire roared, sparks pushed in the wind, black smoke blowing back over the grass, dripping fiery leaves.

Sal leaned heavily against the bumper of the truck, looking pleased with himself. He had had the same expression when he was a child, frying anthills with a magnifying glass. He'd never changed.

Gabe's hands balled into fists. He advanced upon Sal, grabbed his flannel lapels in his fists and shook him. "Why did you do that? Why?" he snarled.

Sal leveled him with the most evil look a human face could countenance. "You found the basilisk. You found its blood—and you gave it to that woman."

Gabe cocked his head. How could Sal have known? He glanced over his shoulder at his fellow Hanged Men, and a couple looked away. Sal had extracted the information from them. Or else, one of them had told him outright.

"That blood was promised to me. And you're going to suffer for it."

The field was burning now, the seed tassels of the grasses popping and sparking. This fire could spread, could cause so much more damage than just to the Lunaria.

Gabe hissed at him: "There is more blood. The snake is still out there."

Sal shrugged. "You boys forgot to follow orders. Now, maybe you'll follow 'em. For whatever short time you have left. I have your complete attention now. Don't I?" He cocked his sallow head.

Gabe hauled off and slugged him. Sal sprawled against the immaculately-washed hood of his truck, spitting blood against the shiny paint. Gabe picked the rancher up and threw him on the ground, twenty feet away from the truck, in the path of the fire. Sal struggled to get up, but couldn't do more than drag himself on his elbows.

Gabe reached inside the pickup to find the keys, and pocketed them. If Sal was going to get back to the house, he'd have to do it on his hands and knees, if the fire didn't claim him first.

The tree was sobbing. He turned.

A soft wind echoed through its branches as they crisped to ash. It was a sound of such sorrow that tears flickered in Gabe's eyes.

The tree was magnificent, still, even in its death. It sighed until all the leaves blackened and curled away, until the fine branches were consumed in smoke, flames licking over the lower branches from which more than a dozen men had been hanged.

By the time the Hanged Men returned with water to douse the fire, the tree was a black husk, part of a trunk and just a few main branches. They'd pumped water into buckets and cattle troughs, dumping it on the fire. But it had to burn itself out, these crooked singed black fingers reaching toward the sky.

Sal was crawling in the field toward home, determined to make it back to his log castle, even if he couldn't drive there.

Gabe's shadow stretched over him. Fury had risen in his chest, settling in his throat. "You had no right."

"It's my land," he gasped. "My tree."

Gabe considered beating him to death, stomping him to bits and burying him in a shallow grave that no one would ever find. He toyed with the idea of burning him, letting him die in sympathy with the tree.

"There's no point in letting him live," one of the Hanged Men, Mitchell, asserted. "There's no tree."

"Do with him as you wish." Gabe said. The image of the smoking tree had hit him too hard; he was tired of dickering with the old despot about which rules he'd failed to follow. If Sal died, another of the Rutherford clan would take over. Could be worse. Could be better. But they wouldn't be alive to see it, not without the tree.

The Hanged Men grabbed Sal and a length of rope, making ready to hang Sal on the last solid branch that remained. Sal kicked and howled and ranted about how he was king of his ranch, and the cops would be down on them like fleas on a dog, but no one answered him.

They strung the noose up, the rope sizzling against the tree. Mitchell jammed Sal's head into the noose and pulled. Sal coughed and sputtered, his eyes and tongue bulging while his feet kicked out into space.

"All of us were hanged by this tree, Sal. All of us." Gabe walked around him, wanting to etch his misery into his brain. "But you will be the only one hanged here who will have truly died. Now that the tree is dead, you'll be dropped straight into the hell of your own making."

Sal didn't go quickly. He thrashed and tried to get his fingers underneath the noose. Then Mitchell made a sharp jerk with his supernatural strength, and Sal's neck finally broke. It was probably a kindness that Sal didn't deserve. But they all remembered their own hangings.

"What now, boss?" Mitchell asked him.

"Leave him. We still have one more night to live . . . and the snake to reckon with. Let's make the most of it."

They packed their gear, took Sal's shiny new truck, and headed down the road.

Not one bothered to cut Sal down from the tree or douse the small fires in the field. The tree was dead. Sal was dead.

All that was left was the snake and whatever life remained in their bodies until they wound down and died.

Petra sat on the steps of the trailer, waiting.

Frankie and Maria, satisfied that she was as prepared as Temperance's meager resources allowed, had left. Sig had found a yellow finch feather stuck to the barbecue, and Maria was determined to braid it into Petra's hair. Some kind of omen or talisman for luck— Petra hadn't really been listening, focusing on how to best cut the fiberglass insulation with the bread knife that she'd found in the kitchen drawer.

But she was ready now.

She was surrounded by all of the gear she'd assembled: bottles of lye tucked back into the cardboard beer containers, the potato cannon leaning up against the dented skin of the Airstream, and the fiberglass insulation stuffed into a plastic garbage bag. A collection of spears constructed from copper pipe, filed to sharp angles at the edges, was tied in a bundle beside her. She'd stuffed the ends with cotton, hoping that a lucky scratch could collect more of the basilisk's blood.

Sig sat beside her, watching the sky darken and the first pinpricks of stars glowing in the ceiling of the night. She rubbed the soft fur of his back, marveling at how it had changed from the coarse fur of a wild animal to the silky coat of a domestic one. The color was still the same—gold ticked with black and grey— but he felt different. He felt different under the fur, too. He had developed a satisfying layer of fat over his ribs and had filled out around his neck. He'd grown a few inches, and he seemed so much more than a pile of legs.

She wondered if she had changed that much. She glanced down at the scars on the insides of her arms. She felt different, inside and out. She'd moved beyond the loss of Des, and come to some understanding of the loss of her father. She understood why he'd done what he'd done: He'd gone looking for magic to cure his illness. As a teenager, she'd never have forgiven him for that. As an adult, she found that she could.

And then there was Gabe. He had given up the future of the Lunaria, and the future of the Hanged Men, for her. She felt unworthy. And she felt responsible for them, the way she'd felt responsible for Des. She couldn't let it turn out the way it had for Des: in flames and death.

And more than that, if she truly admitted it to

herself—she loved him. It wasn't the kind of love she'd had for Des, or for other men in her past. This was different. It was more than fascination, than curiosity. It was a trust, a faith that he was so much more unbreakable than Des. And an admiration for how he'd held on to his humanity for all this time. She wasn't a woman who fell often, but she knew the feeling of the ground when she hit it.

She'd become responsible for a whole lot in a short period of time. And she had to do the right thing. She looked down at Sig.

"For whatever it's worth, I want you to stay here. I love you, and I want you to be safe," she said. "I can take your collar off, and if we don't come back, you can go back to doing coyote stuff." It burned her throat to say it.

He laid his head on her knee. He was so much more than a pet; he was a guide, a lodestone. Sig seemed to know things that she didn't, details of the landscape of Temperance and the spirit world. He was a great big spirit poured into a tiny body.

She wrapped her arms around him. "Thank you, Sig."

He slurped at her cheek, as if to say: *You're not going anywhere without me.*

As the gold began to drain from the horizon, a pang of doubt twisted in her stomach. Would Gabe and the Hanged Men go after the basilisk on their own, leaving her behind out of some stupid sense of protectiveness or a desire to move less encumbered?

A dust plume curled in the distance, and she heard the faraway crunch of gravel. Her heart rose as trio of pickup trucks came into view on the gravel road. It was the Hanged Men—nearly all of them. She counted fifteen of them, perched in the backs of the pickup beds. The trucks drove with no lights. Perhaps they had forgotten, or maybe they had given up on any semblance of attempting to be human for this night.

The first truck pulled up before the trailer. It was shiny new and red except for a dent in the bumper, and Gabe stepped out of the driver's side. He looked as if he was ready for war, in his oilskin, gloves, and a hat drawn low over his glowing eyes. Behind him, she could see the guns piled up in the back of the cab of the truck. Maybe that was why they were running without lights.

"Are you ready?"

"Yeah." She picked up her bags of gear and crossed to the passenger side. Sig ran before her, sniffing at the truck vigorously.

"What's all that?" Gabe nodded at her gear.

"These are for you." She handed him the bundle of spears. "They're copper. Copper is impervious to acid. There's fiberglass insulation and cotton stuffed in the tips, and it should be good enough to gather blood."

"And the rest?" he asked, surveying her packs.

"A way to fight the basilisk. And maybe put it down, once you have what you need from it." She paused, squinting at the moonlight reflected in the truck's hood. "That's Sal's truck."

"Yeah."

She couldn't imagine Sal giving permission for anyone to touch his truck, much less use it for a snake-hunting expedition. She hopped into the cab, Sig bounding over her to sniff at the guns. "What happened to Sal?"

Gabe climbed into the truck and slammed the door. He cranked the engine, and she noticed that it smelled like something was burning. Not the truck—the truck still had that new-car smell. It was Gabe.

His mouth pressed into a grim slash. "It's best if you don't ask."

CHAPTER SIXTEEN

HOME

There was batshit crazy, and then there were the Sisters of Serpens.

The Sisters had made camp around the edge of the snake's cave. They'd found a hillock slightly above the cave, between it and the forest, and had built a fire. Bel had said that the snake liked heat. Which sounded like a really awful idea to Cal, but maybe the snake was too full from its dinner of miscreant bros to bother with them. A couple hours after the first offering, something had churned below the surface of the mud, bubbling in a wave. It snatched the second body down beneath the surface like some kind of a fucking Loch Ness Monster, then vanished. The third body still floated, face-down, on the mud, like a forgotten doll in the gutter. Which was creepy as hell to look at.

Not that he could get away from it or anything. The one time he got up to take a piss in the woods, he could feel the mercury pounding behind his brain. Even though her back was turned, Bel kept him on a tight leash. He was chained to the campsite, just as surely as if they'd tied him up.

He sat morosely in soggy grass, his hands gripping his knees. He watched the Sisters build the fire, chattering among themselves in low whispers. Their excitement was palpable. A couple of them seemed stunned, sitting quietly and staring up at the sky or at the cave. A handful were jubilant, whispering prayers around toothy smiles. Bel was by herself, facing the cave, seeming to meditate.

"It's amazing, isn't it?" Dallas sat down beside him, offered him a granola bar.

Cal shook his head. He had no appetite. After a while, he muttered: "It's what you wanted, isn't it?"

"Yes!" Her eyes shone. "I just can't believe all this is really real."

"You can't believe that there's a man-eating giant snake down there?"

"I can't believe it came true!" She grinned. Dallas had a nice smile for a crazy person.

"I don't get it. Most people get their freak on for Jesus or something. What's the deal with the snake?"

"The snake is ancient, one of oldest allies of women. She is strength, she's renewal. She's medicine and mystery. Snakes guarded cattle and children, temples and priestesses in ancient Egypt. Wadjet was the Mother who defended all of Lower Egypt and its rulers. She was the Eye of the Moon, the Lady of Flame. Under her rule, there was peace."

Dallas took a stick and drew in the soggy dirt. She drew a woman in profile, wearing a crown with a cobra on it.

"Over time, she was demonized. She was cast into the role of Medusa, the adversary. The serpent that tempted Eve. Women were cast as weak, and the snake as the personification of the devil. This is the philosophy that's held sway for hundreds of years. And it's time for it to change."

Cal wasn't going to argue anthropology with her. He had no church to defend. "Well, be careful what you wish for, and all that."

"You don't understand. The Great Mother rewards her followers. She will love us and protect us. You still have a chance."

"A chance at what?" He picked at his boot laces. They were crusted with mud and a bit of dried blood.

"A chance to follow her. To prove yourself. To be safe."

Cal stared at the ground. That was all he ever really wanted out of life. To feel safe. He'd done a whole lot of things to try to feel safe. He'd run away from home, and wound up under Stroud's roof. He sure as hell wasn't going to add worshipping a giant snake with a taste for human flesh to his list of bad decisions. That just seemed obvious.

A roar sounded in the distance. Dallas's head snapped around. The Sisters' bikes were parked at the bottom of the hill—they were silent and silvery. The sound came from beyond them.

Bel unfolded herself from her meditation posture at the edge of the mud. Her spine rolled as if she'd grown a couple of extra vertebrae, and the tattoos on her arms twisted. Cal squinted—was that his imagination? Her voice rang clear and loud over the encampment.

"Sisters! Prepare to defend your Mother!"

She reached to her belt for a knife.

"Oh, shit." Cal groaned.

Headlamps streamed through the landscape. Five men on ATVs stopped at the edge of camp. They wore camouflage hunting clothes and had rifles and shotguns mounted to the racks on the backs of the four-wheelers. A couple of them had video cameras—something about them seemed too slick to be regular hunters.

Cal muttered to Dallas: "What's that thing about not bringing a knife to a gun fight?"

Bel strode toward the first vehicle.

"Greetings, ladies!" the rider bellowed. He was a big man, bearded and jovial-seeming. His teeth were so white that it must hurt when air hit them.

"Are you lost?" Bel asked, cocking her head and parking her hand on her hip.

"I hope not. Name's Arthur." He stuck out a meaty paw.

Bel stared at him, and the paw dropped. "What are you doing here?"

"We mean you ladies no harm. I'm the host of the *Mystery Trackers* television show. You probably have seen us on basic cable. We just got syndicated last season."

Bel stared at him.

"We're the guys who reeled in the world's largest catfish," Arthur supplied helpfully.

She continued to stare.

"Here. I've got pics on my phone. Somewhere." He pulled out a brand-new cell phone and began thumbing through the pictures. Arthur's charm was clearly getting him nowhere. "We're hot on the trail of that Yellowstone Worm, and thought we saw the trail leading here."

"That's what you're calling her? The Yellowstone Worm?" Bel said quietly.

"Until we come up with something better. We were thinking 'Campsite Creeper,' but that's already been used for a serial killer. We're also considering 'The Cryptid Creature,' but we did something like that already with Bigfoot in the Pacific Northwest . . ."

Cal's heart pounded under his tongue. He wanted to shout out at the guy, to warn him and the other dudes to run like hell and not look back. He stood up and opened his mouth to yell . . .

. . . but Bel was faster. A knife glittered in her fist, and she plunged it into the man's camo-covered gut.

The women swarmed into the field beyond. Gunshots rang out as the men grabbed their weapons. Dallas shoved Cal to the dirt, and he heard bellows and shouts. An engine started, then another. One of them must be making a run for it, and the women were giving chase.

Cal peered up. The big guy was rolling on the ground, being stomped by two of the Sisters. Two of the others were trading shots over the shrubbery.

Bel was gone.

Cal's gut lurched. If Bel was killed, who could keep the mercury in check?

And if she was gone . . . maybe he could run.

He climbed to his feet. He got exactly four steps before his feet were kicked out from under him, and Tria was standing on his neck. He gurgled and struggled, clawing at her booted ankle.

"Let him up, Tria. Bel won't like it if you hurt him." Dallas was beside her, tugging Tria's arm.

"He was trying to escape. I saw him." Tria's lip pulled back in a snarl.

"Bel wants him in one piece."

Tria ground her heel into his Adam's apple, and Cal gurgled. He felt the mercury welling up within him. Bel must have gone too far away, too far away to control . . .

The mercury hissed up through his hands, soaking through his pores, wrapping around Tria's boot. She snarled and kicked at him, but the mercury held fast. It curled up her leg, spiraling up her thigh. Tria pulled out her knives and slashed at it, splitting droplets of silver and her own blood to the dirt. The mercury squeezed—Cal could feel it—and there was the sound of bones popping, like chicken bones gone down the garbage disposal.

"Cal, stop it!" Dallas shouted. Her arms were around Tria's waist, trying to support her, but the mercury crawled upward, constricting the woman's waist and lungs. Tria fell to the dirt, slashing and writhing with the mercury.

"I can't!" Cal howled. It was as if the mercury was an entity with its own mind, and it was determined to prove it. He tried to pull away, but the mercury clung to his arms in gooey strings. "Get away from it!"

Dallas scrambled back in horror.

The mercury wrapped around Tria's neck. He could feel through the mercury, as if it were his own fingers. The mercury began to compress. Cal tried to stop it, but he couldn't. The mercury squeezed so hard that Tria's face was beginning to turn red, then purple.

"It's going to kill her!" Cal howled. "Somebody help!"

Dallas rushed toward him, holding a branch like a baseball bat.

A gunshot echoed through the dark, and Dallas

stopped. She looked down at a bloom of red blossoming on her T-shirt.

She staggered and slugged him in the head. Everything in Cal's world went black.

He would not get away.

Bel opened the throttle of her motorcycle, plunging into the forest. The Triumph's engine roared, and the knobby tires chewed into the leaf-strewn dirt. Bel was prepared: the Sisters' bikes were heavily modified to handle road and mud. One never knew when one might have to go into the backcountry to bury a body. It was just a shame she had to chase these cretins. Waste of gas.

The ATV the guy was riding, to her practiced eye, was a stock 110 four-stroke engine. With the two heavy cameras on the back plus a guy around two hundred pounds—it wasn't going above thirty-five miles per hour on this uneven terrain, even if he got a cheetah to push.

Bel could see him ahead of her, a light bouncing in the forest of cottonwood trees. Behind her, the motorcycles of her sisters zinged musically. Her tires slashed through the leaves, spewing yellow fragments of debris and mud into the dark. A June bug slapped into her collarbone, and mosquitoes committed suicide on her headlight lens.

She zipped right and left around the trees, bending through the turns, catching him easily. He glanced back at her in panic. He was the camera guy—he was unarmed and had no idea what to do with a pack of motorcycle chicks on his six.

Bel reached back into an open saddlebag, withdrawing a tire iron in her fist. She drew up beside him, just a bit past, then cast it out. She leaned left, braked and throttled to bank hard away. The tire iron slashed into the guy's chest, causing him to let go of the handlebars. The four-wheeler swerved, caught the edge of a fallen log, and turned over.

Bel circled back, her engine buzzing in her ears. She cut to neutral, dismounted, and walked the Triumph back to where the ATV lay on its back, like a turtle in the road, illuminated by her headlamp.

The rider lay in the saffron leaves, gasping. The tire iron had done a nice job of breaking some ribs, and he rolled on the ground, clutching his midsection and moaning unintelligibly.

Two other Sisters rolled up to a stop, intensifying the circle of light around him.

"What do you want us to do with him, Bel?"

He couldn't be allowed to live. He might tell others about the Mother. "Put him out of his misery. Cover their tracks as best you can. Ditch the machines or hide them, and bring him back for an offering."

The women nodded and began to tear through his packs. If there was any video evidence, they would destroy it. If there was anything there of use to them, they would take it. And the rest would likely wind up in the creek.

Bel climbed on her bike and headed back to the camp. Someone would eventually come looking for these monster hunters. There were more threats coming for the Mother. And she had to look to their own losses, find the best way to protect the Great Basilisk. Before, Bel and her sisters simply hit the road when trouble came sniffing too close. But now, they had another mission: to protect the Mother. And that would require an entirely new strategy, a new way of dealing with the world.

When she returned to camp, her heart sank. The Sisters were gathered around one of their own on the ground. Dallas had been shot.

The boy, Cal, was unconscious beside her. Tria stood over him with a tree branch, ready to whack him if he rose again. She wasn't putting any weight on her left leg, but she was determined not to show it.

Fool.

Bel knelt beside Dallas and pressed her hand to her fallen Sister's sweaty forehead. Dallas's breathing evened a bit, and Bel picked at her bloody shirt to assess the damage.

"How bad is it?" Dallas whispered.

"It's bad, honey." She'd been shot beneath the ribs, and she'd lost too much blood. The dirt beneath her had grown red.

"I won't make it?" Her voice quavered.

"No, dear." Bel put both her hands on Dallas's forehead. There was nothing she could do for the wound and the blood loss, but she could ease her pain. Hypnotic magic trickled from her fingers into Dallas's brow, dulling the sensation. Dallas's brown eyes dilated black, as if she'd spent the evening shooting heroin instead of bleeding out.

"You are a good soldier, Dallas."

Dallas smiled, her lips pale as old bubble gum.

"Do you want me to take you to the Mother?"

"Yes." She exhaled. "I want . . . I want to see *her*."

Bel lifted Dallas into her arms, and turned toward the cave. She carried Dallas down the hillock, waded into the scalding mud with her burden. The mud slid over her knees, down her boots, as she approached the mouth of the cave. It steamed; she did not know if the Mother slept or woke.

"Mother, I have brought you one of your guardians, who has fought off interlopers sent to kill you." Bel's voice echoed in the cave.

She took a deep breath and slogged inside. The mud thinned as she climbed up a slope and around a tunnel, into a hot sandstone cave that caused sweat to prickle out on her skin. Dallas was slippery in her arms, and Bel adjusted her grip. It was dark here, only dim light from the outside filtering in.

"Mother . . ."

Luminous yellow eyes appeared in the darkness.

Bel laid Dallas down on the stone ground before her. Dallas had stopped breathing. "Mother, please give your blessings to this woman who has faithfully followed your will."

She knelt, her slick hands on the dirty floor of the

cave, breathing hard. She knew she smelled of fresh blood, that she was little more than faithful food in the eyes of the Mother.

The yellow eyes peered over Dallas. Scales scraped in the dimness.

The basilisk slid over Dallas's chest and peered into her face. She turned to look at Bel.

"We will protect you, Great Mother. I promise. No matter what the cost."

The basilisk approached Bel. She held very, very still, not even daring to breathe. The snake slid over her shoulder. She was heavy, heavy and muscular and warm as she slid behind Bel's shoulders. The snake rested her head on Bel's shoulder, the tail curling around her waist. Bel could feel every exquisite twitch of scale and bone as she moved, sinuously. Her tongue flickered in Bel's hair, tasting, curious.

Bel was willing to be weighed. Her heart hammered in her chest, and she knew that the Great Mother could feel it. Energy hummed along her spine, and she gasped when she felt the Mother's energy trickling down her back, mingling with her own as it uncoiled.

She caught images that must have come from the Mother's mind. They felt as clear as if she'd experienced them herself, each sensation and color. She sensed the Mother in her true home in the spirit world, a temple in a field. Supplicants came infrequently, but no one threatened her. She hunted, she slept, she napped in beautifully-manicured gardens. A favorite pastime was crawling to the stone roof of the temple and soaking in the sunshine. A priestess would make a fire for her at night, and she would sleep curled around it. Her priestesses would bring her flowers and food, and she would bestow upon them great protection and healing magic.

But someone came looking for her. It was a man, more than a century ago. He came with a crystal to trap her, sneaking into her temple. Once he was discovered, the Mother's priestesses fought hard, but he was a powerful alchemist. Enraged, the Mother chased him. But the alchemist tricked her, causing her to fall through a portal to the physical world. The vessel she was given to inhabit was an ordinary rattlesnake. That was the shape the alchemist had chosen for her, a shape that he thought he could control.

The Mother would not be controlled. She was a powerful spirit, and the body she wore changed, grew too large for its physical cage. She grew the crown on her head to show that she was not to be trifled with, and refused to allow her neck to touch the ground. Venom boiled through her, growing stronger and more powerful. She took up residence in the alchemist's fireplace, determined to find a way to escape.

The alchemist had wanted the Great Mother to act as a guard dog, to spit in the drinks of his enemies. The Great Mother, bearing no great affection for the alchemist, ignored his requests. She killed his servants and destroyed many of his experiments. She would climb out on his metal roof and sun herself, as it reminded her of the temple she'd left behind. The alchemist was furious at her being any place she could be seen.

The alchemist had a mistress, the madam of the bordello in town. Her love for him had been poisoned by his avarice, and she had grown to despise him. Once, she had been charmed by his party tricks and pretty declarations of love. But the mistress had seen what power had done to him, and she was plotting a way to flee. She was with his child, and she had vowed never to raise a man like him.

The mistress felt some sympathy for the Mother. One evening, the mistress left the alchemist's house after a night of particularly brutal ardor. The Mother had slid down the chimney of the fireplace, watching the woman in the darkness as she crept to the door, shoes in hand.

The Mother and the mistress understood each other. They regarded each other in that moment, silently. The mistress crossed the tiled floor of the fireplace, gathered the Mother into her arms. She took the Mother with her, back to the bordello. She and the six prostitutes who lived there intended to take the next train out, heading to San Francisco, in the hopes of finding greener pastures.

The alchemist awakened alone in the night, finding both his mistress and his guardian missing. He took his most loyal men with him, and they laid siege to the bordello. The mistress and her women hid beneath the beds with the Mother, waiting for the glass to stop breaking and the hot lead to cool.

But the alchemist was determined to make an example of the mistress and the others. He set fire to the brothel. The Mother saw to it that the mistress and the other women escaped, and she turned on her old master.

The alchemist was ready for her. He trapped her in a lead-lined box and hauled her out to the wilderness, intending to bury her. The Great Serpent broke the box open, and she and the alchemist fought for three days. He fought her with fire and magical weapons and sheer stubbornness. Eventually, the Great Mother had no choice but to retreat. She sought someplace warm, and she slipped beneath the ground. She found a place, far, far underground, where she could feel the heat of the caldera. And she slept. The Mother had dreamed while she slept—dreams of the world turning in fire, liquid heat. She grew, shedding skin after skin, in that darkness.

But something had disturbed her. The rock had shifted, waking her and collapsing the tiny pocket she'd called home.

And now . . . all she wanted was a new one. Someplace that she would be safe, away from threats. She wanted warmth, a full belly, and the feel of sunshine on her skin. Someplace she wouldn't have to hide.

Home, the basilisk thought, her voice bright and piercing in Bel's head.

Tears slipped down Bel's cheeks. This was the most sublime sensation she'd ever experienced, this communion with the goddess.

I will give it to you, Bel promised. *I will give you a home.*

CHAPTER SEVENTEEN

DROPPING THE LEASH

"**W**hat happened to Sal?"

Petra persisted, as Gabe knew she would. She would not let this go, would not allow him to protect her from any bit of knowledge, no matter how gruesome. Still, he hesitated.

"Sal's dead, isn't he?" There was no judgment or horror in her voice.

"It doesn't matter, anymore."

"What did he do to you?" Her fingers brushed his sleeve. There was so much tenderness and sympathy in that gesture that he cracked.

"He burned the Lunaria."

Her breath sucked in, audibly. "Oh, my God."

"We don't have much time to get the basilisk's blood. If there's still some life in the roots—maybe it will help, if not . . . we have perhaps two, three days."

Petra's fingers had wound in his sleeve. He removed his hand from the steering wheel and twined his fingers with hers.

"We will find it," she said, with what seemed like a deep well of certainty.

He felt the shadows of a great many things, now: worry, anger, even the ghost of love. But not certainty.

Getting into the park proved much more difficult than the last time. The east entrance was blockaded with sawhorses and Highway Patrol cars. A caravan of camouflaged trucks with U.S. government plates had stopped before the checkpoint and was being waved through one by one. Gabe made a U-turn and went back the way they'd come. They turned off on a forest road.

"Mike said the park's closed due to 'seismic anomalies.'" Petra made air quotes around the words.

"I'm sure that's not deterring anyone who's serious about chasing the basilisk. The military's crawling out here." The forest road became a dirt road, then vanished. In the jump seat behind them, Sig made retching noises. Petra reached back to pull him up to the front.

"It's okay," Gabe said. "It's Sal's truck, after all." Funny how the idea of some coyote barf in Sal's pristine truck cheered him a bit.

They stopped in a field for Petra to provide directions. She climbed out of the truck and walked a good hundred yards away from them. This many Hanged Men would likely screw up the Locus's perception of magic; there was no way to calibrate it to "serpent" and exclude "undead." Back in the heyday of Temperance, when Gabe had used it himself, the magnitude of magic seemed to screw with its detection abilities. If there was something stronger than the Hanged Men here, it would likely pick it up.

That wouldn't be hard; the basilisk was much stronger than they were. He didn't want to admit it to Petra, but he felt the loss of the tree deeply; he knew that all of the Hanged Men did. He felt sluggish, dull, as if he were interacting with the world from under a bucket. His shoulder clicked metallically when he moved it, and he couldn't feel his right foot; it had fallen asleep on the gas pedal several times on the way over. The Hanged Men in the back sat slack, like puppets, barely keeping the guns behind their feet from clunking around in the bed of the truck. Things were not good. And he expected them to get much worse.

Ahead, Petra gestured broadly, pointing north.

They gathered the gear and followed her. She held a flashlight in her hand, shining it on the compass, the only light. Gabe didn't like her walking so far ahead, but there was nothing to be done for it. Her star moved steadily ahead over the landscape, with the coyote orbiting around her. The Hanged Men, the ones still able to hold a rifle steadily, swept their scopes over the dark land, watching for anything that might pop out of the wilderness.

They plodded that way for hours, winding through grassland and scrub forests, tracking a creek along a valley. Gabe remembered it—Raven Creek. The creek drained away to a stream, then to mud. As they forded it, the water felt curiously warm. Stream water should be cold, but something was polluting it. Gabe cupped a bit of water in his hand and smelled sulfur.

In the distance, Gabe could see firelight. The star moving ahead halted, then went out. Gabe and his men could still see well enough, and they caught up with Petra within moments.

"Did you lose the trail?" he asked Petra.

She shook her head. She held the Venificus Locus in both her hands, staring at it. A bead of blood spiraled in circles at high speed around the rim. A bit of her blood trickled down her hand to her arm.

Gabe touched her wrist.

"I'm okay. It's just . . . really thirsty." She frowned. She rubbed the blood away on the hip of her pants. "It was leading me there . . ." She pointed at the light. "But then it just went nuts. I don't think it's entirely you guys. I think the basilisk has to be up there . . . and if there's fire, then there are people. And they're in danger."

Gabe squinted at the distant gleam. He took a deep breath. With effort, he concentrated on the feeling of air on wings. A black lump formed beneath his shirt, clawed its way up his collar, onto his shoulder.

It was a raven, albeit a sad one. It had only one good eye and was missing feathers on one wing. But it could still fly. He sent it up, flying low, skimming toward the firelight.

He had to keep above the trees; he had no depth perception, and couldn't risk crushing the bird's body against a branch. From his good eye, he could see the glitter of firelight on mud, where the creek formed an oxbow on itself, and the figures of people.

He swept lower. There were women and motorcycles, and he could smell oil and blood and magic gone stale. In the mud, he could see bodies, lying facedown. One of them was out of the mud, but it was unmoving, with a woman standing over it. No telling if that one was alive or dead.

This couldn't be good.

He winged up, up and over into the night, to rejoin his body.

The raven misjudged the descent in the dark; he was not a nocturnal creature. He careened through a cloud of bats hunting for mosquitoes, missed his target, and swept back for another try.

Petra switched on a flashlight, and he could see better. The raven, all feathers and skidding claws, tried to perch on Gabe's shoulder. He wobbled, and Gabe reached up to grasp him. He melted into the rest of his human flesh, in a slow, lumpy way, like tar melting down his sleeve.

"What did you see?" Petra asked quietly.

"There are campers there. And it seems the snake

has been at work. I counted five bodies. There may be more. There's magic, but I'm not smelling the venom."

"We have to get them out of there."

"They're not running. Monster hunters of some kind, I'd bet."

Petra frowned. "Hopefully, we won't have to fight through them to get to the snake. If they have seen what it can do, and haven't run . . . they must be determined."

"So are we."

Petra wasn't sure the Hanged Men were going to make it.

She didn't say so, of course. When they shambled across the fields, they stumbled in a disconnected way, as if many of them were trying to walk with one foot in this world and one in the afterlife. Their eyes burned even more oddly than usual. Instead of fireflies, Gabe's eyes resembled light reflected in a mirror. She didn't say anything, did her best not to stare. But she could see that something was winding down in them, and she needed to stop it.

She prepared for the confrontation with the basilisk. As the others checked their guns and unpacked the spears, she opened her garbage bag of fiberglass. In this weak moonlight, it looked like cotton candy. She dreaded handling it, the itching of glass splinters, and donned a pair of aluminized welder's gloves. The fiberglass had been separated and cut into pieces. She pulled the part cut like a tunic over her head and set about lashing other scraps to her clothes with duct tape.

"What on Earth are you doing?"

Gabe was watching her, head cocked like one of her birds.

"It's fiberglass. Impervious to acid. I mean . . . it *is* porous. So I wouldn't survive a dip in a puddle with it, but it's good for casual contact." She offered him a chunk, feeling like a kid offering an adult some cotton candy. "Want some?"

He shook his head. "I think . . . you should keep on wrapping yourself in that stuff."

She shrugged and continued suiting up. When she was done, her arms, legs, and torso were covered in itchy pink fiberglass.

Sig looked bewildered.

"Come here."

She grabbed Sig by the collar and looped the fiberglass around his body. She did her best to keep the brown paper side close to his fur. She then set about trying to seal it shut with duct tape while the coyote tried to squirm away, whining piteously.

Gabe watched, and she swore that his shoulders were shaking in laughter.

"Gabe. Either help hold him or quit snickering."

Gabe held the coyote while she succeeded in sticking duct tape to his fur. When she was finished, it looked like she had a coyote dressed in a pink poodle suit. He glowered at her, clearly resenting the loss of the last bit of street cred he owned.

"Hey. You insisted on coming."

He promptly flopped on the ground and tried to tear it off.

"Sig." She didn't have time for this.

She grabbed him one last time and wrapped a piece of welding blanket around him like a cape. The hardware store only had this one, small sample. She wrapped it around his head and fastened it into his collar with the duct tape.

"There. Now you look like a Jedi."

This seemed to be acceptable. Sig snorted.

The Hanged Men were on the move, starting toward the light.

She shoved a respirator on her face and slapped a fiberglass welder's helmet on her head. It wasn't perfect protection against acid, but she hoped she wouldn't have to get too close.

She squinted and pulled the helmet's face shield up. It was hard to see through the clear window of the helmet—it had an auto-darkening feature that made sense for welders, but was pretty useless walking around the wilderness at night. She flipped it down again and squinted at the fire. She could still see it from a distance. Maybe it would work.

She slung the potato gun under her arm, her gun belt over her shoulder, and picked up the bottles full of lye.

"I'm ready to party, Sig."

Sig growled, his cape flowing behind him.

She trotted behind the Hanged Men, feeling a bit like she did that one time in college when she went to a

Halloween party, and she was the only one in costume. That time, she'd gone dressed as Ripley from *Aliens*, with a papier-mâché alien queen glued to one shoulder and a spray-painted Super Soaker gun slung over on the other. This was infinitely more practical, she told herself. Not nearly as badass. But more practical.

But something was off. A flock of sparrows exploded from a tree about a quarter mile away, bursting into noise as if someone had shot at them. Sig whined, keeping close to Petra's legs, his tail slapping her pink-clad legs.

They were crossing a creek, and the water seemed to hesitate in its flow.

"Guys," Petra hissed. "I think a seismic anomaly is happening."

"What do you mean?" Gabe asked, as she tiptoed over rocks, mindful not to get the fiberglass soggy.

"Earthquake. I think a quake is coming. Well, that's what I'd think under normal circumstances. It's possible that the snake's presence is creeping out the wildlife, as well."

Frogs began to bounce out of the stream to the banks.

"When?"

"Don't know. Could be minutes or hours." She craned her head to the horizon.

"We need to get to the basilisk."

They reached the clearing, a shallow hillock before the creek turned into a muddy oxbow. The firelight haloed the silhouettes of women above.

Gabe stepped into the touch of the light. He'd slung his spears and rifles over his shoulder and raised his empty hands. "Hello."

The rest of the Hanged Men lingered out of sight, behind the tree line. Petra could see a lot of machines . . . ATVs, motorcycles. Nice ones, at that. Seemed like more machines than people.

Two women advanced about twelve feet. Petra could see blades glittering in their fists, lowered by their hips.

"What do you want?" one of them, a willowy blond, asked. Her motorcycle leathers were streaked with mud.

Gabe paused, and Petra could see him weighing what to say as his shoulders shifted. "I heard a noise. I thought someone needed help."

Petra held her breath. He was playing it cool. Given that the women were armed, maybe that would put them at ease.

Or not.

The blond woman took two more steps toward him, limping, extending the knife at arm's length. "Look, mister. It's been a long night. I'm going to do you a favor. You have exactly one chance to turn around, go back, and go have a drink someplace other than here."

He cocked his head. "I can't do that, ma'am."

"Then we have a problem."

The blond woman limped down the slope to Gabe, blades flashing in her fists. The other woman was not far behind.

The Hanged Men began to detach from the shadows, their eyes glowing, moving into the firelight. This didn't stop the women—they barely broke stride as they called an alarm to the others.

The blond woman limped to Gabe. He tried to sidestep her, but she was still fast. She looked him full in the face and plunged a knife into his chest. She stood back, panting, clearly thinking the job was done.

Petra muffled a squeak. With the tree dying, would the Hanged Men be vulnerable? Would they succumb to such mundane things as knives and bullets, now?

The blond woman seemed to expect Gabe to fall neatly in a pile on the grass, but he remained standing. He twisted the knife out of his chest and threw it away.

The woman stood her ground, slashing at him with her other knife.

Enough of this dumb-ass, misplaced chivalry. Petra drew her pistol, aimed, and shot at her. The bullet caught her shoulder, spun her around, and she tripped. She landed on the ground in a tangle of bootlaces, still growling and swinging.

The Hanged Men had taken down the second woman, but more were coming over the rise, and these had guns. Petra aimed and shot at the leather-clad figures, catching up to Gabe. He seemed curiously wooden, and she dragged him behind a tree.

"Are you all right?" she demanded, running her fingers over the hole in his shirt.

"I should be . . ."

The Hanged Men always bled luminescent blood,

blood that glowed in the dark. The blood that trick-led from his chest was dull, with barely any shine. He brushed at it with his hand, staring at it.

"I'll be fine," he said, unconvincingly.

She turned back to the fight, though she doubted that he told her the truth. Muzzles flashed as the Hanged Men advanced toward the firelight.

She didn't understand the women, why they fought so hard. Petra moved in the wake of the battle, aiming and shooting where she could get a clear shot. She ducked behind a motorcycle with Sig to reload, and a bullet dinged into its fender. The Hanged Men seemed to be winning as they pushed into the clearing of the camp.

She spied a familiar figure hiding behind the bikes. She reached out and grabbed his collar, dragging him toward her.

"Cal!" She impulsively hugged him. "What are you doing here?"

He blinked at her, seeming dazed or stoned. "It's a long fucking story." He seemed to focus on her fuzzy pink suit. "What the hell are you wearing?"

"Never mind. You look like shit. What . . ."

He pushed her away. "Look, you gotta get outta here."

"Cal, we've got to get the snake, but we'll take you with us, get you some help . . ."

"No. No. No. No." He pressed his fists to his temples, and Petra was reminded of an old photograph she'd seen of Aleister Crowley—there was that look in his eyes. "You can't. You can't help me. Only . . . only *she* can."

"Only who?"

A commotion rattled at the far end of the camp, near a mudpot. A figure walked through the mud, into the altercation.

"Oh. I'm betting you mean *her*."

A woman emerged from the mud, looking like some kind of primordial creature. Her arms were covered in snake tattoos, and her mud-streaked skin had something of a green sheen. Petra had only seen that particular color in very old jade. Her eyes were dark, dilated in the faint light. Plastered to her skin, she wore what looked like the cast-off skin of a very large snake.

"Yeah," Cal affirmed. "Her."

Petra aimed her pistol at her, over the seat of the bike. The green woman turned her obsidian gaze to Petra and began to advance.

"No!" Cal yelped, and he wrestled with her for the gun. "You can't."

"Cal, what the hell?" Petra didn't like the look in his eyes. Silver was beginning to leak around the edges of his irises. She wrenched the gun back, but didn't aim it at the green chick.

"You don't understand," he pleaded. "Bel's the only one who can help me, who can keep the mercury in check."

"Cal, I don't know what's going on here." And that was the God's honest truth.

"You've got to get out of here. You have to get out of here, before she . . ."

The green woman pointed at Cal. It wasn't the glad-handing gesture of a politician pointing at a fictional person at a rally. This was a gesture that Petra would expect to see in a courtroom, when a mobster promised revenge on a witness, or when a voodoo priestess leveled a curse on a soul dumb enough to have taken her parking place.

Cal began to howl. He rolled on the ground as if someone had shot him. Petra reached for him, turned him over, and gasped. The mercury had leaked out of his eyes and crawled over his face, dripping down his neck. It was quickly forming a mask that would surely suffocate him.

She grabbed his shoulders and tried to scrape the mercury off his face with her fiberglass sleeve, but it lashed out, clawing at her with metallic talons. She fell back on her ass, scrabbling for her guns.

The green woman. She had to be behind this. Petra drew down and aimed at her.

"Whatever you're doing to him—stop it now!"

The green woman's black eyes narrowed. "You haven't got any idea what's within him. I just dropped the leash."

Cal flopped on the ground, kicking against strings of mercury tangling around him. "Bel! Help me!"

"Well, put it back on!"

Bel shook her head. "No. He's done."

CHAPTER EIGHTEEN

THE ALTAR OF THE BASILISK

Petra pulled back the hammer of her pistol. "Put. It. Back. On."

She didn't know if she'd really shoot an unarmed person. Probably not. But Cal sounded like he was gargling lead, and he wasn't going to last much longer. There was no choice. She ground her teeth, aimed for her adversary's knee, and pulled the trigger.

But nothing happened. She stared down at her hand. It was frozen. She wrenched down again on the trigger, but *nothing*. Her fingers didn't respond—it was as if she were paralyzed. Her eyes slid to the green woman. No light was reflected in those black eyes. She felt like the ground was shifting beneath her, as if she were standing on a beach and looking past the ninth wave to the horizon.

Her next thought was to duck, but she couldn't make her body move.

"Don't look at her!" Cal howled.

But it was too late. She was under the spell of those coal-black eyes. Numbness was trickling down her neck and arms.

"Priestess!" One of the women in motorcycle gear shouted and threw Bel a shotgun. Bel caught it easily, ratcheted it, and aimed at Petra.

A blur of grey tackled Petra, and she crashed to earth behind the motorcycle.

Bel fired without hesitation. Birdshot peppered the chrome like rain, and a piece of the wad pinged off the top of her welder's mask. Sig stood over Petra, snarling. Beside her, the shot scattered the dirt and zinged into Cal's skin—which was now encased in a metal hide. He was looking a helluva lot like Han Solo in carbonite, and that couldn't be good.

Feeling flooded back into Petra's arms, and she hugged Sig. "Good boy."

She peeked out behind the front wheel, careful not to make eye contact with Bel. She drew down with both pistols, and got one shot off before something rose behind the green woman.

The basilisk. It roared out of the mud with a hiss like bacon grease on cast iron. It loomed behind Bel, eyes glowing, the feathers on its head bristling like a wet rooster's.

Things had gone to shit awfully fast.

Petra slapped her respirator over her nose and the welder's mask down over her face. Through slitted vision, she saw a figure in a dark coat run across the campsite, skidding in the dust beside her. Gabe. There was a bullet hole in the brim of his hat, but he held one of the copper spears in one fist.

"Jeez. Are you all right?" Petra touched the brim of his hat with her clumsy, gloved fingers. It was still smoking where the bullet had singed it.

"The Hanged Men are doing their best, but these women are going to die protecting . . . protecting that. It's got to be some kind of a doomsday cult." The camp was clearing out—Petra could make out gleaming eyes jerking in the darkness and gunfire echoing in the woods.

"We gotta get Cal out of here," Petra said, turning. "If he . . ."

But Cal was gone.

He'd crawled ahead of them, to the green woman, on his hands and knees. Sig darted out from behind the motorcycle, tried to grab his pant leg and drag him back, but he shook the coyote off.

A leather-clad woman revved up on an ATV, slamming into the bike and toppling the frame over on Petra and Gabe. Petra squirmed in the space under the kickstand, and Gabe shoved back with his shoulder, denting the metal, and jabbed his copper spear at the rider. The rider jumped over the wreck and swung at him with a knife. Gabe took the hit in the shoulder and grasped the blade, twisting it away. His adversary reached for a pistol, shot him in the ribs, and they wrestled for the gun.

"Cal!" Petra shouted. She couldn't get a clear shot from here; he was between her and Bel and the snake. She could only make out smears of movement behind the helmet.

Bel aimed her shotgun down at Cal and gazed at him over the sights. "You come to the Great Mother now, on your knees?"

Cal's face was a smooth mirror, reflecting back at her. There was no knowing if he was capable of speech any longer. He reached with one hand up to Bel, the gesture of a supplicant.

Bel smiled.

"You come now, of your free will?"

His fingers strained, and she turned the gun away, reaching for him with her inked arm. "The mercury is now under control. Come to me."

But it wasn't. Cal reached up, his hand a pure silver glove. His fingers wrapped around her wrist, ribbons of silver climbing up her arm.

The snake lashed out, biting him, but came away with a mouthful of mercury. It tossed its head side to side, spewing droplets of poison like a dog with a chili pepper.

Bel struggled, hauling back with all her might, but the mercury held her fast with a claw of metal. She lifted the shotgun and aimed it at Cal's face.

Petra lunged out from behind the bike and fired at the green woman. One bullet struck her in the chest, and the other in the shoulder. Bel flinched, but she awkwardly angled the shotgun over her elbow at Cal's face and pulled the trigger with her thumb.

Petra screamed. Cal's body fell away, tendrils of mercury opening limply around him on the ground like the legs of a dead spider. Where his face had been was a smear of silver, like a crushed aluminum can.

Bel fell to her knees. Where she'd been hit, black blood dribbled over her tank top and down the tattoo ink on her arms. The blood steamed in the dark, but she still clutched the gun in her hands.

The basilisk slipped out of the mud toward Petra, snarling, silver strings of drool sliding down to the dirt. It spewed a stream of venom and mercury toward her, and Petra reflexively threw her arm over her head. She could hear the acid chewing away at the ground around her and braced herself for the burn, but it didn't come.

Through the visor, she saw the snake curl lovingly around Bel's waist. It dragged her away, into the mud, down into a sedimentary cave at the end of the mudpot, and vanished.

"Petra!" Gabe was picking her up off the sizzling ground.

"Don't touch me!" Green venom dripped from

her fiberglass arm. With her other gloved hand, she stripped the soggy fiberglass sleeve off and dropped it to the ground.

"Are you all right?"

"Yeah, I'm just . . . sticky. Is Cal?" She flipped up her visor, tugged down her respirator, and stared at his crumpled form on the ground. His metal hand was splayed open like a pair of scissors, and his head was a wrinkled can leaking silver into the dirt. Sig stood over him, whimpering.

Gabe shook his head.

Petra felt her lip quivering and bit it to still it. Through blurry eyes, she surveyed the rest of the camp. The Hanged Men had defeated Bel's gang. None of the women were still moving; Petra didn't know if any were still alive. A couple certainly weren't, judging by the angles of broken necks and spines.

From the distance, a mechanical roar sounded, a thumping above. Petra's brow wrinkled. "What's a helicopter doing out here?"

"Douse the fire," Gabe ordered. The Hanged Men plunged into the campfire, kicking it over in a shower of sparks. The vehicles left running were shut off, and they retreated to the edge of the tree line, out of aerial view.

"They must be looking for the basilisk. Or else they heard the fight," he muttered.

Holding her breath, Petra waited for the helicopter to fly overhead. It was running dark, no lights, and she could only tell its position by its slightly darker silhouette against the sky and the way it stirred the top branches of the pine trees.

The helicopter churned overhead and disappeared over the woods.

"That's a military helicopter. They want the snake," Petra affirmed. The helicopter swept to the horizon, then turned back in a search grid pattern. "We can't let them have it."

"Then let's get it."

The most injured of the Hanged Men remained behind to keep watch for the military. One of them had a stick run through his shoulder, while another dragged one foot behind him in an oddly-mechanical limp. A third just sat upright with his back against a tree, unmoving. A handful of the others started the ATVs and ran them west, to draw the helicopters away with bright headlights glaring and radios blasting heavy metal music that sounded tinnier as the distance grew.

Petra hoisted the potato cannon over her shoulder, snugged the respirator over her face, and slapped the welding helmet back over her head. She followed Gabe and the remaining Hanged Men to the edge of the mudpot. The Hanged Men fairly bristled with the copper spears, some of them already stained from the fight with Bel's gang.

Sig put one paw into the hot mud and made a face. He hopped back up to solid land and began chewing at his foot.

"Stay here," she told Sig. Thankfully, this seemed like the *one time* it wouldn't be a problem.

She loaded her potato cannon with some more hair spray and a fresh bottle, and they waded into the mud. Petra edged her way in front, figuring that since she had the biggest gun, she should go first. She carried one of the six-packs and handed off two more to the Hanged Men behind her. She wasn't sure she could reload the contraption fast enough. If pressed, perhaps they could throw bottles at the snake, as if it were a trespasser on their lawn.

A deep groan rolled over the site, shivering the surface tension on the mud. Sig whined and flattened his ears as the tree branches stirred.

"Remember that seismic anomaly?" Petra hissed, feeling the hot mud soaking through her fiberglass pants, stumbling in the slop. It was hot, but it could be worse. The cold creek water was mixing with it, cooling it to a somewhat-tolerable temperature. If the mudpot had emerged in the middle of a field, it would have been well over boiling and unable to be forded at all.

But she pressed forward to the mouth of the cave. Hot, sulfurous air exhaled from the darkness ahead, and she could feel the sweat sliding down her back and sticking fiberglass particles to her skin. She hoped that they'd find the snake quickly; it was unlikely she'd last very long in this heat.

Gabe swept a flashlight into the cave, which extended deep into a sedimentary shelf. She could reach the top of the ceiling with her fingers. Bits of sandstone gravel rained down, and Petra felt the terror of being buried alive in this burning, miserable place. It was more miserable and horrifying than her brief glimpse of the underworld had been. Gabe's light shone overhead, illuminating deep fractures in the rock shelf. The bottles in Petra's cardboard carrier clattered together.

This could, quite possibly, be the dumbest thing she'd ever done: pursuing a poisonous basilisk into a cave during an earthquake in the company of a bunch of dead guys, armed with a potato cannon and a six-pack of lye. Never mind her soggy pink fiberglass armor. This was going to be an epic way to die.

The cave ran farther than she anticipated. It didn't feel particularly deep—there were no stalactites, and the level of mud hadn't risen. It was a fresh cave, newly driven up by the tectonic activity below. Bits of broken sandstone and feldspar lay on top of the thick mud in a quivering mosaic. The smell of sulfur became overwhelming, even through her respirator.

"I think—" she began, but was cut off by a deep rumbling.

She turned, feeling the shockwave of the earthquake moving through the mud, bubbling and slopping it up to her waist. She struggled to keep the cannon above the surface as the ground heaved above and below her, and pieces of rock rattled down.

A deafening fracture formed above her, and she lunged forward into the dark, following the pitching beam of Gabe's flashlight. In a roar of thunder, the cave rained shut behind her, flinging her spread-eagled into the mud.

She swore, casting about for the cannon. She found it, grabbed it with her clumsy gloves, but the pack of lye ammo had sunk away.

She waded toward the light glowing against the wall. With a sinking heart, she realized that Gabe wasn't attached to the light. The plastic flashlight floated alone on top of the mud, and she snatched it up with her free hand. She turned the light toward the way she'd come. The sandstone slab had caved in, blocking the entrance. She swept the light back and forth, hoping that Gabe was all right, that the Hanged Men hadn't been crushed. Panic rose in her throat as she realized that she was trapped.

The earth groaned once more, and she jumped when a hand landed on her wrist.

"Gabe!"

He was covered in mud, except for his hat. But she would recognize those luminescent eyes anywhere.

"Where are the others?"

He slogged to the cave-in and pressed his hand to the wall of rubble. "I hope they're on the other side."

The pile of stone creaked and sighed, and it was impossible to hear anything beyond it—to Petra's ordinary ear, anyway. Bits of gravel plinked down on the mud, and she couldn't discern anything else.

Unless there was a hole at the other end, they were buried. Buried with the snake. And the only way to go was forward.

Petra floundered in the mud. It had soaked her fiberglass armor, and the pink protective layer was coming off in pieces. There wasn't anything to be done for it—between the snake, the cave-in, and the heat, things weren't looking real good for her successful emergence into the upper world.

Gabe was at her elbow, seeming to navigate the mud more successfully. Maybe his time in the underworld of the Lunaria had made him more impervious to this kind of hell. And he had so much more to lose—not just his unlife, but the unlife of all the others.

"Look," he whispered, peering into the darkness with his glowing eyes.

She squinted, not seeing anything, and pushed the visor of her helmet up. They had reached the back corner of the cave, and the flashlight beam picked out the silhouette of Bel.

She was propped up against the back wall of the cave, sitting upright on a stone shelf, like a doll. Her black eyes were open and her hands lay bare in her lap. Petra couldn't tell if she was breathing, but she sure wasn't blinking.

Damn it. She'd made eye contact. Petra glanced away. But she felt no paralytic magic stealing over her.

Gabe walked to her and passed his hand over her face. Bel didn't react.

It looked as if that shelf in the cave had been decorated as a kind of altar. Guttering candles that must have been burning for hours spilled wax down the walls, and armfuls of wildflowers had been placed all along the surface. Bits of bone punctuated the nodding yellow toadflax stems. Bel had been carefully arranged among them, like some kind of treasured ornament. Had the snake done this? The snake couldn't build such an altar—this was clearly the work of reverent human hands, but it must have been the basilisk that arranged her here. For the first time, it dawned upon Petra that the thing they were hunting was not simply a raging monster. It was something else—something with intelligence, with sentimentality.

"Where's the snake . . . *oh.*"

Something with wrath.

A rill of movement swam below the surface of the mud, pushing up a cluster of air bubbles.

Shit. Shit. Shit. Her potato cannon was useless under mud. She slung it over her shoulder and reached for her guns with her sweat-slick hands, head pounding. Hopefully, the mud from her swim hadn't gummed up the mechanism . . .

Gabe held his copper spear over his head, eyes narrowed. He plunged the spear once, twice, into the soupy mess. The thing under the mud shrieked and flipped.

Petra aimed at a tail that slipped up over the edge of the mud and fired. In this enclosed space, the shot was deafening, and all sound receded to a roar and a distant ringing in her ears. She shot until the barrel clicked empty.

The basilisk rose out of the mud, jaws open. Petra imagined that it was hissing, but no sound came out of its mouth. Strings of vapor leaked from its jaws, and it spat acid at them.

She felt Gabe's hand on the back of her neck, and he plunged her down into the scalding mud. She sucked in her breath in shock, flailed, and released her grip on the potato cannon as the hot darkness enveloped her.

This must be hell, she realized as she descended. The heavy mud scalded her skin and suspended her movement. She couldn't move, couldn't breathe as the mud invaded the respirator. She could taste the iron in the silt as it pushed through her mask. Gabe's fingers wound in her shirt—he was here, with her, too. She doubted that the monster's acid could penetrate this dense mud quickly, but Gabe didn't need air the way that she did.

When she was convinced she'd pass out, she was yanked up by her collar, gasping. The mud sucked the last of the fiberglass armor from her body. She stumbled back with her ass planted against the altar. Flowers stuck to the mud as she sucked in a breath.

Gabe was fighting the monster. He held the copper pipe spear over his head and had slammed it into the basilisk's right side. For an instant, Petra was reminded of the dozens of renderings she'd seen of St. George slaying the dragon—she'd always had a twinge of empathy for that creature, as terrifying as it was.

But this was not going as well as it had for St. George. The basilisk thrashed and flung Gabe away, the spear still protruding from behind its feathered crown.

Petra spied the potato cannon floating on the top

of the mud. She splashed into the slop, grabbing it. She prayed to whatever weird gods might be listening that the bottle of lye in the cannon's throat hadn't been damaged or fallen out.

The basilisk turned for her and opened its mouth to draw breath and spew venom. She pulled the ignitor, aimed at the basilisk's open mouth, and fired.

Orange flame flashed as the bottle launched and struck the basilisk's mouth. She lost track of the bottle, but it must have gone into its throat and shattered; the basilisk thrashed its head right and left, glass glittering in the mud. It began to foam at the mouth, a pale bubbling like sea foam on a clear afternoon.

Gabe crept up behind it and grabbed the spear. Using the pipe as a handle, he forced the head of the basilisk under the mud. Its tail lashed and thrashed, striking Petra in the leg and clearing the flowers off the altar, shattering the candles. Bel's body slid from the shelf into the mud, staring with unseeing eyes.

Gabe held the spear fast with two hands as the basilisk fought. After some minutes, it began to weaken, then became still.

Petra let out a shaking breath. Her head pounded, and all she could hear was the ringing of gunfire in her ears. But against her back, something stirred—the ground. It shook and quavered, kicking the last of the carefully-arranged bones of the altar to the mud. Pea gravel shivered down on her skull.

"We have to get out of here!" she screamed at Gabe.

The shockwave was moving, more than one. The ceiling slid and fractured as the brittle sandstone began breaking up.

Gabe jammed his foot in the snake's spine and yanked the spear free. He slogged to her side as the ceiling began to cave in.

Petra scrunched beneath the shelf that had been the basilisk's altar. Gabe flung himself in beside her, and his shoulder covered her head. Rock hailed down; she couldn't hear it, but she could feel it as it pounded Gabe's body.

She wanted to speak to him in this moment, to tell him that she was sorry for everything and that she loved him. She yelled it in his ear; she had no idea if he could hear her or if he would survive the roar of the rock to do anything with that knowledge and her shitty timing.

After an interminable time of hot blackness, the shaking stopped. Petra lifted her face against Gabe's chest. She shook him and pointed overhead.

"Look!"

A pinprick of light glistened overhead. A small one, but it was unmistakably light.

"Gabe."

She shook him again, shook him hard. Silt slipped down his collar into her face, and she panicked for a moment, thinking him dead.

But his glowing eyes opened, and his gaze followed her finger to the light.

The light grew bigger, and a coyote nose pressed in.

Sig. He pawed and clawed at the hole, but couldn't get much traction against the larger stones.

They scrabbled out of the pile of rubble, hand in hand. Gabe stood on the altar and jammed the dull end of the spear into the star of light in the ceiling of that little world. Sig backed away, and the crack opened, bringing more grey light and dust.

And blessedly cool air. Petra lifted her face to it, inhaling deeply. Her head pounded; she knew she was close to heat exhaustion, and this was the most wonderful thing she could recall feeling.

Gabe opened the fissure to about two feet, then a large piece of granite fell through, splashing into the mud. The cave crackled with a palpable vibration.

He laced his fingers together, and she stepped into them. He lifted her up to the hole in the ceiling. She grasped the ledge with aching, muddy fingers, and pulled herself through.

The air. She sucked it in, and her breath curled before her. Her whole body steamed in the early morning light. She was on the far side of the oxbow, within view of the encampment. Pale light had begun to filter in from the east, and the sky at the edge of the mountain was beginning to turn pink in a razor-sharp line.

Gabe handed the spear through, and she took it carefully, placing it next to her on the cracked ground. She extended her hand down for him, and he clasped it. He climbed, and she hauled, until he was finally up on the rock outcropping. He fell heavily on the cracked clay. In this finer light, she could see bits of glowing blood smearing his cheek and hands.

She reached out to touch his cheek, frowning. He took her hand and kissed it. He murmured something against her palm, but she couldn't hear it.

Something tackled her, and she winced. Sig. He was washing the mud from her neck, and making horrible faces at the taste. The welder's blanket was still stuck to his collar, and he looked like a superhero dog as he rolled around in her lap.

He turned his head to the sky and barked. She could feel the bark in his chest, and she looked skyward. The helicopter from before. It swept in from the north, blades churning the canopy. It was closer this time, as if it had zeroed in. A searchlight swept from an open door, and red lights that she knew were sights from a gun.

She grabbed Gabe's sleeve and they stumbled to their feet. They ran back to the far edge of camp, where Bel's motorcycles stood in a bullet-pocked row.

Gabe shouted in her ear, over the receding buzzing. "Can you ride one of these?"

"I can drive anything with wheels."

She grabbed the nearest bike—a beautiful Triumph Tiger. The keys dangled from the ignition. She straddled it, flipped the kill switch with her thumb, and turned the key in the ignition. The red start button was easy enough to find, and the bike roared to life. She jammed the spear behind the exhaust pipe. Gabe lifted

Sig under his arm and climbed on the back behind her, one arm around her waist.

She knocked back the kickstand, twisted the throttle, and plunged into the woods. This Triumph was unlike the dirt bikes she'd ridden as a child and the street bike her college boyfriend rode. This one had the springiest shocks she'd ever felt, and the dirt paths felt like pavement under the tires. It wasn't a dual-sport bike—this was something else altogether, customized for whatever adventures those weird snake women had gotten up to. The clutch was smooth, and she accelerated through the gears quickly.

She glanced up at the sky. Dawn had begun to touch the tops of the trees, and a second helicopter had come to join the first. She kept close to the trees, in the thorny huckleberry underbrush that scraped against her muddy legs. Sig rested his head over her shoulder, thrilled to be moving, his tongue dangling in the breeze.

"The other Hanged Men—do you think they got away?" She hoped so—all of the ATVs were gone.

Gabe tapped her on the shoulder and pointed at the sky. Ravens were flying in a black mass south and east—toward the Rutherford Ranch.

Petra circled back to where they'd left the trucks. They were all gone, which gave her hope that every last one had gotten out alive.

She'd reached paved road by the time the sun had crept over the horizon. At this hour, there was little traffic, and she hoped that no one would remark on two mud-caked riders holding a dog that looked suspiciously like a coyote on a spotlessly-clean, bullet-pocked bike.

But there was something about being on the road, feeling the wind dry and crumble away the worst of the mud from her face. The air was cool and dew-damp. It felt as if it was stripping away so much of the fear she'd felt in the last few days: the memory of the basilisk, fear for Gabe and the Hanged Men, even the dark bruises of the underworld still shadowing her face. There was only the roar of the air and the road, the arms around her and the scrape of a paw on her sleeve.

CHAPTER NINETEEN

REMAINS

The road allowed her to forget, for all those miles. She felt that the world had been conquered, that all would be well.

But Petra wasn't prepared for what remained of the Lunaria. Gabe had told her that Sal had burned it, yet she hadn't realized what exactly that had meant.

Where the tree had once stood, an imposing elm at the heart of the field, there was now a black stain of charred grasses. At the center was a blackened timber with broken fingers reaching to the sky. It was as if it had been struck by lightning. A figure dangled from the lowest branch—one she recognized. Sal Rutherford's body twisted in the lazy breeze. It was scorched on one side and crumpled like a paper bag. It made her queasy to look at it.

"Oh, Gabe," she sighed, staring at it as she shut off the engine and they dismounted. Sal was dead. And the old bastard deserved it.

But the tree . . . she scanned it, searching for any sign of life. Sig made no effort to pee on it, which told her that it was bad. There was not a single leaf left on it.

Gabe walked to the burned edge of it with the spear in hand. He gazed at the sharpened edge of the spear, and plunged it as hard as he could into the ground, next to the trunk, deep within its roots. It stood there, like a shining weathervane, looking utterly futile.

She didn't know what to expect. Part of her hoped that the snake's blood would regenerate it immediately, that it would burst into a flurry of green leaves. But the tree remained still, not reacting in the slightest to the sacrifice that had been offered to it.

"What now?" she whispered.

Gabe looked at the ruined timber. "We'll go to ground. We'll wait, see what it can do." He turned to look at her, and it seemed that she was seeing him in the most fragile state she'd ever seen him. He was pale, circles below his eyes, blood and mud smeared on every inch of skin. His hat had blown off long ago, and he looked like some kind of feral creature that needed to find a safe place to sleep and something to eat that didn't need to be chased.

She nodded and stepped up to him. She reached up to take his head in her hands. "I'll come back."

"I know." He bent to kiss her. "I hope to be here, in one piece."

It was a bittersweet kiss. It seemed that all of their kisses were like that—soft and full of a distant yearning she couldn't quantify. When it faded, he pressed his forehead to hers.

"Love you," he said.

She released him, and he bent to open the door to the underworld of the Lunaria. Petra watched him go, until the ground had been sealed shut behind him, as if he'd never existed for the past hundred and fifty years.

Maybe for the last time.

Gabe climbed down into darkness, into the depths of the Lunaria's underground world.

Before, when he'd gone to ground, the roots would reach out to touch him, to acknowledge him in some way. It might be as small as a caress on the back of his neck as the roots lifted him to the ceiling, or as grand as an embrace.

But it was all wrong here, now. The roots were motionless, smelling of burn and gasoline that had sunk deep into the ground. Chill had seeped up from the earth. He touched the roots in greeting, but they were silent and fixed, unresponsive. They must have moved sometime during the burning, spilling out into the chamber, turning and twisting to avoid the fire. They were frozen now in a contortion of agony. Such pain. Gabe couldn't imagine the shriek the tree must have let out, howling underground with no one to hear it. He had long been used to the tree having a personality. Maybe he anthropomorphized it, but he saw the Lunaria, at turns, as playful, serious, and motherly. It could be possessive and controlling, but extraordinarily gentle and loving as it rebuilt the Hanged Men, time and time again, from nothing. It had been a constant, and now . . . now it was gone.

He reached into the rhizomes, climbing up into the mass of still wood. He wormed his way back into the thickest knots, wanting to feel the comfort of the now-brittle roots. He was exhausted, and could go no farther. He leaned his head back in the tangle and closed his eyes. For good or ill, he would stay here. Around him, he was conscious of the other Hanged Men climbing into the dead tree, finding pockets in the stillness to sleep.

As he dozed, a dream bubbled up, from deep in his marrow. It was a fuzzy dream of his hopes and fears for the future, feeling out of focus and drained of color.

He dreamed he stood in the meadow with Petra, listening to the wind scrape through the sage and grass. Behind him, the bare Lunaria stood. It was covered not with leaves, but with the feathers of ravens, turning up like leaves before a rainstorm. The wind whipped roughly through the feathers, breaking the fine barbs and veins.

Rain was sweeping over the mountain, miles away. It slipped down the slope in a dark veil, obscuring the side of the mountain. It smelled like a deluge, a shadow that would send water coursing down into the little creeks and ditches in a flood when it arrived. There was still time before the rain reached them.

He took Petra's right hand, folded it to his chest, and slipped his other hand behind her neck. He kissed her. Her heart beat against his chest, and her skin was warm beneath his hands, warm as sunshine on earth in the summer. He wanted to trace every freckle on her body with his fingers, to learn what made her sigh and what made her laugh. She made him feel alive, as if the impossible were possible, as if he could be with her for an hour or a day.

Her hand slid from his chest, and he looked down at it, cradling it in his. There was a black stain on the palm, like oil. It pooled up in her palm and trickled down her fingers.

Her eyes were dark, dark and black like the smear on her hand.

And the rain came rushing down the mountain, across the field in a torrent. Through all that hissing wind and scouring rain, the stain remained on her hand and in her eyes, unable to be rinsed away.

He knew that what he wanted was impossible. It would not last.

He took her face in his hands and kissed her anyway.

Nothing ever did last. Not the tree, not the Hanged

Men. But if he held on to it, perhaps this moment of his dream would usher him gently into the soft, rotting darkness of the Lunaria's death.

Petra wanted nothing more than to stumble into a bath and a deep, dreamless sleep. But she had to get home. There was a fair amount of gas left in the Triumph, but she was stumped by figuring out how to get Sig on the bike. She drove the bike to the barn and poked around until she found a pair of crates to strap onto the sides. She convinced Sig to perch in one and put a counterbalancing sack of fertilizer in the other. It wasn't elegant, but it would get them home.

Still, she drove slowly on the way. Sig seemed content to huddle in the crate, and she was convinced that he would do just as well with a sidecar . . . if she ever had time to complete that project. She drove slowly in a driving rain that made them both miserable. It seeped through her scalp and clothes, sending mud draining away in runnels. The cold was sharp and brittle, and it was hard to steer on gravel when she was shivering.

At last, she made it home to the Airstream. She moved the bike underneath the tarp that covered the parts of the old bike she was working on. She'd figure out how to dispose of the Triumph later; just getting it out of casual view was enough for now.

She unlocked the door and stumbled inside. She filled Sig's dishes with water and dog food, got a bottle of water out of the fridge, and headed for the tiny bathtub. She hoped to hell that she didn't fuck up the plumbing with a cleanup of this magnitude, but this was going to be between her and whatever plumber had rigged the Airstream in the first place.

She wiped as much of the remaining sludge off her body as she could with towels, figuring the towels were going to be the Laundromat's problem. She peeled off her clothes, leaving a muddy pile on the floor. She took stock of her injuries—scrapes and purpling bruises, mostly. The worst seemed to be an overall scalding from the mud; it looked like she had a bad sunburn. And there was one small spot on the inside of her left arm that looked like it could have been an acid splash, but she wasn't certain. Just one more part of her life that was told on the scars on her arms. There was Des's handprint around her right wrist, the marks where Stroud had bled her, and now a drop of acid from the basilisk.

By the time she'd taken stock, the tub was full, and she scrunched in to sink up to her chin in the luke-warm water. She closed her eyes and tried to slow her breathing, to let the adrenaline drain out of her system. She wanted nothing more than a nap after this. Maybe a good twelve-hour one.

She shrieked as a coyote jumped into the tiny tub, splashing water all over the floor. Sig wasn't waiting his turn. After a couple of attempts to shove him out, Petra reached for the drain and the handheld shower to give him a proper lather and rinse.

After a good half hour, the both of them were clean

and smelling of Maria's homemade rosewater shampoo. Petra eyed the sediment at the bottom of the tub, but it drained perfectly. Petra dressed the last clean clothes she had—a tank top and cargo pants—and fell onto her futon. Sig wiggled his wet hide into bed, and she was too tired to boot him off.

She'd had her eyes shut for a whole ten minutes when someone rapped at the door.

"Fuck." She pressed her face to the pillow. Maybe she could just pretend she wasn't here.

The knocking began again, more insistent. Yep, that was a police knock.

Petra rolled out of bed and padded across the linoleum to answer it. Sig wisely stayed in bed and rolled over to the dry side he hadn't soaked with his wet fur.

She opened the door to find Mike on her doorstep. She looked past him—there was another ranger in a Forestry Service Jeep, and her Bronco was parked in front of the trailer.

"Hey. Brought your truck back."

"Thanks. I really appreciate it."

"We were running out of parking spaces at the station." He made a face.

"C'mon in. What's going on?"

Mike waved at his colleague, but the ranger was on the phone and paced to the edge of the gravel.

Mike came inside and parked himself on a kitchen chair.

"I thought you guys closed the park," she said, digging in the fridge for a couple of cold bottles of iced tea.

"Yeah, well. The Feds are all over us. About everything. They want me to get a written statement from you. And this is your official interview."

"Awesome." She hadn't given a whole lot of thought to embellishing her story. She handed him a drink.

"I did get some of your personal effects back from the scene," he said, putting her truck keys and her cell phone on the table. "They kept everything else."

"Thanks. What do you think they'll want to know?"

Mike shrugged and unscrewed the cap from the iced tea. "I think they're gonna have their hands full, honestly. Shit really blew up last night."

"What happened?"

"Among all the monster-hunting crackpots that have descended upon the park for purposes of fame and fortune were some guys who ran a television show. *Mystery Trackers* or some such."

"Haven't seen it."

"Me, neither. But they all turned up dead."

"Whoa. Did the snake get them?"

"No . . . that's where shit continues to slide down the slippery slope of weird. We think they were killed by a biker gang. A cult, really."

"You have enough people out here to have cults?" Petra took a drink and tried to look blank, though her heart was racing.

"This isn't ours. This is a gang that the Feds had some limited intel on. The Sisters of Serpens. They're into some funky stuff—black magic, murder, some racketeering. They apparently showed up here in search of the snake. Looks like they had one hell of a gunfight with parties unknown. The Feds will interrogate the ones who are left, but they're tough cookies. I don't think they'll get much."

Petra nodded. "What about the snake?"

"They're looking." He took a swig of his tea. "Listen, I know that you know more than you're saying about this."

She frowned, but remained silent. She was a shitty liar, and they both knew it.

"But I think I know you well enough by now to know that, whatever you were up to . . . it was on the side of the angels, okay? So. I'll watch your back as much as I can with the Feds."

She looked down at the table, took a deep breath. She wanted to tell him the truth. But she couldn't. "Thanks. It's complicated. But I promised someone I care about that I wouldn't get anyone else involved."

"I can respect that. Just . . . can you tell me something, for my own peace of mind?"

"I'll sure try."

"That snake . . . is it still a threat?"

She could see it in him, that needing to know. He needed to protect the people in the park, and that was entirely fair.

"I don't think you need to worry about the snake, ever again."

She wound up sticking to her guns with respect to the official statement that she scribbled out on notebook paper. She said she'd fled when the snake had killed Phil and Meg had fallen. She reiterated that she'd gotten a nose full of the vapor, passed out on horseback, and apparently woke up at Sal's ranch. She didn't deviate, didn't elaborate. If any of the higher-ups wanted more details, she'd come up with something better, later.

She jumped when her cell phone rang. She answered it as she scribbled: "Hello."

"Ms. Dee?"

"Yes."

"This is the Phoenix Village Nursing Home. We've been trying to reach you."

Her pen stilled. "Is my father all right?"

"Yes . . . he's awake, and he's asking for you."

She sucked in her breath. *What? How?* "I'll be right there."

She shoved the paperwork back at Mike and reached for her truck keys.

"Where are you going?"

"My father—at the nursing home. I'll let you know later." She left him behind to lock up and sprinted out to the Bronco.

Petra made record time to the nursing home, pushing the Bronco's engine until the old car roared like a proper dinosaur.

Could it be? Could her father be having a window of lucidity? And had she missed it, mucking about in the backcountry with snakes and undead guys?

She skidded through the doors of the nursing home, past the arrangements of silk flowers and a mop bucket surrounded with yellow caution placards. She skipped the front desk and rushed straight to her father's room.

The door stood open, and her father's wheelchair was sitting before the window, as it often was in the afternoons. A nurse was standing at the foot of his bed, taking notes.

"My dad . . ." Petra began, breathless.

The nurse intercepted Petra, leading her out into the hallway by her elbow. "Before you talk to him, you need to know some things. His lucidity comes and goes. He seems pretty with it, now . . . but he goes off on delusions, talking nonsense about snakes and the underworld and doves. The doctor wants to do some testing, some psychological testing and a brain scan. Would that be okay with you?"

"Yes, yes, of course. Can I see him now?"

"Sure. Just don't . . . don't expect too much, okay?" She patted Petra's arm. "He's not going to be the guy you knew when you last saw him."

"I understand." Anything more than staring out at the parking lot would be a gift. Even one word. Petra nodded and went in. She pulled up her usual chair beside her father's.

"Hi, Dad."

His chin moved toward her—the first time she'd seen his head really move in response to stimuli. His mouth turned upward, just a bit.

"Hi, sweetheart." His voice was thin, like worn gauze.

He recognized her. She leaned forward to give him a hug. He felt light and fragile as a bird in her arms.

"How do you feel?" she asked as she released him.

He squinted, as if he was focusing on something fuzzy. "The umbilicus. You remember?" It seemed to take him a great deal of effort to speak.

It had been true. All of it. She touched his cheek. "Yes, Dad. You and me and Sig and the raven."

"You cleaned up."

She looked down at her tank top and cargo pants. Not fancy, but at least, she wasn't covered in goo. Her hair was still damp as it hung against her freckled cheek. "Yeah. That was first on the order of business."

"You brought me back." His eyes shone. "The raven was a powerful thing. Much more than I thought."

She grinned. Her chest felt like her heart could burst inside it.

"Listen . . ." He leaned forward, and his thin hand grasped hers. "You didn't just bring me. You brought something else."

Nothing could dampen her joy. "What?"

"Stroud. You brought Stroud back through."

CHAPTER TWENTY

SHELLS AND VESSELS

Petra's father lapsed into mumbling about wanting biscuits and gravy for breakfast. Moments later, he drifted off to sleep, leaving Petra to mull his words.

She wasn't certain what she thought. The idea of Stroud—whether on the spirit plane or physical world—invoked a visceral sense of terror in her. If he had returned somehow, some way . . . he would have it in for her. Revenge would be on his bucket list. She'd have to figure out how to deal with it. Later.

She returned home, to bed, finding that Sig had not budged a muscle. She locked the door, propping up a chair beneath the knob. She slept for the rest of the day with Sig's ass in her armpit, awakening only to the sound of her phone ringing.

"Damn it, Mike," she groaned, pressing her face to the pillow. She hauled herself up to answer her cell.

"Hello."

But it wasn't Mike. It was Maria. "You're back. Are you okay?"

"Yeah. I think so."

"I'm so glad."

But something was wrong; her friend's voice trembled. "Maria, what is it?"

"It's Frankie. He's in a trance at the Eye of the World. I can't wake him up." A sob caught at the end of her words.

"I'll be right there."

Petra dressed and headed out the door with a sleepy Sig in tow. They drove back to the reservation, with early evening light streaming over the land in a haze of orange. She parked in Maria's driveway and ran into the field that stretched between the house and the Eye of the World.

Two figures were huddled there in the falling light. Frankie was sitting on a rock, cross-legged, with his hands in his lap, eyes closed. Maria had wrapped a blanket around him and was rubbing his shoulders.

Sig crept up to him and licked his hand. When he got no response, the coyote sat down, whined, and slapped his tail on the ground.

"What happened?" Petra panted.

"He said he was coming out here to meditate. I mean, that's usual for him. It was just a few hours, but he didn't come back for supper. He never misses supper when it's stuffed peppers, you know? So I went out looking for him, and . . . he's just in a trance. I can't get him out of it. I've tried splashing him with water, pinching him . . . nothing seems to work." Maria eyed the turquoise pool. "I even took a drink of the sweetwater, to see if I could follow him, wherever he's gone. But nothing happened, and I don't know what else to do."

Petra knelt by the water's edge. "Let me try it." The water slipped down the back of her throat, tasting like tea and minerals. She expected that nothing would happen, as usual. But she had to make the attempt. She sat down on the ground at Frankie's feet, trying to ignore the chill of autumn radiating up through her ass. Sig took a slurp of the water and crawled into her lap, his legs sprawling over her knees.

"I think that maybe we should call somebody . . ." she began. But the word became slippery, and her words ran together with the orange of sunset. She sucked in her breath and tried to gather her equilibrium, but the world faded.

Autumn's brilliance was replaced by a soft, pearly grey. A diffuse mist surrounded Petra; she couldn't identify a light source from where she stood, but a dim glow seemed to filter from somewhere above. Beneath her feet stretched silty mud the color of slate. It felt like a thin concrete that hadn't set, with a wash of water over it. She couldn't make out the horizon from here—just the fog and the mud.

"Why is the spirit world always sticky?" she wanted to know. And she wasn't dressed for this nonsense—she was wearing, of all things, a sleeveless white dress. The last time she'd worn a white dress had been at her baptism as a child. At least she was barefoot; that made the mud somewhat easier to deal with. It was actually lukewarm, and her toes splayed as they squished in it.

Sig was beside her. He nosed around the slop, his nose wrinkling. If he had an answer to her question, it wasn't a pleasant one.

"Frankie!" Petra called out into the grey.

There was no answer. But Sig found some light, sketchy tracks in the mud. They looked like a bird's—three front toes and one back one, large, with a ten-inch stride. These weren't raven tracks; these were the steps of a big wading bird.

They followed the tracks in the mud. Sig had a smear of mud on his nose, and the hem of Petra's dress was grey by the time they caught up with the bird: a blue heron, standing at the edge of the filthy water.

She squinted at the heron. "Frankie? Is that you?"

The bird cocked its head and answered in Frankie's voice: "Oh, it's you."

"Were you expecting someone else? Maria tried, but couldn't get here."

"No, it's fine." He ruffled his feathers, as if convincing himself. "It's good that it's you, because, well. You're responsible for this." He gestured toward the grey water, beyond a stand of scraggly reeds.

Petra sucked in her breath and took a step back. The basilisk lay in the water, motionless and curled in on itself, with its tail in its mouth. Sludge water lapped over its scales, dulling the iridescence of the ouroboros, still as a creature carved from granite.

"What the hell, Frankie?" She automatically reached for the guns at her waist, but there was no gun belt and no guns on her hips in this jaunt to the spirit world. Her hands came back empty.

Sig insinuated himself between Petra and the snake, hackles rising.

"Relax." The heron whacked Sig on the back of the head with his wing. The coyote yelped and looked offended.

"What's wrong with it, Frankie?" She had given no thought to the basilisk's afterlife; she'd been fixated on stopping its rampage and getting its blood. It had not occurred to her to wonder what would happen . . . afterward.

"Well, it's stuck." The heron folded his wings back. "Lascaris summoned her out of the spirit world a hundred and fifty years ago and poured her into a snake body. When she was killed in the physical world, she had nowhere to go. She's now here . . . in limbo. She's trapped, and she can't move on."

Petra looked at it. "Move on to where?"

"She really belongs back at her home. She's not

a creature of our world. When you bring a creature from the spirit world into ours, disaster follows."

Petra felt an unexpected pang of sympathy. The basilisk was likely the only one of her kind. She wasn't evil—she was a force of nature unleashed. She couldn't blame the basilisk for lashing out against humans, any more than she could blame a bear for an altercation with a human holding a box of donuts at the park. The snake was what she was, and she just didn't belong in Petra's world.

She took a deep breath. "So. How do we send her back? Preferably, without getting killed?"

"A good start would be getting her out of that mud."

Petra regarded the snake with narrowed eyes. "That sounds like a colossally dangerous thing to do."

"Hey, you did it. Can you live with yourself if you leave the last basilisk in spiritual limbo forever? I mean, I'd do it myself, but . . ." He shook his feathers like jazz hands. "No hands."

She made a face. What Frankie said was true. Her father had been trapped in a limbo of his own for years. It seemed only right that she try to balance the scales.

She stepped into the gooey stream, and it soaked into her dress. About two feet of water stood on top of the heavy silt. She waded out to the basilisk.

Her heart hammered as she approached. Surely, the basilisk could sense her slogging in the mud with its preternatural senses, and was playing opossum? But the snake's body just rolled limply with the turbulence, floating like a pool noodle. Petra steeled herself and reached for the middle of the body. It felt warm and supple, but incredibly heavy. The serpent didn't react, and that gave her courage. Using all of her might, she dragged the snake backward in the mud with a sucking sound, stumbling against the weight. The basilisk gave no resistance as she hauled, the tail sliding free of her mouth. Petra slogged in the mud and water, hauling the serpent to where the heron stood. The tail and the body still remained in the water, but the head made it to the mud beside the heron. Petra rested her hands on her knees and panted. Sig trotted back and forth, growling at the snake and nosing at the scales.

"Okay, so now what?"

"We need to take the snake home." Frankie pointed with his feathered wing beyond the mist. "Her temple is beyond the gate. Thataway."

The mist had drained away around a rock arch about fifty feet up the muddy beach. It looked as if it could have been a naturally-occurring structure, except for the carvings in the dark basalt. There were humanoid and serpentine figures writhing on it—it dimly reminded Petra of Dante's Gate to Hell. But as she squinted, she thought the figures might be dancing. It was hard to tell in this half-light. But it looked like there was tall grass beyond it, and she'd never pictured hell with grass.

"Blergh." Petra reached for the limp snake. She was easily five hundred pounds of dead weight. With each clumsy attempt to get her hands around the slippery creature, Petra was convinced that she would awaken and tear Petra's head off. But the head just lay there, eyes open. As she looked closer, she saw a transparent film over each eye. Perhaps the basilisk was pretty thoroughly comatose. Petra hoped so.

"That's it," Frankie said, fluttering before her. "Put your back into it, girl."

"Frankie, shut the hell up." She was tripping over the hem of her ridiculous dress and was in no mood to put up with his mansplaining. Heronsplaining. Whatever.

"I'm just trying to boost your morale," he huffed.

She was unable to wrestle the snake from the water. She sank up to her knees in the mud, sliding backward with each effort to bring the limp body to shore.

"You can't give up," Frankie told her.

"She's too heavy." Petra gasped. She cast about, looking for materials she might use to build a sledge or get some leverage. All she could come up with were a few handfuls of reeds and some broken sticks.

"There has to be another way, Frankie."

"Well. You *could* wake her up."

Petra's eyes narrowed, and her pulse thudded in her throat. "Assuming that I thought that was a good idea . . . how do I do that?"

"Look in her mouth."

She balked. "Um. She'll eat me."

"Possibly," Frankie admitted. "But can you live with yourself if you leave her this way?"

The snake, half-dragged out of the water, looked like trash washed up on the beach. There was something incredibly sad about her limp and dirty form that caused a lump to form in Petra's throat. Such a rare and deadly creature—reduced to this. She couldn't walk away, no matter how badly this was destined to play out.

Steeling herself, she knelt in the sludge before the snake's still head. She reached out to place her hand on the basilisk's nose, flinching. The snake didn't move, her lifeless gaze not shifting.

Petra jumped when Frankie landed in the shallow mud beside her.

"Jesus, Frankie."

"Quit flirting with her and get in there!"

Petra grabbed the snake's jaws and pried them open at the snout. Such a creature had jaws that could crush her, but the mouth opened easily, like a suitcase. A forked tongue slid over sharp fangs, dangling coldly against Petra's wrist. The basilisk's mouth smelled like rotten cold cuts.

"I don't see anything, Frankie."

"Keep looking."

She peered into the dark maw. At the back of the snake's throat, she spied something that glistened. She braced the bottom jaw open with her knee and reached in with her right hand, feeling the cold damp of the basilisk's flesh around her arm.

After a moment of fumbling, she grasped something solid. She tugged it out, the snake's fangs scraping her arm on the way out. She landed on her ass in the mud, blinking.

In her hand, she held a bottle—a beer bottle. It was identical to the one that she'd loaded in the potato cannon, full of lye. This one was capped, with liquid sloshing around inside it.

"Good work!" Frankie cheered. "Look!"

Sig snarled beside her, and Petra's head snapped up.

The snake was awakening. Scales began to move, muscles twitching, the spine undulating. The basilisk turned sleepily, as if still dreaming, her tail curling in the water. The transparent scale over her eyes flickered away, and the creature coiled up, lifting her head from the ground.

Oh, she was screwed. Petra scrambled up the filthy beach on all fours toward the arch, slipping and sliding in the muck. Sig pressed against her leg, growling.

Petra found her footing and ran toward the arch. She had no idea what was beyond that portal, except that the grass was likely to be surer footing than the mud. She lurched through the arch with Sig at her heels.

A dreadful hissing sounded behind her. The basilisk whipped through the mud, racing after her, far too fast to escape. Petra threw her arm around Sig to shield him.

The heron fluttered to Petra's side and whacked her hard with his wing. "Calm down, for Chrissakes."

"Frankie!" she hissed.

The basilisk slid through the portal, past Petra, into the grass. It seemed to look beyond her, at something that made its eyes dilate in fascination. Petra could see no other prey, just grass and sky. Once through, the snake stopped, writhing, and collapsed to the ground. It seemed that her skin was too tight, and the green scales were splitting open.

"What's happening?" she whispered to Frankie.

"She's shedding the form she was forced to wear on Earth," Frankie said. "You're about to see what she truly is."

The snakeskin ruptured open, and something shining tore through the husk of the snake body. It was a lustrous green, the color of jadeite dishes, speckled in black. The creature turned and twisted free of the snakeskin on the ground beside it. The new shape was serpentine, still, but much larger—it had a pair of clawed feet, and damp wings as large as parachutes unfurled in the mist, veined with gold.

"Oh, my God," Petra breathed.

The creature turned to face her. She still had golden eyes of the basilisk, the general shape, and the feathered crest. But she was so much more—magnificent. She spread her wings and shook them, extending her face to the sky. The force of her wings pushed the mist away, sounding like the thunder of sails in a stiff wind.

There was nothing for Petra to do but cower before this amazing creature. The basilisk was as near a dragon as anything she'd ever seen in a picture book. Tears sprang to her eyes. To have the privilege to see such an awe-inspiring sight . . . if she was devoured now, she knew that her life would have been worth it, to see this.

The basilisk faced her, toes digging into the long

grasses, tail spiraling. She brought her massive head level to Petra's.

"I'm so sorry," Petra said, mouth dry. She knew that these would be the last words she'd ever utter. There was no use explaining about anything, about fear and the Hanged Men and threats to the general public. There was no point in it.

The basilisk stared at her with her slitted golden eyes, so close that Petra could hear her breathing.

After many long minutes, there was a sound from the field. A cry—a chorus of them.

The basilisk turned, and a reptilian expression of joy spread across her face.

Petra's gaze slid to the field. There were women in the field, women in white cloaks and tunics, running toward the basilisk. Behind them loomed a great stone temple, hewn of the same dark basalt as the arch. Cheering, the women came with open hands, dozens of them.

The basilisk bounded away, plunging into the field like a puppy. Petra sank to her shaking knees. As the basilisk ran to the women, Petra cringed, half-expecting that there would be a massacre that would paint the tassels of the grasses red.

But, no. The basilisk knelt in the grass, opening her wings. The women clustered around her, embracing her. Her neck and tail curled around them, lovingly.

And Petra realized what the basilisk was. In this corner of the spirit world, the basilisk was a treasured goddess. She was precious and adored. The women pressed their hands and faces to her jadelike hide, crying and laughing.

"She's home," Petra whispered.

The basilisk swam through the field, with the women in white. A warm breeze stirred the grass, and they walked together, the women singing, to the temple. Petra watched until the basilisk had climbed the temple steps and gone inside. There was a lump in her throat that she couldn't swallow around. Even Sig seemed reverent. He sat beside her, watching intently.

"You done good, kiddo," Frankie said. He patted her with his wing.

"What now?" she managed to ask.

"You go back, back to your world and Maria. Tell her that I love her." He took a couple of steps away and peered up over his long beak into the leaden sky.

"You're coming back with us, right? You can't stay in a trance. You've missed supper," she said lamely.

"Sweetie, I've gotta fly," he said. He turned back to Sig. "You take good care of this one, okay?"

Sig barked.

And Frankie flapped his wings, once, twice, then took off into the sky. He tucked his feet beneath him and soared up.

"Frankie!" she shouted.

But he didn't come back.

Petra's eyes snapped open.

She was sitting on the cold ground, shivering. Sig

had rolled off her lap onto the ground and turned his head up in alarm. The sun had drained out of the sky, leaving cold purple twilight in its wake.

There was the sound of sobbing. Maria. Her face was a mask of tears.

Petra looked up at Frankie. Maria was patting the old man's cheek. Frankie was sitting in his trance posture, unmoving. And he fell over, like a rag doll, his hat falling into the water.

"Frankie!" Maria screamed.

Petra crawled on all fours to him. She grasped his wrist for a pulse, then his throat. Sig nosed his chest, whining.

There was nothing.

"Frankie!" Petra shook him.

He didn't come back.

CHAPTER TWENTY-ONE

AWAKE

The paramedics said that Frankie died of a stroke.

"As far as ways to go, it was a peaceful death," one of the medics told Petra as they loaded Frankie's body into the ambulance. He was a young man from Maria's tribe who had grown up three houses down. "We will take good care of him."

Maria had fallen into a soft shock. The paramedics had wrapped her in blankets and offered her a ride back to the house, but she refused. She walked back with Petra, Petra's arm over her shoulder and Sig plodding on her other side. The stars had been scattered overhead in a brilliant jewel box of glitter, and the women and coyote slowly moved under the weight of all those stars. Maria kept pausing to look back, as if the ghost of Frankie would be standing beside the pool.

"I had . . . no idea he was at a risk for stroke," Maria said. "I mean, sure, he was overweight and drank a lot, but I didn't think of it as an *immediate* risk. I should have made him go to the doctor more often."

"Maria. You couldn't make him do anything."

"But I'm—I was—his niece. I was responsible for him. I should have called the paramedics sooner. I assumed he was off . . . gallivanting in the clouds or whatever he does on the other side when he gets bored with life here." She rubbed her drippy nose.

"You couldn't have known that this was the last time. You can't be everyone's social worker, especially in more than one plane of reality."

"He was my last living relative." She stared up at the stars.

"I'm so sorry," Petra said, feeling helpless. There were no good words for this, nothing to say that would make anything better.

"Did you . . . did you see him in the spirit world?" she asked.

"I did." Petra felt guilty, at that. Maria should have been the last one to see him, to speak to him in this plane or any other. "He said that he loves you, but that he had to fly."

Maria smiled. "Was he . . . was he a man or a woman in the spirit world? I always hoped that he would have found the body he wanted."

"He actually . . . he was a great blue heron. I think he would have slapped me with his wing if I'd been impertinent enough to peer at his tail feathers."

Maria laughed through her tears. "I can see that, somehow. Damn it." She dissolved into sobs again.

The house was dark. Petra turned the lights on as they entered. Pearl hopped down off the kitchen table, making a series of inquisitive *mrrps*. Sig lay down on the floor beside her and made whining noises. They seemed to hold a conversation as Petra ran a bath for Maria.

Maria said little else that evening. Petra tucked her into bed, intending to sleep on the couch. But Maria caught her hand and asked her to stay. She tucked herself into the other side of the bed and pulled up a quilt that smelled like lavender. Maria fell into a fitful sleep, while Petra stared at the ceiling for hours, listening to the clock tick in the next room.

Eventually, she dreamed, dreamed of walking with her father in the underworld. He was talking about wanting to go to a Waffle House, because there were apparently no waffle irons in the spirit world, and he missed them. There were only pancakes. When she asked him why, he said that he didn't know the reasoning, that it was just a rule. Mike walked by in her dream, hauling a wagon of confiscated waffle irons and writing tickets. Cal sneaked up to the wagon when Mike's back was turned and stole a waffle iron, and she tried to talk to him. But he just gave her a sad look and scurried away. She felt a deep pang of mourning for him, and wondered if anyone else in the world would notice he had gone missing, that his shy smile had vanished.

Maria drifted past her, wearing a white dress, calling for her uncle. There were no herons in this dream, only ducks. Maria sorted through the ducks, but none of them was blue. One of them spoke, telling her that Frankie had gone home. But Maria insisted that he was not home yet, that he had missed supper.

Petra searched for Gabe in her dream, but couldn't find him. Her father told her that it was completely inappropriate to date an undead man, unless he had a waffle iron and knew how to use it to make snake waffles.

Clearly, her subconscious was overwhelmed.

She awoke in the middle of the night, finding Maria still as a stone and snoring softly beside her. Sig and Pearl slept at the foot of the bed, nested together like spoons. She made no move to disturb them, just watched the elderly cat turn over and knead Sig's belly in her slumber.

Frankie was gone. Really, truly gone. Tears slid out of the corners of her eyes and trickled behind her ears onto the pillow. She had somehow expected that if Frankie were to pass away, it would be in some spectacular bar fight with six-shooters or a car chase involving cops and a cliff. Something that would have made a great story. But he had slipped away so silently. Had he somehow known? Had he felt that stroke curdling in his body, and walked away to the spirit world to spend his last hours communing with the basilisk, to fix Petra's fuck-up?

And she felt guilty that her father had returned to this world—at least, some of the time—just as Maria had lost her only living relative. Still, her father's return gave her a bright spot of hope. She'd come here, to Temperance, to search for him. And now, she had both his spirit and his body together. She could speak with him. She had so many questions she couldn't wait to have answered. So much she didn't know about all that time he had been absent from her life. And about his own alchemical experiments. Where had he gone? What had he seen? What secrets did he know that he could share with her?

She cried for Cal, too, feeling the pillow growing cold and soggy around her face. That poor kid didn't deserve anything that had happened to him. He'd been a victim from the start, despite his good intentions. She wished that she could have done something—anything—to help him. Clearly, she'd done the wrong thing by taking him to the hospital, and that had ignited a chain of events that had ultimately led to his death. He had trusted her, and she had failed. That knowledge settled heavily in her chest. Her best hadn't been good enough. She would carry that with her for the rest of her life, she knew.

And she thought of Gabe and the Hanged Men, her fingers brushing her lips as she remembered him kissing her. He was not human, sometimes not even close. But he *felt*. And he loved her. If the Hanged Men could survive, that would be enough. She would make sure that it was enough. They *had* to survive. She couldn't face the idea of Gabe rotting underground, passing from this world without so much as an acknowledgment from the world above.

Maria's neighbors had visited the back porch in the darkness before dawn. By the time Maria awoke, there were piles of offerings at her door: casseroles in insulated carriers, flowers, cards, even a beautiful pink agate as big as her fist with a note on it—Frankie had apparently found it and given it to a little boy. The boy was all grown up now, and was giving it back. Frankie, for all his eccentricities, and for not being a blood member of the tribe, had been loved. By the time Maria was dressed and staring into her coffee, a knock sounded at the screen door. Petra answered it, seeing Mike on the other side.

"Hey. How is she?"

"Holding up, I think?"

"It's a shock." He rubbed the back of his neck as she let him in.

"Yeah. I just . . . I thought he had a lot more mileage left in him. He was an old man, but he was tough as nails, you now?"

When Maria saw Mike, he wrapped his arms around her, and she sobbed into his jacket. He stroked her hair and held her hand as she told him what happened.

Petra busied herself washing dishes in the sink. It was the only concrete thing she could think to do to help. Pearl assisted by sitting on the countertop and supervising.

"You gotta watch over her, okay?" Petra said to the cat.

Pearl looked sad, patting at the bubbles. She would miss Frankie just as much as Maria would—that much was clear.

Maria came to her and said, "You don't have to stay."

"Are you sure?"

Maria nodded. "I'm okay, now. It's just . . . a lot, you know?"

"I'll come back later tonight, if you want. Should I pick up anything for you?"

"I'll have food coming out of my ears for the next few days. And I think Mike will stay with me."

"Good." Petra dried her hands and kissed her friend's cheek. She was heartened to see the two of them together. She'd never pried about their history. But they were both good people, and she hoped that they would figure out a way to be good for each other.

The roads were empty and still this early in the morning, and a thick mist clung to the ground, as though it were left over from her trip to the spirit world. The whole land seemed to sleep, to be holding its breath for some inkling of the future.

She steeled herself and headed toward the Rutherford Ranch.

If the Hanged Men were gone . . . Petra shuddered

to imagine what she would find. In the chamber beneath the Lunaria, would Gabe and the others be
hanging as corpses tangled in dead roots? Would that
eerie light be forever gone? Would she never get the
chance to fully understand Gabe, to explore the what-
might-have-beens?

There was no sign of life on the ranch. There were
no lights on at the house or the barn on the high
ground. A dense, pearly mist had gathered from the
sky and hugged the lower land, obscuring the world
beyond the barbed-wire fence. She took the Bronco off
the gravel road, through the fields. Her headlights reflected shadows of grass and the ghosts of fog before
her, nearly useless.

She stopped where she thought the Lunaria was,
but could see nothing before her. She hoped she had
the right spot, but it seemed as if there were nothing
there, as if the tree had been entirely erased from the
land. The tree wasn't visible from the road, and she'd
have to hunt for it even on a clear day. But this sense of
obliteration chewed at her.

She hopped out of the truck and pulled out the Venificus Locus. She scraped some blood from a scratch
on her elbow into the device and squinted at it with a
flashlight. The bead of blood moved, sluggishly.

And she followed it. She whistled to Sig and plunged
into the mist. The Locus led her to the burned spot in
the center of the field. Sal's corpse was gone, but the
tree remained, a broken hulk against the grey sky.

A lump rose in her throat. She didn't know what

she'd been expecting. She'd been hoping that the basilisk's blood would have regenerated the tree, that it would rise from the field in full, leafed-out glory . . .

But there *was* something there. She crept forward to see where the copper spear had been plunged into the roots. A tendril of green wood wrapped around the shaft of the spear, with dewy green leaves at the crest. The sapling had grown around it like a caduceus, tiny branches reaching up to the sky. It was only about five feet tall, but it was *alive*.

And the Hanged Men had to be alive, too. Hope swelled in her.

After about ten minutes of hunting, pacing, and swearing while she stared at the blackened ground, she found the door in the grass that led to the Lunaria's chamber. Lifting it open, she found a charred tangle of tree roots below her; it was as if the tree had moved during its burning, but it provided better footing for the descent. She climbed down and was able to convince Sig to jump into her arms.

Sal's body lay on the ground. It looked like someone didn't have time to dig a proper burial hole, and had just shoved him down the hatch to hide him. His neck was bent at an unnatural angle where he'd been hanged, and the severed rope trickled off into the darkness. She walked around him, sweeping the light ahead of her. The Lunaria's roots were still and black. None of the golden light dripped through their vessels, nothing of the shimmering biomass that she had known before showed itself. A single golden taproot from the sapling dripped down from the ceiling, like a stalactite, holding nothing.

The Hanged Men dangled from the dead rhizomes of the old tree, like empty fruit. She swept her light at their split and broken faces. The men always rotted at night in the Lunaria's embrace, but they'd also always regenerated by morning. But these decomposed faces were still, and the bodies were missing limbs, stubs of bone tangling in the roots. She forced herself to reach out and check for pulses, but there was nothing. No sign of life. The ripe smell of decay overwhelmed the soft scent of earth and the stench of burning.

There hadn't been enough magic in the blood to restore them. There was just the sapling of the tree, and nothing more . . . the realization of that finality suffused her chest and burned her eyes.

The Hanged Men were dead.

All these men, gone forever.

She searched among them for Gabe, staring at each of their decomposing faces, trying to identify teeth and jawbones as her stomach churned. She couldn't find him. That didn't mean he wasn't here—maybe she didn't recognize him in this mass grave, under the soft blanket of decay. She ran from body to body, her heart in her mouth, sweeping the light back and forth, trying to imagine what each of these corpses would look like with a thick layer of flesh.

She finally stopped, crouched, and pressed the heel of her hand to her brow, sobbing. He was gone. All of them, all that mysterious magic of this wild land, gone.

Sig sidled up to her and licked her cheek. She threw her arm around him and cried into his ruff. He pressed his chest to her shoulder and whined.

It was over.

Gabe had given the blood of the basilisk to her—and that blood might have saved them. She was acutely aware of the blood thudding in her temples and the hot tears on her skin. She was alive, painfully, horribly alive. All the men were gone. And Gabe . . . she would never have the chance to return to the Stella Camera with him. She had begun to hope for something more with him, and that hope shriveled violently in her chest like wadded-up paper.

Eventually, she forced herself to her feet. This would be the last time she would come here. It would be too dangerous to return, since someone would eventually come searching for Sal's body. She plodded down the tunnel that she knew led to the Stella Camera. She wanted to see it, one last time, and putting one foot in front of the other was all she could do now, this numb shuffling.

She wound her way to the Stella Camera, wiping her drippy nose. The mist from the ground had soaked deeply in here, and she could make out only the faintest glimmer of the salts in the filtered grey light from above.

This place. Once upon a time, it had churned with possibility. She wondered if anyone would ever find it again.

Sweeping the flashlight beam around the room, salt

glittered, and the black lake lapped at the shore. A lone figure stood at the edge of the lake. Her heart slammed against her sternum.

"Gabe?"

He turned. His eyes did not gleam in the dark as they usually did.

She dropped the flashlight and rushed to him, lifting her hands to his face. His flesh felt solid under her fingers, unmarked, and warm. But there was no pulse of sunshine beneath his cheek. "You're alive."

He kissed the tips of her fingers. "I am."

"I went to the Lunaria, and when I didn't see you there, I thought you were dead. Like the others."

"I . . ." he began, looked away at the water, and back at her with dark eyes. There was something confused and helpless in them. "There was only enough magic to restore the tree, and me. Just me. I don't know why. Maybe because I was the oldest and the strongest. The rest . . ." He rubbed his hand over his face, and it remained over his mouth, his eyes glistening with tears. "They're gone."

She grabbed his face fiercely, pulling his forehead down to meet hers. "You are alive. That's miraculous. And I'm so glad for that." Her gaze fell on his neck, exposed by the undone last buttons of his shirt. She trailed her hand down his neck. The scar around his throat was gone, obliterated, as if it had never been there.

"You don't understand. I'm alive." He grabbed her hands. "But that's all. I'm not . . . magical anymore.

There are no more ravens. No glowing blood. No blocking bullets." He held up his hand, and it bled dull red from a scratch. "I scraped my hand climbing out of the roots. I . . ." he faltered, staring at it with an expression of horror and wonder.

She breathed it in, the totality of that knowledge. "You're human."

"Yes."

She kissed him hard, wanting to drink in every bit of him. He responded by tangling his fingers in her hair, cradling the back of her head in his wounded palm and sliding his other arm around her waist, pressing her body to him. She felt his heart pounding against her chest, a real, aching pulse.

He was alive. She was certain.

And, for now, for this partitioned moment in time, so was she.

Cal rolled over, feeling for all the world like someone had whacked him in the head with a baseball bat and hit a homer with his skull. He groaned and retched, feeling the mercury sliding over his skin, cold against the bruises. Plastic stuck against his skin, and the world was dark around him.

Bel. Bel had shot him. In the face. And he was still alive. *What the hell?*

He reached up to his face with shaking fingers, tracing the lines of metal around his chin and cheekbones. The mercury had formed a helmet over his head, he realized. It was dissolving now, retracting back under his skin.

Despair lanced through him. Bel was his last hope, and she was done with him. He lifted his head. Plastic stuck to his arms and nose. He tried to pull at it, but it wouldn't give. It was sticky and . . . oh, my God. He felt a zipper.

He was in a body bag. A fucking body bag.

Whimpering, he wriggled right and left, clawing at the zipper. One of his broken fingernails caught the top of the zipper, and he worked it down enough to get his pinky finger into the gap. He was able to draw it open enough to get some cooler air in his face.

And light. He lifted his head out of the bag.

Oh, Jeez.

He was in the back of what looked like a refrigerated restaurant truck, the air conditioning humming as the refrigerant dribbled out of the blower. A fluorescent light shone overhead, and it illuminated at least a dozen other body bags, stacked haphazardly in the space. A full bag had been thrown over Cal's legs, and he jerked free of it, curling up in a ball. He was alone with the dead.

He had to get out of here.

He crept to the back of the truck, pressed his ear to the cold metal. No voices outside. Maybe he had a shot at running.

There was a red release button on the inside of the door. Sucking in his breath, he hit it and thrust his shoulder at the door.

The door popped open easily, sending Cal sprawling on the ground with the wind knocked out of him. It was brighter here than in the truck—he registered that it was daylight, but not much else. Scrambling to his feet, he fled into the nearest cover—forest. He wheezed and waded into the underbrush, praying that nobody had seen him.

He ran until his breath finally seized up, driving him to his knees. His stomach cramped, and a string of silver slipped out of his mouth, forming a puddle in the yellow leaves. He panted, staring at his reflection in the quicksilver. The mercury moved under his skin. His nose got longer, cheekbones grew more pronounced, his cheeks thinned, as the mercury slid under his bones and moved the contours of his face. His skin ached and pulled over the swelling.

His own face disappeared. He saw another familiar face in its place: Stroud's.

He jerked back. It had to be a trick of the light. Had to.

Hello, Cal. It's been a long time. Stroud's voice echoed in his skull.

Cal pressed his fist to his forehead. "You're not real. You're dead. This can't be happening."

Look at me.

Cal peered into the quicksilver mirror. Stroud's unmistakable visage looked back at him, under the filthy shock of Cal's own black hair, all sharp angles and the prominent brow. Silver flecks crept into his irises, metal sliding into soft tissue.

I am here. Within you.

Cal whimpered. He rubbed at his face with his palms. The mercury dented under the pressure of his hands, but sprang back and reorganized in Stroud's image, like a candle melting and being remolded.

Behind him, he could hear people walking in the woods, the crackle of radios. Cal scuttled around in panic.

Run. Don't let them catch us.

"Well, maybe they'd shoot us, and this would be over," he whispered back at the voice.

No. They'll take us apart, molecule by molecule. They'll keep us alive, tortured. Is that what you want? Or do you want to be free?

Cal climbed to his feet. He leaned forward and backward. Part of him wanted to run to the people, relinquish control over his own life. He'd been in charge of his young life for years, and he had to admit that he'd done a pretty shitty job of it. Maybe it was time to let someone else be in charge, someone with a badge and some legit authority.

Cal. You will never see sunlight again if they catch us. And I will fight them. Their blood will be on your hands.

No. No more killing. He couldn't face that. He fled. He tried to run away from the voice in his head, the horrible memory of Stroud he wanted to forget. Weeds slashed at his pant legs.

He'd struck his head. He must have. Or else had a schizophrenic break. People just didn't hear voices. It wasn't real, couldn't be. Maybe when his concussion faded, the voice and the hallucinations would, too. That was his most rational hope, and he clung to it.

I'm real, Cal. I'm in you—in your cells and your DNA. And I'm not leaving you, ever again.

Cal sobbed.

ACKNOWLEDGMENTS

Thank you to my amazing editor, Rebecca Lucash, for the opportunity to let Sig romp and stomp around Yellowstone. I'm very grateful for your invaluable editorial magic and insight.

Heartfelt gratitude to my awesome agent, Becca Stumpf, for always holding the door open for new ideas. Thank you for your support and advice throughout these many creative processes.

Special thanks to Caro Perny, Publicity Guru, for all of your amazing promo work for this series.

Many thanks to all the motorcycle gurus for sharing their awesome knowledge: Stephanie Hoover, Aaron Mezger, Bill Tardy, Samantha Groom, Justin Reed, Colin Blain, Brad Lenk, Jay Hobbs, and all of Spite. Thank you, road warriors!

Much gratitude to Marcella Burnard for all the beta reading. I owe you a whole bunch of catnip.

ABOUT THE AUTHOR

Laura Bickle grew up in rural Ohio, reading entirely too many comic books out loud to her favorite Wonder Woman doll. After graduating with an MA in Sociology-Criminology from Ohio State University and an MLIS in Library Science from the University of Wisconsin-Milwaukee, she patrolled the stacks at the public library and worked with data systems in criminal justice. She now dreams up stories about the monsters under the stairs. Her work has been included in the ALA's Amelia Bloomer Project 2013 reading list and the State Library of Ohio's Choose to Read Ohio reading list for 2015–2016. More information about Laura's work can be found at www.laurabickle.com.